"I'd really like to know, Sam. What have you done wrong that leaving is going to fix?"

"How about everything? It was a mistake to pretend I might be able to have something like a normal life."

"I suppose last night was a mistake, too."

"No."

"It wasn't a mistake, but you can still just walk away from it as if it didn't happen."

"I'm not going to stay just so we can agonize over what we aren't going to have. You want to cry? Fine. That's the way you handle things. But it's not how *I* handle them."

"Oh, that's right. You're a *man*, aren't you? And men don't cry. And they don't get hurt, and they don't get scared. And they don't *feel*. How long is it going to be before you admit that men—real men— are human beings, and that they do get hurt and scared? Or maybe you plan to keep running away from it forever...."

Dear Reader,

The Silhouette **Special Edition** selection has seldom been more satisfying than it is this month. For starters, beloved **Nora Roberts** delivers her long-awaited fourth volume of THE O'HURLEYS! *Without a Trace* joins its ''sister'' books, the first three O'Hurley stories, all now reissued with a distinctive new cover look. Award-winning novelist **Cheryl Reavis** also graces the Silhouette **Special Edition** list with a gritty, witty look into the ironclad heart of one of romance's most memorable heroes as he reluctantly pursues *Patrick Gallagher's Widow*. Another award-winner, **Mary Kirk**, returns with a unique twist on a universal theme drawn from the very furthest reaches of human experience in *Miracles*, while ever-popular **Debbie Macomber** brings her endearing characteristic touch to a wonderfully infuriating traditional male in *The Cowboy's Lady*. Well-known historical and contemporary writer **Victoria Pade** pulls out all the stops (including the f-stop) to get your heart *Out on a Limb*, and stylish, sophisticated **Brooke Hastings** gives new meaning to continental charm in an unforgettable *Seduction*. I hope you'll agree that, this month, these six stellar Silhouette authors bring new meaning to the words **Special Edition**!

Our best wishes,

Leslie Kazanjian
Senior Editor

MARY KIRK
Miracles

Silhouette Special Edition

Published by Silhouette Books New York

America's Publisher of Contemporary Romance

To all those who,
by chance or fortune,
are facing life for the second time.
And to the nurturers and care-givers,
who teach us all how to love.

SILHOUETTE BOOKS
300 East 42nd St., New York, N.Y. 10017

ISBN: 0-373-09628-3

First Silhouette Books printing October 1990

Books by Mary Kirk

Silhouette Desire

In Your Wildest Dreams #387

Silhouette Special Edition

Promises #462
Phoenix Rising #524
Miracles #628

*coauthored as Mary Alice Kirk

MARY KIRK,

born and raised in Baltimore, Maryland, labels herself "a true daughter of the working class." She studied piano for thirteen years and holds a degree in American Studies and history; however, it was when she began penning fiction that her creative energies found their focus.

Mary says she writes novels to reflect her "profound respect for the capacity of the human spirit to survive and flourish. As a writer, I also feel very much a part of the ongoing dialogue among women who are questioning what it is they want in life and love, and I strive to present the most hopeful visions this dialogue offers." Her last Silhouette Special Edition novel, *Phoenix Rising*, won the *Romantic Times* Reviewer's Choice Award.

She is married to a biology and horticulture teacher, with whom she shares the pleasure of raising their two sons.

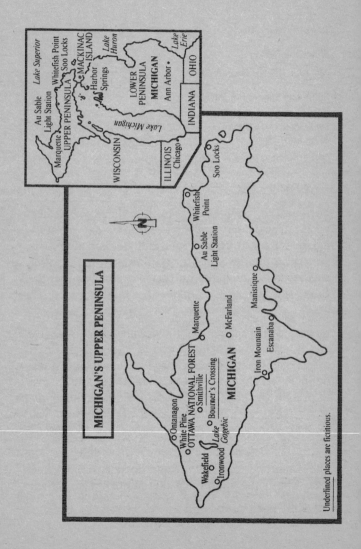

MICHIGAN'S UPPER PENINSULA

Ontanagon
White Pine
OTTAWA NATIONAL FOREST
Smithville
Bourner's Crossing
Wakefield
Lake Gogebic
Ironwood
Marquette
McFarland
MICHIGAN
Iron Mountain
Escanaba
Manistique
Au Sable Light Station
Whitefish Point
Soo Locks

Underlined places are fictitious.

(inset map)

Au Sable Light Station
Lake Superior
Whitefish Point
Soo Locks
MACKINAC ISLAND
Lake Huron
Harbor Springs
UPPER PENINSULA
Marquette
LOWER PENINSULA
MICHIGAN
Ann Arbor
Lake Erie
OHIO
INDIANA
Lake Michigan
WISCONSIN
ILLINOIS
Chicago

Chapter One

The rain was cold on Kate's face. It was colder still as it soaked through her jacket and jeans. It turned the pain she was suffering into misery and the misery into tears that ran down her cheeks to mingle with the rain.

Huddled against the tree whose roots had tripped her, she looked up at the wind-twisted maples and birches that dominated the Michigan forest. Their tender new leaves offered scant protection from the deluge, which she knew would only get worse. This was no spring shower but a storm out of the northwest off Lake Superior. It had blown in without warning, turning the fair afternoon sky into a mass of roiling black clouds. Hurrying along the rutted dirt track to beat the storm had been useless; all her haste had accomplished was to make her careless enough to trip and fall.

Kate grimaced and squeezed her eyes closed. The ankle was bad. Her fingers trembled as she gently poked the thick cotton sock covering it, and she winced at the sharp pain that accompanied the tentative exploration.

A loud crack followed by a wrenching groan brought her gaze flashing up in time to see an old hemlock, less than fifty feet away, split wide open. Cleaved in two, the dying giant crashed earthward, wreaking havoc on neighboring trees as it fell. In the next instant, when a switch of maple leaves stung her face, she cried out, inching her way around the tree trunk in a futile search for shelter.

She told herself she was being childish, letting a storm frighten her, but circumstances were rapidly undermining her confidence. She was alone and in pain. Her left ankle was swelling rapidly. It was storming violently. Lynn and Erik Nielsen, whose house she'd just left, lived a half mile south; Bourner's Crossing, where she lived, was two miles north. And crawling the distance in either direction would be impossible.

Maybe a fisherman would find her, or a park ranger patrolling his section of Ottawa National Forest land. How long would it be before anyone missed her? Maybe tomorrow morning, when she didn't stop by the office, Doc would wonder where she was. More pessimistic speculation had her waiting two or three days. But what would she do that night, as the temperature dropped, to keep from freezing in clothes that were soaking wet?

With the wind howling and the rain beating upon her, Kate stared at her foot and tried to stop crying. She didn't mind crying over sad movies, happy occasions or tragedies in other people's lives. But these tears made her uncomfortable. They were an expression of her own helplessness and pain, an echo of the queasy, panicky feeling growing inside her. And she fought against them, hoping that if she could control the tears, she'd control the panic.

It didn't work.

Kathleen Morgan, eldest of six Morgan children, rarely wallowed in self-pity and never gave in to hysterics. But she was on the verge of indulging in both when a male voice, coming out of nowhere, pushed her over the edge.

"What the *hell*—"

She screamed, recoiling, before she'd even gotten a look at the figure looming over her. When he moved a step closer to hunker down beside her, she tried to scramble away, wrenching her ankle in the process.

"Ouch! Oh, Lord—"

"Hey, it's okay." His voice was deep and gravelly and harsh over the roar of the storm. "What are you doing here? Are you hurt?"

She struggled to speak past the lump in her throat.

"Look, lady—" the man laid a hand on her arm "—we've got to get out of this storm! There're trees going down!"

Kate tried to blink the blinding wind and rain out of her eyes, but she got only a glimpse of the man through a dense gray curtain. Lean thighs encased in black denim, broad shoulders hunched inside a worn leather jacket. A face of sharp lines and dripping wet hair.

His hand tightened on her arm. "Did you hear me? We've got to get out of this!"

"Can't walk," she croaked. "My ankle. It's twisted." His eyes slid away from hers, zeroing in on the injured limb. "I was on my way h-home from the N-Nielsens'. They live down the road, and Erik . . . Erik has a truck. He'll help if you—Oh!"

The wind shifted, blowing a sheet of rain in their faces, and Kate shrank farther against the tree. The man swore, standing abruptly to shrug out of his jacket and drop it around her shoulders.

"Oh, th-thank you, but . . ."

He snatched her knapsack off the ground, slung it over his shoulder, then reached down to her. "Give me your hand! I'll carry you."

Kate saw how quickly the pounding rain soaked his chambray shirt and noted irrelevantly, "You're going to get cold."

He gave her an exasperated look. "I'll survive. Now, come on, before we both drown!"

"But it's too far for you to try to carry me, and Erik—"

"For God's sake, lady, shut up and give me your hand! We can argue later!"

Kate's breath caught in her throat, and she flushed with embarrassment. He was right; she sounded ridiculous. But she wasn't thinking very well, and it seemed a great effort to shove her concerns aside enough to hold out her hand and let the man enfold it in his grasp.

His hand was strong and warm despite the cold, and he pulled her upward in an easy motion.

"Honestly," she began, "I could wait while you go—" Her suggestion died abruptly when he drew her arm around his neck, slipped his arm under her knees and lifted her.

She gasped. "Are you s-sure about this? The pack's heavy, and I'm not exactly...l-little! Let me hop or— Oh!"

He tossed her slightly to shift her weight, and her arms locked in a death grip around his neck.

"It's all right, honey," he said. "You let me handle this." And without further comment, he began walking down the mud-washed track.

Kate was too stunned to utter another word. *"It's all right, honey? You let me handle this?"* No one ever talked to her like that. She wasn't used to being "handled." She was used to doing the handling herself. Still, amid her pain and the punishing torrent, she was relieved he wasn't giving her choices she was incapable of making.

Kate closed her eyes and buried her face against his shoulder. Soon enough he'd realize he couldn't carry her far and would want to put her down. Not that she was overweight, but the ample curves on her five-foot-six-inch form could not, in her estimation, be considered insignificant. He didn't put her down, though, and after a minute or two, she stopped worrying that he would slip or drop her.

He didn't move like a man who was unsure of himself. He didn't feel like one, either. His body was all lean muscle on a tall, broad-shouldered frame. He moved carefully and as quickly as the wind and the rutted, slick track would allow, carrying her not easily but with confidence. Slowly, as they traveled, some of that confidence seeped into her. It came in the form of heat. Heat radiating from his body into hers, through their rain-soaked clothing. She felt it in her arms, wrapped around his shoulders, in the thigh and hip he held firmly against his ribs, and in her breast, cushioned against his chest.

After what seemed a long time, the man stopped walking. Kate lifted her head and saw through the rain that they'd reached a small, cedar-shingled hunter's cabin, one of many scattered throughout the forest.

"I'm going to put you down," the man warned, setting her on one foot, her back braced against the cabin. Her hands clutched his shoulders, and he gave her a questioning look. "Will you be okay?"

She nodded, but the instant he moved away, her knee buckled and she slid to the ground. He grabbed for her, but she waved him off. "G-go on. I'm f-fine."

She wasn't fine; that was obvious to both of them. But he left her sitting there to reach for the door. It was locked, and he rattled the handle, slamming his shoulder against the stout pine several times before giving up. Moving to the window to the right of the door, he yanked hard on the shutter until it finally banged open. Then, giving the window a cursory look to see that it was locked, he stood back and put his booted foot through it.

Kate winced at the sound of shattering glass, then watched anxiously as he reached inside and unlocked the window, sliding the frame up until he could climb through. He did so with long-legged ease and, an instant later, opened the door. This time her arms went around his neck unhesitantly as he lifted her, carried her inside and kicked the door closed behind them.

The sound of branches scraping across the roof combined with the clomp of heavy boots as the man strode across the plank floor. Maneuvering in the semidarkness to a couch in the center of the room, he started to lower Kate onto it but stopped when she tensed.

"By the f-fireplace," Kate rasped.

He put her down on the braided rug in front of the cold hearth, and she hugged her ankle close, shutting her eyes against the pain. Her relief at being out of the wind and rain was palpable, but for the first time Kate realized how badly she was shivering. Her teeth were chattering, and she couldn't clamp her jaw tightly enough to make them stop.

A sudden slam made her eyes fly open, though she had to strain to see across the room. Her rescuer had closed the shutter against the driving rain and, in doing so, had cut off the only dim source of light. She could just make out his shadowed form as he grabbed something from the day bed along the opposite wall, then moved toward her, his boots crunching on broken glass.

Dropping to one knee in front of her, he started to drape a blanket around her shoulders. But then he hesitated and finally tossed the blanket aside. "Got to get these wet things off," he muttered, "or the blanket won't do much good."

Right, Kate thought. But she couldn't make her muscles do what she wanted, and he wasn't wasting time letting her try. Without asking permission, he pulled his wet jacket from her shoulders, then went to work on the buttons of hers.

She struggled to speak. "I'm K-Kathleen Morgan, but people call me K-Kate."

"Sam Reese," he replied, pulling one sodden sleeve, then the other, off her arms. "Hell, you're soaked to the skin. Look, Katie, I know this is kind of short acquaintance, but..."

Above all else, Kate was practical; she knew this was no time for modesty. Besides, it was nearly pitch dark in the cabin. She wasn't entirely at ease, but she didn't offer a word of protest as Sam Reese's long fingers skimmed down the buttons of her cotton blouse, leaving gaping fabric in their wake. He yanked the hem out of her jeans, then lifted each hand in turn to loosen the cuffs. The darkness didn't hinder him, Kate noticed, and she appreciated his tactful comment when his hands slid inside the sopping blouse to peel it off her shoulders.

"Now, I'm just going to close my eyes, here, and..."

"I'm... f-freezing," she whispered.

"Honey, you're not just freezing. You're in shock."

"Uh-uh."

"Uh-*huh*."

"Not y-yet." But almost. Over a twisted ankle and a storm! It was mortifying.

Kate's shirt slapped onto the floor in a wet heap, and in the next instant Sam had reached behind her and unhooked her bra—one-handed. In the dark. She might be cold and hurting, but she had enough sense left to realize she was being undressed by an expert. When his hands skated down her hips and discovered her jeans were mostly dry to her thighs, she was relieved. Even putting modesty aside, she couldn't have coped with having them pulled off over her ankle.

The wool blanket was thick and scratchy and warm as Sam rubbed it over her bared back and shoulders.

"S-Sam, you know…you're not exactly…c-catching me at my b-best."

"Is that so?"

"I promise, I'm u-usually a lot d-different."

"You telling me these goose bumps aren't permanent?"

"I'm really… v-very efficient."

"Well, Katie, we all have our off days. You sit tight while I try to hunt up some matches and get a fire started."

Sam drew the blanket around her, and she clutched the ends together between her breasts. Fire. That sounded like salvation. She'd been in this cabin before and knew it had heat and lights, but the power came from a liquid gas generator located outside. Weather conditions being what they were, a fire was the easiest, fastest way to make heat.

"In my pack," Kate said. "F-flash…light. And m-matches."

"Good girl," Sam murmured, dragging the pack across the rug toward them. "I was beginning to wish I hadn't quit smoking."

As he unbuckled the straps and began sorting through the knapsack, Kate tried to concentrate on him rather than the pain. He was on his knees, only inches away, and with every shallow breath she took she caught the scent of him—an unembellished male scent that blended with the smell of his wet leather jacket beside her and the wool around her shoulders. In the face of physical discomfort, her senses focused on those clean, honest scents and found in them something immensely comforting.

A beam of light shot across the room as Sam switched on the flashlight. He used it to find the matches, then turned to the fireplace. There was wood piled beside the hearth, and when he began arranging logs, Kate almost asked him to find her aspirin first. But if he was half as cold as she was, fire was more important.

Gritting her teeth and telling herself she could wait a little longer, she searched for something to say to keep her mind off her ankle.

"Did you know about this c-cabin? Or did we get l-lucky?"

Sam answered without looking at her. "I'm renting it."

"You're renting this place?"

"Right."

"So, how c-come we . . . had to break in?"

"No key. I stopped to look around before I went to meet the owner—a man name Fournier."

"Yes, I know Steve."

Sam shot her a quick glance, and Kate added, "I kn-know everybody around here." His replies hardly encouraged conversation, but she persisted out of her own need. "S-Steve's my brother-in-law. He's m-married to my sister, Cressie."

Sam's "humph" was unimpressed as he broke kindling to stuff under the logs he'd stacked.

Kate closed her eyes briefly, then tried one more time. "Where are you f-from?"

"Detroit," he said, then reached for the matches to light the fire.

The tip of a wooden match scraped briefly on the side of the box, then flared. He waited an instant, his hand cupping the flame until it steadied, then touched the match to the kindling in several places before tossing the charred remains onto the fire. He only had to repeat the procedure once; the logs, being seasoned and dry, caught quickly, and soon tongues of fire licked at the hardwood.

Eager for heat, Kate wiggled closer and reached for her knapsack. Sam turned to find her struggling.

"What do you want?" he asked.

"A black case. It's in the b-bottom. Somewhere."

She let him take the pack from her, and he produced the case in seconds, snapping it open, then giving her a startled look at the sight of her stethoscope, blood pressure cuff and other medical equipment.

"You a doctor or something?"

"A nurse practitioner. And a n-nurse midwife." She was having trouble preserving her modesty and rooting through the bag at the same time. "Please. Do you see the aspirin?"

"Got it."

"Give me th-three."

Without comment, Sam uncapped the bottle and tapped the pills into the palm she'd stuck out of the blanket. She groaned when her uncontrollable shaking made two roll onto the floor.

"I'm sor—"

"Hush," he said, steadying her hand with his own as he shook out two more. His hand closed over hers, curling her fingers around the tablets, then he waited until she had them in her mouth before recapping the bottle.

"What's in here?" he asked, already unscrewing her Thermos.

Kate answered with the aspirin on her tongue. "Coffee."

He wouldn't even let her try to handle the plastic cup but held it for her as she drank to swallow the pills. Caffeine might not be the best cure for a bad case of nerves, but she was desperate enough for its warmth that she reached with both shaky hands for the cup.

Sam hesitated. "You sure?"

"No, but it f-feels good. Hot."

He held the cup out to her but didn't let go when her fingers trembled against it. Instead, his hands covered hers to hold it securely. Slumped and shivering, her eyes closed, Kate concentrated on the way the heat from both the cup and Sam's strong, steady hands seemed to travel up her arms to warm the rest of her body.

It should have felt strange, she thought vaguely, to sit there, nearly naked and less than half coherent, while a stranger touched her with such familiar ease. But it didn't feel strange at all. It felt right. Right and natural, the way it should feel when circumstances defeated pretense and formality, and people were forced to trust each other in a hurry, under stress.

She knew the feeling well. She'd experienced it treating gunshot wounds in victims of hunting accidents and stitching cuts in unlucky hikers and fishermen. It was at its strongest when the isolation of the northern wilderness necessitated that she deliver the baby of a woman she barely knew. The sudden, intense intimacy. The bond that formed at those needful times between two people whose only common ground was their essential humanity. Yes, she knew the feeling.

But she'd never experienced it from this side of the fence. She was always the helper, the rescuer, the strong, reassuring one who, hopefully, made everything all right again. To be treated as she might treat a patient contradicted Kate's view of herself entirely, and under less dire circumstances she probably would have balked. Having reluctantly accepted the situation, though, she discovered it wasn't so bad. In fact, if she thought about it too closely, it might even make her cry. For having Sam Reese hold her hands to help her get warm was, very simply, the nicest thing anybody had done for her in a long time.

Slowly, Kate's shivering lessened. Sam felt the change, too, and withdrew his hands. Taking a ragged breath, she opened her eyes to discover the coffee wasn't sloshing in the cup. The pain in her ankle was atrocious, but she felt better. Still a little rattled, but together enough to remember she wasn't the only one who was cold and wet.

Holding the cup out to Sam, she spoke in a voice closer to her own. "Here. Pour yourself some. And you should do something about your wet shirt."

"I'm okay," he said, taking the nearly empty cup from her and setting it aside.

He was crouched in front of her, one side of his face bathed in firelight, the other side in shadows. He couldn't be called handsome, Kate thought, but she found the rough-hewn planes of his face compelling. Lines fanned out around his eyes and creased the corners of his mouth, carved in skin bronzed by the sun. Like his harsh-edged voice, his features were distinctly masculine—a thin, straight nose and high, sharp cheekbones beneath which his face was long and a bit too hollow. In contrast, his mouth was generous, with a fullness to the lower lip that made it disturbingly provocative. His hair swept back from a high forehead and was medium brown streaked with blond. She guessed he was close to forty.

"Feeling better?" he asked.

"A little. Thanks." She tried to smile as she met his gaze.

His eyes were clear gray. In the firelight, they were almost colorless, like prisms that in one instant reflected light and in the next, absorbed it. A second later, though, the sparkling irises darkened to a muted pewter, and Kate felt cheated. For a moment she'd seen something in the depths of Sam Reese's eyes that belied the tough image he projected.

He rose to drag two straight chairs from the kitchen table to the fire, then draped Kate's garments and his jacket over them to dry.

"What about your jeans?" he asked. "Do you want to try to dry them out, too?"

She shook her head. "I wouldn't dare take them off over this foot.... Sam?"

He glanced at her, and she tried another smile, this time revealing a hint of dimples. "I behaved like a perfect fool back there. I'm sorry."

He lifted one shoulder in a loose shrug. "Don't worry about it."

"I *was* worried. And I'm very glad you showed up."

With a nod of acknowledgment, he walked away.

Kate wanted to ask him not to leave her. The throbbing in her ankle was bone-deep, and talking helped keep her from coming unglued. Her eyes followed him, her fingers knotting the wool chafing her breasts, as he scouted the farther reaches of the cabin. The purpose of his search became clear when he pulled a broom from a closet in the corner of the kitchen.

"So, are you in the area to fish?" she asked, her tone brittle with forced cheerfulness.

Sam crossed the room and began sweeping up the broken glass, giving her a brief, "Maybe."

"Lake Gogebic is practically next door, and it's the best place for walleye. But just about any direction you go, you'll find water to throw in a line."

"Hmm."

"Then again, if you're a hiker, you can't go wrong, either. Of course, this is our slow season—and the snow melted early this year, too. People come to the Upper Peninsula to see fall colors or to ski—or to hunt. About the only thing now is fishing. Are you going to be staying long?"

"Depends."

"On?"

"On how long I decide to stay."

"Oh."

Leaning the broom against the wall, he studied her from across the room. Then, slowly, with what appeared to be reluctance, he came over to stoop in front of her. His eyes were full of an emotion she couldn't begin to read, and he seemed to be deliberating as he worried a corner of his bottom lip with his teeth.

Finally he asked, "Is it bad?"

His directness startled her after his vague, terse statements.

"Your ankle," he said, when she didn't answer. "Do you know how bad it is?"

Her gaze fell from his, and she tried to muster some breezy assurance. "Oh, it's nothing an ice pack won't cure."

It was a ridiculous lie. Her ankle was obviously swollen, her hiking shoe biting into the flesh around it.

Lifting her gaze, she said tentatively, "You know, I would like to get this shoe off, but...well, do you think you could lend me a hand?"

For a moment Sam neither moved nor spoke, though his eyes darted from her face to her ankle several times. Then, abruptly, he surged to his feet and pivoted away, reaching for the poker hanging beside the fireplace.

"You'll do better yourself," he replied, giving the logs a shove. "I'd just wrench it worse."

His refusal struck her as odd in light of everything else he'd done for her, but Kate wasn't about to push. Maybe he was squeamish about injuries and medical things.

Gamely, she tucked her blanket so it wouldn't fall open, then stuck her hands out from under it to begin working at her wet shoelace. It was soon obvious, however, that her short-trimmed nails and shaky fingers couldn't untie it. She kept trying, but pain and frustration and raw nerves were driving her to tears.

"Cut it."

Kate's eyes were brimming when they snapped up to collide with Sam's. He was standing beside her, an open pocketknife lying across his outstretched palm. She looked from the knife to him in pain and confusion, not understanding how a man could sound so hard and cool when his eyes said he was anything but. Understanding even less his almost anguished expression when his gaze dropped to her ankle.

Was he that squeamish? If so, why did he torture himself by watching as she took the knife from him, slipped the blade under the lace of her shoe and sliced it? And why did he hover over her as she whimpered through the agonizing process of working the shoe off her foot? Finally, when her hand slipped on the wet leather and she gasped at the sudden jerk, he made a low, strangled sound and strode away.

His behavior was definitely odd, but then again, she'd seen enough men, especially macho types like Sam Reese, turn to jelly over medical emergencies. As she sliced her cotton sock from shin to toes with Sam's knife and peeled it off, she had only a vague awareness that he was pacing the room like an animal paces a cage.

By the time her injured foot was bare, Kate felt sick to her stomach. Besides that, she was beginning to think about the ramifications of this accident. She wanted to believe it was only a sprain but feared it was worse. In any case, she was facing a trip to the hospital for X-rays, days in bed with her foot elevated, and maybe weeks of hobbling around on crutches, dragging a cast.

But she didn't have time for beds and crutches and casts! Laura Graff's baby was due in ten days. And she'd promised Marion and Steve she'd stay with the kids one evening soon so they could get out. And there was Bert Andrews, with his new high blood pressure medication, who had to be closely monitored. And she'd promised Alison Lenox she'd talk to her biology classes next week about prenatal development...

Kate groaned at the long list of obligations. Some of them were part of her job, but many she'd agreed to simply because she enjoyed doing things for people. Yet here she was with a messed-up ankle, and there wasn't a thing she could do about it except worry.

"Doc's going to strangle me," she murmured, giving voice to her anxious thoughts.

"Aren't you allowed to get hurt or sick?"

She glanced up to see Sam standing on the other side of the hearth. Uttering a short laugh, she replied. "To tell you the truth, I don't know. I've never tried."

"This Doc guy—who is he?"

"Dr. William Cabot. His office is in Bourner's Crossing. I've been working with him for about three years."

"And he's the slave-driver type?"

Kate shook her head. "No, Doc won't really be mad at me. But he's an older man, and he depends on me to handle most of the emergencies. I also do all the prenatal care, and I deliver babies for women who can't make it to the hospital, and...well, things like that."

"You mean, you do the legwork."

She cast a woeful glance at her ankle. "As much as I dislike your choice of words right now, yes."

"So maybe he'll have to get somebody to help for a while."

"I wish it were that easy. But look, it's my fault I'm in this mess, and I'll figure it out. Now, tell me the truth, Sam, are you really from Detroit? Because you sure don't look it."

His face went blank at her shift in topic. Then, slowly, one side of his mouth sloped into a smile. "How does somebody *look* like they're from Detroit?"

"Oh, I don't know. You *sound* like you're from the Midwest. But I'd have said you lived somewhere hot and sunny."

He raised an eyebrow, and she directed a look at his hair. "It's the tan and the beachboy blond streaks. I remember, in the summer, my sisters and I would smear lemon juice all over our hair, trying to get it to look like that. Except it never worked." With a toss of her head, she caught her thick, long braid in her fingers; it was dripping wet, and she looked at it, dismayed. "We had to settle for plain, ordinary brown."

There was a brief silence, then Sam drawled, "I don't know, Katie. Plain and ordinary can be real nice ... under the right circumstances."

His lazy, sultry tone got her attention. Her eyes flashed to his, and she blinked, certain she wasn't reading him right. The harsh lines of his face revealed nothing, but those gray eyes told her things his expression did not. She knew with every feminine instinct she possessed that she wasn't mistaken; his gaze still held an odd wariness she didn't understand, but it also held interest—frank, sexual interest that was made even plainer as his eyes slid over her blanket-wrapped body in a slow perusal.

Kate flushed, her gaze skittering away. She wasn't accustomed to being eyed so openly. Men always seemed to look at her as a big sister or a friend—which often meant their shoulder to cry on. They almost never looked at her *that* way. And the not-so-subtle message in Sam's appraisal was even harder to believe given that she must resemble a drowned rat.

Squirming a little inside the blanket, she busied herself by working her waist-length hair out of its braid. It was imperative to keep talking, although she wasn't sure anymore if it was to keep her mind off her ankle or her eyes off Sam Reese's sexy mouth and its unsettling smile.

"So, are you really from Detroit?" she asked.

"Yes. But I haven't lived there in a long time."

"Am I right? Do you live somewhere hot and sunny?"

"It's definitely hot and sunny in the Mojave Desert."

Kate's fingers, caught in the tangles of her hair, stilled. "The desert? What do you do in the desert?"

"Nothing, right now."

"Well, what *did* you do?"

He paused before answering. "I flew planes."

"Oh, you were a pilot!"

"I *am* a pilot."

He said it with such vehemence she felt as if she should apologize for her ignorance.

"Were you—" She stopped to correct herself. "*Are* you in the Air Force?"

Sam shook his head. "I was in the Navy. But I've been out ten years."

"So you fly commercial planes now?"

It took him so long to respond that Kate looked up. He was staring at her, and he didn't look happy.

"You know, Katie," he said, "you're awful damned nosy."

Heat rose in her cheeks, and she began an apology. "I'm sorry. I don't usually babble like this, but—"

"But your ankle hurts."

There it was again. That reminder that, regardless of what he said, he understood. He was willing to cooperate, up to a point. Then something would happen—maybe she was asking questions he didn't want to answer—and he'd balk.

Well, we all have our secrets, she thought. He's as entitled to his as I am to mine.

"The aspirin helped a little," she mumbled, glancing toward the shuttered window. "Listen, maybe the rain's let up.

You could probably go get Erik now, and I'm sure he'd take me—"

"It's still pouring," Sam interrupted her. "When the storm's over, I'll take you home."

"But I've already put you to a lot of trouble, and—"

"Katie."

"It's getting late—close to dinnertime, anyway—and—"

"Katie, stop it."

She sucked in a quick breath, and her eyes flashed to his.

"You haven't been any trouble. I just don't—" He broke off, his eyes reflecting indecision. An instant later, he scowled. "Listen, I'm a little touchy about answering questions. I've been doing a lot of it lately. I know why you've got to keep talking—and, believe me, I'm sorry as hell about your ankle—but I'm not much of a talker. Okay?"

Kate supposed that scowl could be darned intimidating, and she suspected Sam intended it to be. But it was too late for that. He'd carried her out of the rain and undressed her and helped her get pills into her mouth. He'd held her shaking hands around a hot cup of coffee in unquestioning silence until she was warm. There was no way she could be intimidated by Sam Reese. And he must have realized it, for gradually, his expression softened.

"Forget Nielsen," he said. "I'll take you home."

Kate hesitated only a second or two before giving him a single nod of acceptance. She held his gaze a moment longer, but when he turned away to stare into the fire, her eyes slid over him and she suddenly registered that his hands were rubbing his crossed arms—and that his shirt was till wet.

"You're cold," she said.

His right hand, wrapped over his left biceps, stopped moving. "I'm okay."

"Where are your things, Sam? If we're going to be here a while longer, you should put on a dry shirt."

He shook his head. "My Jeep's around back, but I'm not going to unload it in this deluge."

"I guess everything'd be wet by the time you got it in-side," she agreed. "But your shirt would dry faster if you hung it with the other things."

He shrugged off her concern. "I'm fine."

"You're not fine. You're cold."

When he didn't answer, Kate sighed. "Sam, I feel bad enough, causing you all this trouble—and don't tell me I didn't. I was a pain in the neck when you found me, and you've got a broken window to fix because of me. I'd feel better if I didn't think you were freezing."

His head turned, and she met his gaze with an encouraging look. "If you're worried I'll faint at the sight of a man's naked chest, forget it. I grew up with three brothers. And in my line of work, believe me, hairy chests are the least of what I put up with."

He didn't respond to her attempt at levity but continued to look at her with that wary, closed expression. Then, sud-denly, he yanked open the buttons of his shirt, tore the wet garment off, and flung it over the chair with his jacket. Without pausing to glance at her, he grabbed the poker and squatted in front of the fire to give the blazing logs a few good jabs. He made a production of it, shifting logs until streams of sparks were flying up the chimney.

But Kate was hardly aware of Sam's actions. Her eyes were wide with shock, riveted to his lean torso.

Scars. Flat, shiny scars. They mottled his right side—chest, ribs, back, and upper arm. All were the result of burns. There was another scar, though, that wasn't from a burn, and it commanded her attention, making her ache simply to look at it. A single arc that began over his heart, swept under the curve of his right pectoral and around his rib cage, ending at his spine. It was a surgical scar, one she was certain must have resulted from a monumental effort to repair internal injuries.

Kate's first thought was to wonder what had happened to him. Her second was to regret persuading him to take off his shirt when he clearly hadn't wanted her to see the marred flesh. Her third was to note that it would take a lot more than scars to diminish all that unashamed virility. Scarred or not, Sam Reese was quite a man.

"Is there a grocery store in Bourner's Crossing?"

Kate hardly even heard the question. She was studying the pattern of crisp hair, muscled contours, and scars on Sam's chest. He was stooped down across from her, stuffing her medical bag and Thermos into her pack, and when she didn't answer, his hands fell still.

"Have you changed your mind about fainting?"

Her eyes flew to his and locked for the space of a heartbeat—long enough for her cheeks to stain red.

"No." She dropped her gaze. "No, of course not."

A minute of strained silence passed before he resumed the packing.

"I'm hoping I don't have to drive a lot farther tonight to find a store that's open," he said. "Is there one in town?"

"Uh-huh."

"What time does it close?"

"Whenever Mrs. D. calls Mr. D. home to dinner."

Kate realized how worthless her answer was; she also realized she was staring at the place the line of dark hair running down his flat belly disappeared into the top of his jeans. There was a scar just to the right of it that . . .

Her eyes flickered upward, and when she found him watching her, her blush deepened at being caught—again. This time, though, she held his defiant gaze. *I dare you to say what you're thinking*, his eyes seemed to say. And manners dictated that she keep her mouth shut.

But Kate was no actress. Even when she was at her best—which she certainly wasn't—it would have taken more talent than she possessed to pretend she didn't see the scars. And her understanding of pain and her abiding respect for the fragile nature of life made it impossible not to ask, "Sam, what happened?"

Something dark flickered in his eyes, but he applied his attention to buckling the straps of the knapsack as he spoke. "I ran into some trouble with a plane."

"You mean you . . . crashed?"

"That's the general idea."

His tone was so lacking in emotion Kate could almost hear him adding, *But it was no big deal.*

"How long ago was it?"

"A little over a year."

Not long enough for burns to lose their angry look, nor for him to sound even half so dispassionate about it. At least, Kate thought, she now understood why he'd been upset about her ankle; given what he'd suffered, it was easy to see why pain—even someone else's—would bring back agonizing memories for him. As she tried to imagine what those memories must be like, her eyes coasted over him again, her expression an unconscious reflection of her thoughts.

"Cut it out."

The sharp order snapped Kate's head up, and her eyes locked with Sam's angry ones.

"Listen," he said. "I don't need you or anybody else feeling sorry for me."

Actually, the thought of feeling sorry for Sam Reese was laughable. He stirred a welter of emotions inside her, but pity wasn't one of them. Still, Kate knew what he must have seen on her face, and she had to explain.

"I wasn't feeling sorry for you. I was feeling, well, bad, I guess. Not about the scars, though. I promise you, Sam, I've seen worse."

His scowl was suspicious, but he seemed to believe her.

"It must be my nurse's instincts," she went on. "Looking at you, I can't help thinking about how badly you must have been hurt." Her eyes traveled over him, and she shivered. "A plane crash! Heavens! It's hard to believe you survived at all."

There was a flash of silence before Sam muttered, "Yeah, well, maybe I didn't." And with that, he grabbed her clothes off the chair and tossed them into her lap.

Kate stared at the clothes, then at him. Then she frowned. "What is that supposed to mean—maybe you didn't?"

He buttoned his half-dry shirt as he answered. "Nothing. Forget it."

"You're here, and you're alive, aren't you?"

"Yeah, right. Look, the rain's stopped." He picked up his jacket, nodding toward the door. "I'll bring the Jeep around front while you get dressed. Or, uh—" his eyes skimmed over her "—do you need some help?"

His tone wasn't suggestive; the offer was sincere, for all its reluctance. But it wasn't dark anymore, and she was no longer simply the stranger in need he'd helped undress an hour ago.

Kate turned to look at the fire. "No, thanks. I can manage."

He walked to the door, stopping when he'd opened it to glance over his shoulder. "Listen, Kate," he said, "I'm a nasty bastard to be around lately. Don't take it personally. And don't try to make sense of it, either. Not much about life makes sense, anyway. Take my word for it."

And then he was gone.

Chapter Two

Sam stood with his back to the closed cabin door and heaved a sigh. He stared at the greening, rain-drenched forest, listening to the silence, smelling the wet dirt and leaves, willing the tension out of his body. Slowly, his jaw relaxed. Gradually, the trembling in his hands stopped, and his heart, which had been racing for the past hour, settled down to a quieter beat. He felt like he'd won a war.

Well, okay, maybe only a battle. But that was progress. Total victory would have been if he'd been able to keep Kate Morgan from knowing the battle was even being fought.

Sweet, dimple-cheeked Katie Morgan, with her big brown eyes and her soft, sexy body and her "plain, ordinary" hair that fell all over the place in masses of rippling waves. Yeah, she was plain and ordinary. Like hot apple pie with vanilla ice cream. Nothing fancy or exotic, but rich and luscious and so damned good you kept wanting more. A man could get hooked on that kind of goodness.

Sam grunted softly and glanced at the door. He wouldn't have to worry about getting hooked. He wouldn't even count on being given a taste. Because no matter what he thought of her, Katie probably thought he was pretty strange. And he couldn't blame her.

Frowning, he trudged through the mud and last year's fallen leaves toward his Jeep, parked behind the cabin. His only comfort at the moment—and small comfort it was, too—was that nobody, Katie Morgan included, would ever guess the cause of his odd behavior. Not in their wildest dreams. The only way they'd find out was if, by either word or deed, he told them.

Words were easy to control; he could ration them out as he saw fit. Deeds were a different story. His impulsive actions over the past few months had all but ruined his life. And that's why he was here. He had to take charge of things again. Get a handle on what had happened to him, on what he'd become.

First, he'd unwind a little. Relax. Put some space between him and all the people who'd been bleeding him dry. Not that he held it against them, but enough was enough. And he'd forget about all the others—the ones with the endless questions, and the ones who'd looked at him, shivering-in-their-shoes scared. Then, when he was feeling less harassed and scattered and more like himself again, inner battles such as the one he'd fought this afternoon over Katie Morgan wouldn't be a problem.

And neither would flying.

That's all he needed—some time to get himself together. After seven months stuck in a hospital and another four spent fighting with the Federal Aviation Administration, he could finally think about flying again.... God, it had been so long.

Climbing into the Jeep and tossing his duffel bag into the back to make room for Katie, Sam started the engine. He stopped, though, in the act of releasing the brake, to look around. The air was clear and chilly with the passing of the storm, and the late-afternoon sky, through the trees, was a splashy array of blues and pinks. Rain dripped off the old hemlock beside the cabin, splashing occasionally on the canvas top of the Jeep. This was the big woods. Tall, straight

aspen and shapely birch and maple stretched over mile after mile of rolling hills. The place felt clean, immutable.
Safe.

If he wanted it to stay that way, though, he was going to
have to be more careful than he'd been in the past two
hours. He'd come too damned close to giving in to Katie's
big, brown, tear-filled eyes. Her little sounds of pain had
about destroyed him. The worst part was, he'd have to listen to those sounds until he got her home—and he'd have to
ignore them.

Sam's hand fell from the steering wheel, and he slumped
in the seat with a sigh, figuring he'd better plan his defense
before he had to face her again.

Okay. So, he'd gotten here this afternoon, and the first
person he'd run into was a nurse. The local doctor's assis-
tant. Yeah, he'd walked straight into that booby trap. And
she was sweet and sexy, and the idea of spending about a
week in bed with her was damned appealing. But no matter
how sweet and sexy she was, and no matter how hard it was
to deny the urges that had tormented him since he'd found
her sitting there, nursing her ankle, he was going to keep his
urges—all of them—to himself.

With that thought, Sam's mouth twisted in a dry smile.
As far as his baser urges were concerned, he didn't think he
had anything to worry about. Ten to one, Katie was married with a bunch of kids. He could see her with some big
lumberman, the kind who'd flatten any guy stupid enough
to let his eyes drift below her chin. So all he had to do was
take her to town, turn her over to her husband and leave.
And, hell, she'd still be a damned sight better off than she'd
been when he'd found her.

Between now and then, he wouldn't try to get to know her
or give her any reason to think he wanted to make friends in
the area. Because in order for his plan to work, he needed
to foster the idea that he wanted to be left alone. Let the lo-
cals think he was a recluse—"that strange guy who moved
into Fournier's cabin. Never speaks to anyone when he
comes to town. Goes about his business and disappears
again. Oh, he's polite enough. Just strange."

Sam wasn't a recluse, and he didn't like the idea of going weeks without talking to anyone. He didn't like being thought of as strange, either. But he needed the isolation—and the peace—this cabin and these woods offered. If letting people think he was strange was what it took, he'd put up with it. What he couldn't put up with was worrying that maybe they were right.

Perched uncomfortably on the seat of Sam's no-frills Army-surplus Jeep, Kate grabbed for a handhold as they started toward town. The storm had turned the forest road into a river of mud and potholes, some of which half-swallowed the Jeep's tires. Sam wasn't making any concessions to the terrain, though; he was attacking the road as if the Jeep were an armored tank.

Kate cast a sideways glance, wondering if she dared ask him to take it a little easier. His jaw was set, and his mouth was turned down at the corner. He hadn't spoken three words since he'd come into the cabin to get her, and she decided she'd rather put up with the jarring ride than ask him anything.

What on earth made him so touchy? She didn't believe he was really the nasty bastard he'd called himself. In fact, she'd seen enough of the person beneath that crusty exterior to know Sam was actually a very nice man. A nice man with a problem.

Clearly, he'd been through some rough times. He'd had a terrible accident, which must have had something to do with his leaving his job—whatever that job had been. He didn't like answering questions, because he'd been doing a lot of it lately. He wasn't here to fish or hike. And she had a gut feeling he might have come simply to seek shelter, like a wounded animal slinking off to a cave to lick its wounds.

Turning her back on someone in pain went against every instinct Kate possessed. She should do as he'd told her—not take his remarks personally or try to make sense of them. She should let him work out his own problems, stop worrying about a man she barely knew. Yet the only thing that kept her from trying to cheer Sam out of his black mood was that she was exhausted from her own pain and didn't have the energy to be anything more than polite. Besides, at the moment, it was all she could do to stay in her seat.

"Ouch!" The word escaped Kate's lips as the Jeep bounced in and out of a pothole and her left foot hit the floor.

Sam muttered something crude, then shot her a quick look. "Sorry."

She wasn't sure if he was apologizing for hitting the pothole or swearing—he seemed to have a flair for both—although he did slow down to navigate the road more carefully.

"It's okay," she replied, every muscle tensed for the next jolt. Short of sticking her bad foot across Sam's lap, she tried every conceivable position the confined space allowed, but nothing was comfortable.

Sam's frequent glances told her he was aware of her dilemma. Finally, when she moaned in defeat, he passed a hand over his jaw in an impatient gesture and spoke.

"You okay?"

"I'll manage," she replied with a tight smile. "It's not that far."

"What the devil were you doing walking from this Nielsen house, anyway? It's a long way from town."

"It's only about two and a half miles. Up here, that's around the corner." Kate locked her hands together under her left knee to keep her foot suspended. "I have to drive most places, so I like to walk when I can."

Sam grunted, then lapsed into silence. A minute later he asked, "Are you going to have that ankle X-rayed?"

"I think I'll have to," she replied.

"Where's the closest hospital?"

"There's a small one in Ontonagon and a bigger, new one in Ironwood. They're both about fifty miles."

Sam kept his eyes on the road, but Kate could see by the tautness of his features that he was shocked.

"But you must have ambulances closer than that," he said.

"We used to, over in Smithville, about ten miles from Bourner's Crossing. But they got cut out of the county budget."

"Great," he murmured. "So now people just die, huh?"

Sam had picked up quickly on one of her own worries, but it startled her that it so clearly upset him, too. As her arms quivered with the strain of supporting her leg she drew her ankle onto her lap and attempted to explain. "People who've lived here all their lives are used to being isolated. They don't think anything about driving twenty miles to shop or fifty miles to the doctor. And folks are generally prepared for emergencies. The loggers have field radios, and nearly everyone has phone service now. But it's true, sometimes things happen, and we don't make it. That's the risk of living here. If you live in a city, you'll be near the hospitals—but then, you're taking other kinds of risks."

With a sharp turn of the wheel to avoid a fallen limb Sam spoke angrily. "So you're saying that to get your ankle X-rayed tonight, your husband will have to drive you fifty miles to a hospital and back."

"Yes. Except I don't think I can face going tonight. Tomorrow will be soon enough. And it won't be my husband taking me because I'm not married." She frowned at his quick glance. "That surprises you?"

Sam looked away and shrugged.

"Did I say something to make you think I was?"

He hesitated, then shook his head. "No. I just had you pegged as a home-and-family kind of woman."

His disgruntled tone made her think he wasn't happy to have the image dispelled. No more happy than she was to be caught off guard by his perception of her. He was right: she was a home-and-family woman. One with a home but no family to put in it.

Kate was saved from having to comment when the forest track came to a dead end at Main Street in Bourner's Crossing.

"Which way?" Sam asked.

"Turn left and go straight through the intersection."

She gave him the directions, knowing she should feel relieved—as relieved as he looked—that the ride was nearly over. She ought to be glad she'd soon get to lie down. She ought to be glad to be rid of Sam Reese, with his puzzling moods and his testy personality. Yet she wasn't glad, and any relief she might have felt was mingled with disappointment.

Silly woman, she thought. The butterflies in her stomach were only the result of being around a man whose every look and gesture carried a latent sexual message. She shouldn't take those messages any more personally than anything he'd said. Still, it was a good thing he was a stranger, passing through—not the kind of man she would consider getting involved with. Because if she saw much of Sam, she suspected, the butterflies might get out of hand.

Bourner's Crossing, Michigan, population two hundred and thirteen, occupied a few dozen acres in the middle of Ottawa National Forest. It was, literally, a crossroads town, but neither of the roads in question appeared on any but the most detailed map. Unlike the rocky, mountainous coast along Lake Superior, the land surrounding the town rolled in gentle hills or lay in marshy fields. Like all of the Upper Peninsula, it was veined with rivers and creeks. A few dairy and cattle farmers made their living off the heavy soil, but the plan of the National Forest Service was to allow the wilderness to reclaim much of the developed land; many roads weren't being maintained, and farming, which had filled the economic gap when the iron mines had closed years before, was being replaced by controlled logging and a booming recreation industry.

The town of Bourner's Crossing had seen its last dairy farm go under three years before. The townspeople, and those who lived close by, were mostly either lumberjacks, small-business people who catered to the year-round needs of sportsmen, or sawmill workers.

The mill on Larry Bourner's property was located on Bourner's Mill Road, which crossed Main Street at the town center. Both were the wide dirt roads common to the

Upper Peninsula. On the northwest corner of Main and Bourner's Mill sat the post office; on the southwest was Ed Davenport's general store; across from Davenport's was the First Lutheran Church, and on the remaining corner was Gibson's gas station and small-motor repair shop.

In addition to Main and Bourner's Mill, a narrow dirt track cut into Main by the Williams's house. Called simply the old lake road, the track wound its way in a southeasterly direction through the forest, providing local access to the eastern shores of Lake Gogebic. It was upon this timeworn trail that Sam and Kate arrived in town.

"Now what?" Sam wanted to know when they'd crossed the town center.

"My house is the last on the right," Kate answered. "The gray one with the red pickup parked in front."

She gave Sam a brief look. A muscle in his temple flexed as he clenched and unclenched his teeth. He'd grown silent again, and Kate wished to heaven he'd done as she'd asked—gone to Erik Nielsen for help, rather than put himself out when he clearly didn't want to be put out.

Sam parked behind Kate's pickup and, without a word, removed her from the Jeep and carried her up the front steps, into the small one-bedroom cottage. As he ducked through the narrow hall on the way to the bedroom, she persuaded him to give her a few minutes alone in the bathroom, where she managed to maneuver in the confined space on one foot. The effort left her quivering, though, and she was glad he appeared to catch her the instant she called, before she fell and made things even worse.

"Is the place we passed—Davenport's—the food store?" Sam asked, lowering her onto the patchwork quilt that covered her double bed.

"Yes," she replied, "but I'm sure it's closed. You can fix supper here and take some things with you for breakfast."

He started to protest, but she stopped him. "Sam, I haven't got enough fight in me to argue. The refrigerator's packed. Fix yourself something. All I want is my nightgown and robe out of that closet, and the pills in the corner kitchen cabinet called— No, wait, I'll write it down." She grabbed the pad on her bedside table, made the note and handed it to him. "If you just get me those things, I'll be fine."

Sam looked at the piece of paper then asked, "Are you going to call Doc Cabot to look at that ankle?"

Kate shook her head. "Doc's in Wakefield tonight, visiting his brother. I'm not going to bother him."

Sam's forehead creased in a dark scowl. "You should call somebody to help you."

Kate pushed her hair out of her face with a trembling hand. "It's nice of you to be concerned, but, really, I'll be all right until tomorrow. Believe me, I'm not going to be stupid about this. It's too important that I be able to get around."

When she looked at him, his gaze dropped to her ankle. He stood there glowering at it for several seconds. Then, abruptly, he turned toward the closet opposite the bed. He found her robe and gown hanging on the inside of the door and, snatching them off the hook, tossed them to her. Then, without a glance in her direction, he left the room, mumbling something about getting her pills.

Kate stared at the empty doorway, feeling confused and unaccountably sorry that she'd met Sam Reese under such abysmal circumstances. In spite of his reticence and strange behavior, he was the kind of man a woman wanted to impress.

Sam strode through Kate's house, found the kitchen and automatically slapped the light switch. But when he reached the cupboard, instead of opening it, he lay both palms flat on the counter, let his head drop forward and drew a long, steadying breath.

The ride had been harder than he'd expected, and things weren't getting any better. He'd thought he had it all figured out, but Katie disarmed him at every turn. He had to get out of here. Soon. The war wasn't over yet, and he knew from experience he could still lose.

He also knew that worrying about it would weaken his defenses. Confidence was crucial. Panic would doom him to failure. He had to *think* his way through this. He couldn't *react* like some green kid caught in his first street fight. The crucial thing to remember was that Katie's life was not in danger. She only had a messed-up ankle.

So he'd get her the pills. Then he'd fix her something to eat—and himself, too. It was the logical thing to do. He'd see to it that she let someone know she was incapacitated. Then he'd leave.

It was a good plan. He wasn't being cruel. He was just being practical, trying to survive.

Sam straightened to locate the pills amid the cabinet's variety of medical supplies. When he heard the phone ring faintly in Katie's bedroom, he hoped it was a neighbor, somebody she could tell about her predicament. Grabbing a glass out of another cabinet, he filled it with water and headed toward the bedroom, arriving in time to see Katie hang up the phone.

She had put on her nightgown and robe. Her discarded clothing was in a heap on the floor—except her jeans, which were bunched above her injured ankle. She'd obviously been trying to get them off, and her expression of pain and frustration nearly wasted him then and there.

"Sam, I need your knife again," she said, her voice raw.

His steps slowed as he approached.

She made a tiny exasperated gesture. "These jeans are too narrow at the hem to go over the swelling."

He set the glass and the pills on her bedside table and reached into his pocket, producing the knife and opening it for her. She took it from him without a word. As she started to slip it under the thick hem, though, he saw her hand tremble, and he reached out to cover her fingers with his own.

"I'll do it," he said, crouching in front of her. "You'll cut yourself that way."

He couldn't blame her for looking surprised. Hell, he'd acted like she had leprosy when she'd asked for help taking off her shoe. She handed him the knife, though, and her murmured thank you sounded relieved. But when he slid the blade under the cloth and saw how badly his own hand was shaking, he had to wonder which of them was in worse shape.

It would be so easy, Sam thought as his hand brushed her tender skin. So easy to give her what she needed—what he needed, too, to satisfy the gut-wrenching ache inside him. But then she would know. And that alone was enough to harden his resolve.

With a few careful movements, he sliced through the fabric binding Kate's ankle, parting the leg of her jeans up to the knee. Then he paused to ask, "Do you want to try to salvage these?"

When she didn't answer right away, Sam glanced up. Her lower lip was caught between her teeth, and her eyes were squeezed closed. She let out a shuddering breath and opened her eyes to look at him.

"No. Just get them off."

His gaze fell to her mouth. Her lower lip was purple and swollen where she'd bitten it—probably to keep from screaming—and he knew he had to hurry up and get out of that room.

The sound of tearing cloth filled the silence as Sam worked the blade through the length of denim. When the waistband parted and the rent cloth fell to the floor, he closed his eyes briefly and took a shallow breath. Then, in one swift motion, he flicked the knife closed against his thigh, pocketed it and stood. Turning away, he shoved his hands into his back pockets and cast his gaze over the cozy, feminine bedroom.

"Was that a neighbor on the phone?" he asked, barely recognizing his own voice.

"Yes," Kate answered, easing her legs onto the bed.

She'd arranged two pillows at the bottom, on top of the quilt, and he watched as she cautiously lowered her injured ankle onto them. The ankle was a mess—bruised and swollen to the size of the sensually curved calf above it.

Sam cleared his throat. "So, are you going to get some help tonight if you need it?"

Reaching for the pill bottle, she replied, "Ruth Davenport's going to stop over later, but I'm hoping I'll be asleep. I really don't feel like talking to anybody."

His eyes followed her movements as she took a white pill out of the bottle and swallowed it with the water he'd brought. "I'm going to fix supper. What can I get you?"

"Nothing. I'm not hungry."

"You sure?"

She nodded, lying back on the pillows piled behind her. "Thanks, Sam. The only other thing I want is an ice pack. There's one in the cabinet where you found the pills. Could you—"

"I'll get it."

He did so, quickly. And he delivered it to her, turned around and left without pausing to see that she got it arranged properly.

As Sam rummaged through the refrigerator in Kate's bright kitchen, he thought somewhat desperately about walking out the front door and driving away. But he couldn't. He had to get through this trial by fire. If he didn't, he'd only face another such trial somewhere down the line with no more ability to handle it than he had now. Which was next to none.

Granted, the particular battle he was fighting was harder than most. Katie was a nurse, and his conscience was bothered by the thought that people depended on her. Besides that, he was having a damned hard time ignoring his attraction to her. He wanted her. And he wanted to help her. And it wasn't clear how much wanting he could stand before he gave in to it, one way or another.

Sam settled on scrambled eggs and leftover baked potatoes that he could fry up in a hurry. He had finished the meal and was washing his plate when the back doorknob rattled. With his hands full of soap, he turned to see a small, gray-haired woman enter, the key still in her hand.

The woman looked startled by the sight of him, but before he could explain his presence, she smiled.

"Oh, you must be Sam Reese. Kate told me about you. I'm Ruth Davenport. My husband Ed and I own the general store."

Wiping his hands on a dish towel, Sam said a polite greeting and shook Ruth's hand.

She met his gaze with a worried look. "Mr. Reese—"

"Sam."

"Yes, thank you, Sam. I want you to know how glad I am you were there to help Kate when she needed it. Storms off Superior can be bad business, and once in a while we lose somebody with winds like we had this afternoon."

"I can believe it," he said softly.

Ruth nodded. "And Kate would have been in even worse straits tonight, since it's supposed to drop down close to freezing. I'm sure she's thanked you, but I want to thank you, too—for Bourner's Crossing. She means a lot to all of us."

Sam started to brush off Ruth's gratitude, but she peered anxiously around him. "How is she? Does she need anything?"

"I think she's asleep."

"Oh. Well, I'll just go and check."

Sam was washing the skillet he'd used when Ruth returned.

She bustled into the kitchen, snatched the butter dish off the table to put away, and let out an exasperated sigh. "That girl!"

"Is she all right?" Sam demanded, his battered nerves reacting instantly to Ruth's tone.

"She's fine. Well, she's not fine, of course, but she's sound asleep. I didn't disturb her." Ruth shut the refrigerator door, then proceeded to take Sam's place at the sink, plunging her hands into the soapy water as she went on to say, "Kate amazes me, that's all. She works herself to the bone, doing for others, but do you know, if Sarah Winfield hadn't called me to say she saw you carrying Kate in the door, and if I hadn't called to see what was wrong, I bet she wouldn't have said a word to anybody about being hurt if she could've helped it."

Sam didn't doubt it. He'd heard Katie himself, lying through her teeth about how there was nothing wrong with her ankle an ice pack wouldn't cure. No, Katie wasn't a complainer.

"Not that she ever *needs* help," Ruth continued, scrubbing at the potatoes and eggs stuck to the cast-iron skillet. "She's as capable and dependable as the day is long. Comes from all those years of taking care of her family."

A warning light went off in Sam's head. He knew he shouldn't listen to any more of this, but simple male curiosity about the woman who'd stirred his senses made him say, "Her family?"

Ruth was glad to satisfy his interest. "Kate's mother died in childbirth when Kate was twelve and left John Morgan with six children, including the new baby. Kate's the oldest, so you see what I mean that she comes by her knack for taking care of others honestly. And a sweeter, nicer girl you'd never want to meet. Of course, I imagine you've already found that out."

The bottom had dropped out of Sam's stomach, and he offered no resistance as Ruth plucked the dish towel out of his hands to dry the skillet. Nor did he interrupt as she went on.

"Cal Drinker, in Ontonagon—he's Kate's family doctor and a friend of Bill Cabot's—Cal says if it hadn't been for Kate, John Morgan would've had to split up the children between his brother down in Grand Rapids and some cousins back east. But they got a neighbor to take care of the baby and the next youngest during the day, when Kate was in school. The rest of the time, that girl kept things running smooth as clockwork. Cal says they'd never have made it without her." Pausing, a wet dishrag poised over the stove top she was about to wipe, Ruth murmured, "I hope things around here don't fall apart without her."

Then she gave Sam an anxious smile. "I imagine she's just sprained her ankle some, don't you think?"

Sam's stomach was churning. "I'm no doctor, Mrs. D., but I'd guess it's broken."

"Oh, dear." Ruth dropped her rag on the stove and turned to face him. "I should call Bill Cabot. Kate said not to, but—"

"I don't think one night's going to make much difference," Sam assured her. "And Katie said she couldn't face riding to the hospital for an X ray tonight. She's had a pretty rough day."

With her brow wrinkled, Ruth shook her head. "This could be bad. Laura Graff is due in a couple of weeks, and if this baby comes as fast as the first one did, Kate will end up delivering it. Of course, could be somebody besides Laura, too, since Bill and Kate are the only ones delivering babies in a hundred square miles, outside the hospitals."

Ruth's frown deepened. "I know Kate's been keeping an eye on a few folks who live outside of town. Lord knows what'll happen if there's an accident at one of the campgrounds. Kate and Bill between them have picked up the pieces since they took the ambulances away—filling in till the ambulance gets here. But Bill isn't up to traipsing over the countryside—arthritis, you know—though, knowing him, he'll try to do it, anyway."

So much for problems and solutions, Sam thought. Taking a step backward toward the doorway, thinking he'd better get out while he still could, he began, "Well, listen, Mrs. D.—"

"Goodness!" Ruth shuddered. "The more I think about it, the worse it looks. I guess you don't know until you face losing someone how indispensable they've become. And Kate's gotten to be Bill Cabot's right hand—or I guess I should say his right knee, since it's his knee that gives him the most trouble."

"Yes, well . . ." Sam cast a glance toward the doorway. "I'm sure you'll all work out something. But, listen, I'm a little worried about getting back out that road in the dark. I think I'd better get going."

"Now, hold on." Ruth's anxious frown disappeared instantly, replaced by a no-nonsense look. "There's no point in you leaving town without the things you're going to need in that cabin. Kate told me you were asking about groceries, and Ed said to send you over to the store. He'll meet you there.''

Sam's heart was pounding as he thanked Ruth and said goodbye, leaving her in the kitchen to put away the dishes. He strode through the dining room, grabbing his jacket as he passed the chair where he'd left it, managing to get three feet from the front door. Then, most unwillingly, he came to a stop.

He stared at the door, his forehead and upper lip beaded with sweat, his insides twisted in knots. Move it! his mind screamed. Get out of here—now! But he couldn't move, and he had that feeling in his gut he wasn't going to make it.

Dammit to hell! Why did it have to be her? Why, of all people who could have been hurt in that storm, did the one he'd found have to be the town nurse? The one person nobody could do without. Pregnant women who might not make it to the hospital. People hurt in the woods. Accidents happening where the old doctor might not be able to get to them. Yes, people needed Katie, and it was going to make their lives miserable—if not downright dangerous—if she couldn't do her job.

And what about Katie? What about the woman who'd taken over raising her brothers and sisters when her mother died? She'd gone on to make a career of taking care of people, but who was taking care of *her*? How was he supposed to turn away from her? How was he supposed to fight this thing inside him that urged him to give her back some of what she gave to others?

How could he justify walking out that door?

The answer came in hard, absolute terms: He couldn't.

"Ah, hell," Sam muttered, rubbing his face, then the back of his neck. What was one lost battle, anyway? God knows, there'd be others—others he'd have a better chance of winning than this one.

Whirling away from the door, he walked purposefully toward Kate's room. When he got to the doorway, he paused, and the tortured expression on his hard features softened as his gaze swept over her, lying there on the bed.

Her eyes were closed, and her hair lay fanned across the pillow. He'd never in his life seen such hair—a curtain of toasty golden-brown ripples—and it framed a face that maybe wasn't beautiful but couldn't have been any sweeter or more honest. A small, turned-up nose and soft, rosy lips and a stubborn little chin that all went so well with her warm brown eyes. Her bathrobe was long and pink; it tied at her waist and, above the belt, lay open far enough to reveal little rows of lace across the top of her white flannel nightgown. The nightgown had pink flowers on it, too, and Sam couldn't remember any woman he'd known wearing a nightgown like that. But then, he hadn't known many women like Katie. And it fit her just right.

As he stood there, his eyes taking in the lush, womanly curves of her thighs and breasts, the torment and the gutwrenching ambivalence drained out of him. The decision was made. He wasn't going to fight it anymore. And, oddly enough, looking at Katie, he didn't feel like he'd lost a battle. No, for once, this just might end up being a pleasure.

Half awake, Kate sensed someone in the room with her. As exhausted as she was and as groggy as the pill had made her, the pain wouldn't let her fall asleep. She opened her eyes but couldn't quite focus on Sam, standing at the foot of her bed. He looked so tall, she thought, in her low-ceilinged house.

"I thought you'd lef'," she said, slurring the edges of the words.

"Not yet," he replied. "You're supposed to be asleep."

She yawned. "I am. Mostly...Sam?"

"Hmm?"

"T'morrow...when you go t' Cressie and Steve's t' get your key..."

"Yes?"

"Would y' tell Cressie I won' be out? She'll have t' bring the baby in t' see Doc."

"They have a sick kid?"

"Uh-uh. A new one. She's due for a three-week check."

"I'll tell her. Listen, Katie, about tomorrow...I'll run you down to Ironwood."

She looked at him, blinking in surprise. "Sam, you don' have t' do that. There's lots of people—"

"I'll take you to the hospital."

"But—"

"No buts."

"Okay, but—" Her breath caught, then left her in a sigh. "Well, I jus' don' know what t' say."

That bought her a crooked smile. "Try, 'Thanks, Sam. I appreciate it.'"

There was no arguing with this man. He was more bullheaded than she was. With a tiny smile, Kate repeated his words.

"That wasn't too hard, was it?" he said softly.

She yawned again. "Sam, you've been awful nice. I really do 'preciate it."

"You're a nice lady. You don't deserve to hurt."

Something in his tone caught her attention, something very determined, but her mind was too foggy to figure it out. It was getting harder and harder to keep her eyes open.

She let them drift closed on a whisper. "I guess it was my turn."

"Is that how it works? We all take turns hurting?"

"Seems like it...sometimes. Other times, seems like there're people who get..." She trailed off, half asleep, then finished, "...more than their share."

"Which is why it's a good thing there are people like you around to take care of them."

"Sam, you really are a nice man... Don' know why you preten' t' be so... What are you doing?"

"Just looking. Relax."

He'd lifted the ice pack from her ankle, and she felt the brush of warmth as he laid his hand on her swollen, chilled flesh.

"I won't hurt you, Katie."

"Doesn't hurt. Feels good. Kinda funny, though."

"You've had an ice pack on."

"Hmm. Makes your hand feel...hot."

Very hot. So hot, it almost burned. But it was a pleasant sensation, completely absorbing and not at all painful, and she sighed at the luxury of being touched with such tenderness. Who would have thought, she mused, that a man like Sam Reese could be so tender? Who would have thought, after all the hard things he'd said, that he could express—or even feel—such compassion? Oh, but he did feel it, and he somehow made her feel it, too, in the simple touch of his big, strong hand.

It seemed an eternity passed. Surely she'd slipped off to sleep and was dreaming. It was a lovely dream, filled with scenes of happy times, childhood memories she hadn't thought of in years. Sunshine on Lake Superior. Walks in the red-gold world of an autumn woods. Her mother's laughter.

The best memories, though, were the babies. Images of her much younger self holding her brother Josh, when he was an infant, sent a wave of pleasure wafting through her. But there were other babies, too—tiny little strangers, still wet and naked from their mothers' bodies—and one after the other, the memories of helping those new beings along their journey into the world flashed through her mind. What a gift it was to hold those precious pink bodies. What a humbling, thrilling moment when they slipped, helpless and wrinkled, into her hands. The touch. The flesh-on-flesh contact. She felt it even then, along with the awe and reverence that went with knowing she was the first—the very first person to see, to know, to feel the new life.

She clung to those memories. Those most treasured memories. They were what she lived for—what she couldn't do without. They were also what broke her heart.

Kate sighed, vaguely aware that she wasn't dreaming anymore and that Sam had taken his hand away and replaced the ice pack. And she sighed again, sorry that he'd stopped touching her, yet filled with the oddest floating sense of well-being.

"You go to sleep, Katie," he said. "I'll see you in the morning."

"Okay. But you won't like me any better."

"What kind of nonsense is that?"

"T'morrow. I'll be a wreck again. You won't like me any better than t'day."

"Honey, I liked you fine today."

"Didn't. Made you mad."

"It wasn't you, Katie. I told you that. Now go to sleep."

She had little choice. With a final, shuddering sigh, Kate gave up her last hold on awareness. Not, however, before one final irrelevancy had crept through her mind.

He called her Katie. She'd never liked the name, but she hadn't bothered to correct him. Of course, he'd call her anything he wanted, regardless of what she said. Still, there was something about the way he said *Katie* that made her inclined not to dislike it. He made it sound different. He made it sound . . . special.

Chapter Three

Doc, I promise you, I haven't lost my mind. Last night that ankle looked like a watermelon." Kate sat on the edge of her small kitchen table, her left leg extended below the hem of her denim skirt as she offered the ankle for inspection.

Bill Cabot's pale blue eyes studied the appendage through the thick lenses of his black-framed glasses. Clucking his tongue, he shook his head. "Well, Kate, what can an old man say? Ruth Davenport called at seven and sent me scampering over here before I'd even drunk my coffee. She had me believing gangrene had set in, and here I find you bouncing around as if to say the woman's gone senile on us."

"I don't know about gangrene," Kate said, chuckling, "but it's true, I couldn't have walked last night if my life had depended on it. Doesn't make a bit of sense."

Wiggling her bare toes, she flexed the ankle in every direction, but it didn't hurt any more than it had an hour ago—which was not at all. She'd woken up and jumped out of bed before she'd even remembered the injury. Yet the swelling was gone. Her skin was a healthy pink. There wasn't a bruise anywhere in sight, and if she hadn't found yesterday's disheveled clothes neatly arranged over the shower rod this morning—including the ruined jeans—she'd have wondered if she'd dreamed the entire incident. Somehow her ankle had recovered overnight, and while she found it awful darned strange, Kate wasn't one to look a gift horse in the mouth.

"I think you were looking for an excuse to get a whole, uninterrupted night's sleep."

"Hmph!" Kate hopped off the table, tugging down her plum-colored knit top as she picked up her empty coffee mug to carry it to the sink. "I'll remember that the next time you ask me to take your calls because your knee's bothering you."

"You'd doubt my word about my knee? Shame on you, girl!"

"Besides," she scoffed, "I haven't got a reason to complain about night calls. There aren't that many."

"You wouldn't complain if there were. Which brings me to something I've been meaning to discuss with you." Setting his coffee mug down on the bright yellow place mat, Doc turned in his chair to wag a finger at her. "You're a workaholic, Kathleen Morgan. Worse than I am. And that's saying a lot."

Kate put the milk in the refrigerator as she replied. "I'm no such thing. I just like what I do."

"Ruth told me you fixed dinner for Sarah Winfield three nights last week."

"Gretchen Brown and I agreed to help Sarah out in the evenings, but Tommy came down with chicken pox last Monday, and Gretchen couldn't do it."

"And yesterday morning you went grocery shopping for Laura Graff."

"For pity's sake! Laura's nine days from her due date. David can't take off work to shop, and Mr. D.'s closed by the time he gets off. I was just being neighborly."

"Maybe. And maybe you need something to occupy your time besides taking care of your neighbors."

Kate groaned, swiping toast crumbs into the sink with a sponge. "Doc, please, let's not start that again. Tell me how your talk went with the supply house. I used the last disposable glove yesterday, and I'm almost out of Ringer's lactate. Are we going to get our order soon or not?"

"Don't change the subject." Doc arched one bushy eyebrow. "You aren't seeing Scott Gibson anymore, are you?"

Kate had known the question was coming, and she braced herself for the worst as she answered. "No."

"Good."

She gave Doc a startled look.

"Scott's a good sort," Doc explained with a sigh. "But he's got no grit—no *spirit*. He'd never have known what to do with a willful woman like you. You need a man who knows his own mind."

Kate couldn't resist a smile. "Scott knew he liked my apple pie."

"Hmph. And what did *you* get out of it?"

"Well . . ."

"I'll tell you what you got." Doc tapped his fingertips on the tabletop for emphasis. "Every other Friday night at eight-thirty, Scott walked out your door—after you'd fed him supper—and you got a buss on the cheek like the ones my brothers and I gave Aunt Letty when we left her house after Sunday dinner."

"Doc!"

"Don't look at me like that, girl. You know Sarah Winfield sits over there watching everything that goes on in this town—not that there's much to see. I can't imagine Scott's notion of a good-night kiss made Sarah any dizzier than it made you."

Kate gasped, but her indignation soon turned to mild reproach—which then became a soft chuckle. "Doc, you're terrible."

He smiled, a little too smugly. "That's what my Lydia used to say. But I never did think it made sense to waste time beating around the bush. And you don't have time to waste. Not unless you're planning to settle for lukewarm pecks on the cheek for the rest of your life."

Kate wasn't *planning* to settle for a passionless existence, but sometimes she was afraid that was how it was going to work out—pecks on the cheek or no kisses at all. Still, if she'd really resigned herself to that, she'd have been married long ago. Scott wasn't the only man she'd known who'd liked her apple pie. The problem was, she didn't want to marry someone who was more interested in her cooking—and in how well she listened to him talk about himself—than he was in her.

All her life she'd attracted men who wanted her to tell them what to do, and when and how to do it. They wanted her to be nice, not sexy. Gentle, not passionate. And, honestly, how passionate could a woman feel about somebody she constantly had to reassure? Her girlfriends in college had told her it was her own fault men looked at her not as a lover but as a shoulder to cry on. She had to "assert her sexuality," they said. Learn to flirt and be more mysterious. Stop being so straightforward—and straitlaced. Well, so, she'd tried. And the results had been disastrous.

At thirty-one, Kate was a lot less unsure of herself than she'd been at twenty-four. She realized her mistake with Rick Sommers had been one of naïveté, poor character judgment and confusion over the difference between passion and love. She also knew that just because she'd made one mistake didn't mean she had to make another one. But there were moments...moments when she thought of the men she'd dated since Rick, moments when she thought about how lonely it could be sometimes—how many mornings she made breakfast, wishing there were someone to share it with, how many winter nights she lay in bed, watching the snow pile up against the windows, wishing there were a warm, strong body lying next to hers... At moments like those, she wondered if maybe the pain she lived with as a result of that one mistake had made her too careful. Too wary.

Maybe she was too picky, too. But then, what good would it do to marry a man like Scott Gibson? She wouldn't be alone anymore, but she'd be more lonely than ever.

"Well, I've had my say on the subject. For now, anyway."

Kate breathed a sigh of relief when Doc levered himself out of the kitchen chair, hitching his trousers over his belly and picking up his black bag.

"I've got to go fight with that smart-mouthed clerk at the supply house," he said. "Tell him to get that order out here before we have to start tearing sheets for bandages. And Bert Andrews is coming in at nine. Are you going to see that new niece of yours?"

Kate uttered a bewildered laugh. "Last night I didn't think so, but I guess I am after all."

"How was the Nielsen girl yesterday? You got there, didn't you?"

"Yes . . ."

Doc's thick gray eyebrows drew together. "Something wrong?"

"I'm afraid Lynn's doing too much," Kate admitted, following him as he headed for the front door. "She's nineteen years old, she's never been sick a day in her life, and she's having a hard time accepting the idea that pregnant ladies get tired quicker."

"Hmph." Doc's comment was to the point. "She ought to get out of that ramshackle hole she's living in, with no phone and no decent road, until this baby's born."

"That would be best. But she feels she has to help Erik. My guess is, if he doesn't get the camp in shape to open by deer season, they'll lose it. And since he's doing all the work, it's slow going."

Reaching the front door, Doc shook his head. "The place is a mess. Has been since Andy Tibbs abandoned it. It takes a pair of foolish kids to think they can make something of it again."

Kate sighed. "Lynn and Erik are just young and naïve. They've got to prove everything to themselves, the hard way."

"Well, we all know how that goes," Doc muttered as he turned the doorknob. "Maybe you should have her—"

Standing back, he opened the door wide. "Well, what's this? Kate, you've got a visitor."

"Sam!" Kate's cheeks dimpled as her lips curved into a welcoming smile. "Good morning."

Sam hesitated on seeing her, gave her a quick once over, then scowled as he mounted the last step to amble across the wide front porch.

"Katie, what are you doing on your feet? I expected to find you in bed, groaning."

"Me, too." Her smile deepened as she held open the screen door and motioned him inside. When he brushed past her and she caught that straight, leather-and-soap male scent, the butterflies set to fluttering in her stomach. They added a hint of nervousness to her voice as she said, "Sam Reese, this is Dr. Bill Cabot. Sam's the man I told you brought me home last night, Doc."

"The man who *carried* you home," Sam corrected, his eyes still traveling over her as he shook the older man's hand. "Good morning, sir. Katie, what the hell are you doing standing on that ankle? Trying to ruin it for life?"

"It's all—"

"Doc, last night this woman had an ankle you'd have thought was—"

"Sam, it's all right!" Kate put a hand on his arm, and his gaze shot down to meet hers.

"Look," she said, letting go of him to walk halfway across the room. With a whirl on her toes that made her calf-length skirt ripple out from its gathered yoke and her braid wrap around her shoulders, she turned to meet his stunned look with a grin. "My ankle's fine. No swelling. No pain."

His eyes narrowed. "Come on."

"Really." She nodded. "But I'm glad you're here to tell Doc I'm not crazy. He thinks I made the whole thing up."

Suspicion was etched into every harsh angle of Sam's expression. "I don't get it. That ankle was a mess. I saw it myself. At least... Well, hell, who am I to say?"

With a final look at Kate's bare feet as she walked toward him, he shook his head. "Sir, Katie's not making anything up. I came to take her for an X-ray. I thought she should go last night, but she was set on waiting."

"I'm not doubting you, Sam," Doc told him. "And Kate would be the last person I'd expect to hear crying wolf. But joints are funny things. I've been prepared to put a cast on more than one ankle I was sure was broken, only to find it wasn't. Just count your blessings—you don't have to make the trip to Ironwood this morning."

"Thank goodness!" Kate exclaimed, then immediately felt a pang of disappointment when she realized that meant she wouldn't be spending the morning with Sam.

In the clear light of day, without pain blurring her vision, it was impossible to ignore the charged, intensely male energy he transmitted or to deny how much he stirred her senses. Nor could she keep from noticing how well his jeans hugged his long legs and stretched across his narrow hips. His jacket was unzipped to reveal a dark T-shirt molded to his chest, and as her gaze skimmed over him, the memory of that chest, with its strangely alluring mixture of tanned flesh, muscle, crisp hair, and scars brought a flush to her cheeks.

At the same time, another memory intruded—Doc saying Scott Gibson's kisses hadn't made her dizzy. No, Scott hadn't made her dizzy. But Sam Reese could. If he wanted to. If she let him.

She was being a complete fool, Kate knew, even considering such a thing, because she wasn't about to get involved with an out-of-work stranger who wouldn't even say how long he'd be in the area. Still, she couldn't keep the disappointment from coloring her tone as she said, "I'm sorry, Sam. But it looks like you came in this morning for nothing."

"Oh, maybe not," Sam drawled, and the long, slow inspection his eyes made of her said he had a good idea what was going through her mind. "As long as I'm here, you can show me the way to your sister and brother-in-law's. I still have to pick up my key."

Flustered by his frankly approving look and the unexpected surge of electricity passing between them, Kate lowered her gaze. "Well, sure. That'll be fine."

Doc cleared his throat and took a step toward the door. "If I don't get over to the office, Bert'll have the place reeking with cigar smoke just to spite me. I'll let you know how I make out with supply house, Kate." Stopping on the top porch step, he turned to look at Sam, standing beside Kate in the doorway.

"You going to be doing much fishing while you're here?" he asked.

"Some, maybe," Sam replied.

"Hmm." Doc studied him. "You got business in the area?"

"No, sir."

"No? Hmm. Well, then—"

"Sam's on vacation," Kate said, responding to a sudden impulse to protect him from questions she knew he didn't want to answer. Hugging one side of the door frame with both hands and leaning forward to give Doc a meaningful look, she added, "And he doesn't need busybodies like you and me spoiling it with a bunch of questions. So why don't you go nag Bert Andrews to give up his cigars, and tell that supply clerk to get our order here, like he promised three weeks ago, and let me get to work. I've got a million things to do."

Doc frowned, then started down the steps. "You watch out for this girl, Sam," he tossed over his shoulder. "She's a bossy one."

"Oh, you—" Kate began, but her affectionate scolding was cut off by Sam's earthy chuckle.

"Don't worry," he called after Doc. "Katie already knows how poor I am at taking orders." Then, with a slight pause, his voice dropped low to finish. "Then again, I can think of some things I wouldn't mind hearing her say she wanted me to do. . . . No, I wouldn't mind at all."

His meaning was unmistakable, and Kate's cheeks burned as she stared, unseeing, at the empty front walk. Dear Lord, no man had ever made her such an obvious proposition.

And on such short acquaintance! It was unnerving—and a little frightening. It was also wildly exciting. But for a woman who was used to thinking she inspired men's appetites, not their passion, it was mostly confusing.

Kate felt Sam's gaze upon her. She tried not to look at him as she turned, mumbling something about getting her shoes so they could leave. But her eyes skittered upward briefly, and then she was trapped, unable to look away from or to deny the hot message his clear gray eyes conveyed.

The rules had changed. Yesterday was a bad dream. Today she was at no disadvantage that would protect her from having to deal with this. He wanted her, and if she didn't want him, she was going to have to tell him so directly. But with her knees feeling so rubbery and a flush of sensual awareness curling through her, Kate couldn't utter a word.

"Get your shoes, Katie, and let's go," he said softly. "Ed Davenport tells me they're expecting another storm tonight, and I've got a window to fix."

Chapter Four

Kate's sister Cressie lived with her husband, Steve, in an old farmhouse three miles east of Bourner's Crossing. Kate spent the short ride telling Sam how Cressie had met Steve when he'd flown seaplanes on Lake Superior, using her father's marina as a port of call for his fishermen clientele. For various reasons, the main one being Cressie's fear of flying, Steve had sold his two planes and taken a job with the National Forest Service. The money from the sale bought the newlyweds two houses—a dilapidated farmhouse and a hunter's cabin—and they'd made enough improvements to live in the cabin for a year while the farmhouse was being renovated.

"Seems like a damn shame," Sam commented, pulling to a stop in the Fourniers' side yard.

"What does?" Kate asked.

"That a man would give up his planes for a two-room cabin and a rundown farm."

Kate looked at him askance. "I don't think that's quite the way Steve saw it. Besides, he never really gave up planes.

At least, not to Cressie's satisfaction.'' Climbing out of the Jeep, she reached into the back for her knapsack, then stopped, her eyebrows rising at the sound of Sam's muttered oath.

He was standing on the other side of the Jeep, staring toward the field beside the red barn, where a trim, single-engine airplane basked in the morning sunshine.

Kate's knowledge of planes could be stated in one sentence—they went up, and they came down—yet she knew there was something special about this particular old military plane decked out in its camouflage paint with yellow tail and wing tips.

"I think it's called a T-34 Mentor," she said.

Sam replied with an affirmative grunt. "Right, but what's it doing in the middle of nowhere? There can't be more than a couple hundred of them in civilian hands."

"Steve bought it at an auction," she explained. "He's spent the past year taking it apart and putting it back together, with a bigger engine and bigger fuel tanks and all sorts of updated instruments that cost a fortune. The plan was to make money selling it, but when he finished it last month, he said he wanted to fly it in air shows. Cressie went through the roof."

Still looking at the plane, Sam shook his head slowly. "If he's done as good a job on the inside as he has on the outside, that plane's worth a bundle."

"Steve's had offers," Kate admitted. "In fact, I think he's considering one. Since he took a part-time job at Gibson's Garage, and since they've got a new baby, he doesn't have much time to fly."

Watching Sam's back, Kate saw his shoulders rise and fall in a deep breath. Then, abruptly, he turned away, walking around the front of the Jeep to take Kate's knapsack from her.

"I should warn you about Francis," Kate said, as they headed toward the front of the house.

Sam glanced down at her. "Francis who?"

"Cressie and Steve's two-year-old. He's deaf, and Cressie's a little—"

"Deaf?" Sam stopped in his tracks.

"Yes, and Cressie's sensitive about it, so—"

"What happened to him?"

Kate paused briefly to let him catch up; then, casting a glance toward the tall porch windows of the white frame house, she spoke quietly. "About eight months ago he had a viral infection. It didn't seem like anything too unusual—just a bad stomach thing—but it left him hearing-impaired."

Sam's hand shot out to stop her when she started up the front steps. "Can't they fix it?"

"Nerve deafness is permanent," she answered, her voice heavy with regret. "There isn't a specialist in the world who could do anything about it." She started up the steps again, whispering over her shoulder, "Cressie gets nervous sometimes, in front of strangers, so I thought I ought to warn you. Just in case."

A young woman with short brown hair and brown eyes that matched Kate's met them at the front door. Cressie had been expecting them, but not together, and Kate's explanation of the day before led to Sam's apology for the broken window and his assurance that it would be fixed that afternoon. Cressie wasn't worried about the window; she was too upset over Kate's being hurt, and she showered Sam with gratitude as she ushered them into the living room and gave him his key.

They stood talking in the large, toy-cluttered room until a small, rosy-cheeked face appeared around the edge of the doorway to the foyer. Kate saw Francis first, and she opened her arms to him with a smile as he came running toward her.

Scooping him up, she planted a kiss on the top of his curly blond head. "How's my sweetheart?" she asked, chuckling. "And how are you and your new sister getting along?"

"Not too well, I'm afraid," Cressie answered, her eyes darting nervously from the little boy to Sam.

Kate noted Cressie's discomfort but decided the best plan was to ignore it. "Oh? How come?" she asked.

"He doesn't understand why I can't just put April down whenever he wants me to do something for him. And it's so frustrating, not being able to explain it to him. I suppose I should try, but I just don't know how, or what good it would do, when he can't—''

"Has he held her yet?" Kate asked.

Cressie's expression was horrified. "Oh, no! I mean, I don't think he should." Hesitantly, she added, "Do you?"

"Sure," Kate replied easily. "He'll need help, of course. But I'm sure he'd be tickled to hold her. It would make him feel important—like you trusted him."

"Well..." Cressie looked at Francis doubtfully as he snuggled in Kate's arms. "I guess if you think so..."

"So, are you ready to be a big brother?" Kate mused as Francis examined the thick braid hanging over her shoulder. "When you're a little older, I'll explain the pros and cons of being the oldest to you—except you'll probably have them all figured out on your own. Won't you, my smart little friend?"

She put a finger under Francis's chin to lift his face to her. He looked at her intently for a moment, then placed one stubby finger on her left cheek where her dimple lay hidden. It was a game they'd played before, and Kate grinned in compliance with his request. The dimple magically appeared, and Francis made a pleased sound as he touched the small indentation.

"Francis." Kate spoke slowly, setting him down so she could "sign" the words. She'd been teaching herself to sign and was pleased that Cressie and Steve were, too. "This is Sam," she told Francis, indicating the man standing beside her. "He's a friend of mine."

Francis's gaze followed Kate's gesture, and he promptly gave Sam a wary scowl. When Kate looked up, she understood why. Sam, who had been silent since Francis had run into the room, was scowling at Francis just as warily. Kate stared at him in disbelief. Why on earth would he frown like that at a child? How insensitive could he be?

But Sam *wasn't* insensitive. And as though she'd willed him to shape up and prove it, his piercing look softened. Slowly, with a sparkle creeping into his prismlike eyes, he gave Francis a broad smile.

"Hi, buddy."

The little boy hesitated, then smiled back. And an instant later he let out a sound that, in spite of its harsh, unmodulated tone, couldn't have been anything but a laugh.

The sound tugged at Kate's heart. Despite Cressie's overprotectiveness, Francis was an especially friendly child.

"He doesn't talk," Cressie explained to Sam. "He knew a few words when he was one, but then he caught this terrible virus and—"

"I told Sam already," Kate announced gently. "Cressie, where's April? I should see her soon, because Sam wants to fix that window before it rains tonight."

"She's upstairs in her crib," Cressie replied. "Let me bring her down."

Kate shook her head, smiling. "Why don't we both go on up, and I'll examine her where she is."

"All right, but let me put Francis in his room."

When Cressie stepped forward to pick up her son, Kate put a hand on top of his head, saying, "Maybe we can persuade Francis to keep Sam company."

"Oh, no, Sam won't want to—"

"What do you say, Sam?"

His expression said he thought she'd lost her mind. His features were rigid with shock, and if she hadn't known better, she'd have said he was scared. Scared of a little boy? Sam?

"You and Francis will be all right while I examine the baby, won't you? It'll only be about fifteen or twenty minutes."

Sam's lips drew into a straight line, and Kate saw his throat move as he swallowed.

"Sure," he rasped. "Sure, we'll be fine. Won't we, buddy?"

"Oh, Kate, I don't know...."

Kate grabbed the advantage while she could, bending to explain to Francis in both words and signs, "Sam wants to see your blocks. Will you show them to him?"

Then, pointing toward a pile of wooden blocks, she grabbed Sam's hand and pulled him in that direction, her eyes never leaving Francis. The child followed with a bright-eyed look—he adored his blocks—plopped down on the floor and tilted his head way back to look at Sam.

"Have fun!" Kate dropped Sam's hand and flashed him a smile as she turned and stepped lightly toward the foyer. When she reached Cressie, hovering in the center of the room, she linked an arm through her sister's elbow to coax her along. "Come on, Cress, let's see that little girl of yours."

Kate didn't look back, but as she followed Cressie up the stairs she prayed like mad that her instincts about her sexy but puzzling stranger weren't wrong.

It was another lost battle. Sam had known it the minute he laid eyes on Francis. Kids got to him every time. He didn't mind that so much—kids got to everybody, didn't they?—but it was starting to feel like he'd jumped out of the frying pan into the fire. He'd come up here to get away from all this!

An instant later, his mouth slanted in a dry smile. It served him right, getting the hots for a nurse. He could have been holed up in the woods right now instead of sitting in the middle of a pile of blocks. It occurred to him there might be some sort of weird irony to this scene. Like someone—or Someone—was telling him that, if he thought he could go hide in the woods and forget what he was supposed to be doing, he had another think coming. That wasn't part of the deal.

But, dammit, he wasn't trying to squirrel his way out of anything; he was just trying to survive! And, by God, he could *still* hide in the woods. He wanted anonymity? Ha! With Francis, it was guaranteed. The kid couldn't talk.

Sitting cross-legged on the floor opposite the round-faced, blue-eyed child, Sam picked up a block and placed it atop the tower Francis had constructed. The toddler looked at him, his blond lashes and curly hair shining in the sunshine coming through the window.

Suddenly, with a whack of his chubby hand, Francis sent the block tower flying, an act accompanied by excited, incomprehensible chatter. He grinned broadly at Sam, who grinned back in approval. And together they began constructing the tower again. They built it two more times, each time with Francis taking great pleasure in destroying it, before Sam decided he'd established what they called rapport with the child.

He began looking for a way to make his next move. But before he'd figured it out, Francis scrambled to his sneaker-clad feet and toddled over to the bookshelf beside the couch. Yanking a book from it, he toddled back to climb into Sam's lap, perching himself sideways on one muscled thigh so he could open the book across his own small lap and still look up at Sam.

Sam blinked, thoroughly disarmed, a flash of awkwardness making him uncertain. But then, while he was wondering what to do with his arms, a strange, warm feeling stole over him, the child's boldness and trust taking a chunk out of the wall he'd spent years constructing around himself. It felt good having Francis's sturdy little body close to his. Letting instinct take over, he put an arm around the small, straight back. Francis promptly moved closer, sliding his diapered bottom higher up Sam's thigh. Sam tucked him closer. And when Francis craned his neck to look up at him, he smiled, lifting his hand to ruffle the child's blond hair.

It was as easy as that. Sam nearly laughed, thinking this was going to be a piece of cake.

Francis looked at the book, pointing to something he liked. Sam nodded, turning pages slowly with one hand, all the while stroking the silky locks on the small head, his fingers tangling gently in the curls, tracing them as they curved around the child's right ear, resting lightly there ... lingering. . . .

Lingering as the sunshine poured through the lacy-curtained windows to warm the air, to warm the pages of the book upon which it fell, to warm the golden curls on a little boy's head and the flesh of a man's strong, gentle hand . . .

* * *

Kate pronounced her new niece healthy and flourishing, then, giving April to Cressie to nurse, packed up her things and went to "check on the boys." Halfway down the stairs, she heard Sam's voice. At first she thought he was reading to Francis—an activity Francis enjoyed if there were pictures to look at. But then she realized Sam was making up the story, and it surprised her not to hear blocks clattering or other impatient sounds indicating Francis was bored with the sound-oriented exercise.

What surprised Kate more, however, was the sense of drama, the feeling, in Sam's gravelly voice. By the time she reached the bottom of the stairs, she herself was caught up in the story, whether or not Francis found it interesting.

"And, you know, Francis, it was a dream come true," Sam said. "Oh, sure, the boy had flown other planes, but *this* was the one everybody said was the greatest revolution in aviation in decades! And it was a beauty. Nothing like anybody had ever seen. A hundred feet wide and only thirty feet long, and shaped like the wings of a huge white bird. Nothing stuck out on it anywhere—no engines, nothing. They'd buried everything inside, so it all sort of blended together in this giant, sweeping curve. And you just knew it was built to punch holes in the sky that hadn't *ever* been punched before..."

Moving to stand by the arched doorway, Kate remained silent, blatantly eavesdropping. She knew Sam would close up instantly if he realized she was listening, and for some reason it seemed very important that she hear this pilot's fairy tale. She was stealing a glimpse of the inner Sam Reese, a glimpse she suspected he rarely gave anyone. In fact, he wasn't giving it to anyone now. Not knowingly. Whom was he speaking to, after all? A deaf child.

Leaning against the wall, Kate closed her eyes, wondering at the openness, the intensity—the joy—in Sam's voice.

"Well, Francis, that boy was pretty excited. But he was smart enough to play it cool, because if he'd acted *too* excited, they'd have thought he wasn't taking the whole thing seriously. And he took it seriously, all right. Wringing out a plane for the first time always gets to you, and the boy knew he'd be testing the creases of a *brand-new* kind of envelope. Nobody knew where the outside of it was or how far it would stretch. So, naturally, the boy was a little nervous—not scared or anything like that, but nervous. But he wasn't about to tell anybody, because he wanted them to think he was . . . well, a man.''

Is that what it took? Kate wondered. You had to be a man to want to do what Sam's fictitious young hero was about to do? It was certainly true that the thought of flying a plane no one had ever flown made *her* stomach knot, but she very much doubted it had to do with gender.

''Well,'' Sam continued, ''the big day came. The boy climbed into the cockpit and started down the runway. And, I tell you, that big white jet went up just as smooth and nice as if it were an angel lifting off for heaven. It was something else, going almost straight up. All that sky, and those piles of white clouds, and above the clouds, nothing but deep blue space . . .''

Sam paused, and Kate heard him sigh.

''The timing was perfect. It was just before dawn, and he was over the water flying at sixty thousand feet. So he rolled off into a dive and leveled at ten thousand feet into an eastward cruise and shot *right* into the sunrise. Well, I tell you, it burst on him all at once, and for a couple of seconds it blinded him. It's not like it is down here, all pink and gold and kind of mellow. Up there it's . . .'' Sam trailed off again, then continued with a soft, nearly wistful inflection. ''Up there is where you get to see the white light. It's so clear. So . . . pure. And I'll tell you a secret, Francis. Once you've seen the sunrise from up there, you almost know what it's like to be looking at the gate to heaven. . . .''

The gate to heaven. Sam painted the picture with clean strokes that lent the image a simple beauty. When he fell silent, Kate thought he must be finished, but then he began again, this time on a quiet, strangely solemn note.

''But, of course, the boy didn't know anything about heaven. He just knew he wanted to fly that plane forever. He hated the thought of coming down because . . . well, he was kind of alone, you see. But up there, being alone didn't matter. In fact, it was better that way. He was in charge, and he didn't have to worry about anybody letting him down or making him feel bad. When he was flying, he felt good inside. Happy, and kind of peaceful. The boy wished sometimes that it could be that way down here. But it never was. And so he kept on flying. He flew every chance he got until . . . until the day he died.''

Sam ended abruptly. So abruptly that Kate felt an almost physical pain. It might have been only a fairy tale, but it seemed to her that Sam had instilled in it an intimate view of himself—a view that made her want to cry. Then, however, he spoke in a matter-of-fact, nearly lighthearted tone, and the tightness in her throat gradually lessened.

"Has your dad ever taken you up with him in the Mentor?" he asked Francis. "Maybe not, huh? You're a little young yet. But I'll bet you've got a plane somewhere in this toy box, haven't you? I mean, what decent toy box hasn't got at least one plane in it? Let's see.... Ha! I knew it.''

Hearing the clatter of Sam rummaging through the toy hamper, then his satisfied declaration, Kate smiled.

"A P-51 Mustang,'' Sam announced, sounding positively reverent. "This is one neat little fighter, Francis. A mite slow by today's standards, but back in World War Two it was a real razor blade in a fight. Like this, see? Brrrrr...''

Kate was impressed with the authenticity of Sam's audio effects. She could almost see the plane climbing, banking, diving through the air. But she blinked, then frowned in puzzlement when Francis added his own buzzing drone—a second engine to Sam's single-engine plane.

"Hey, that's the idea,'' Sam said. "Here. You take the controls. Come on, now, there's a German Bf 109 at two o'clock! Go for it! Brrrr...''

How odd, Kate thought. And how disappointing. For a minute it had seemed as if... But no. Francis obviously thought Sam was playing a spitting game, blowing out air and letting his lips vibrate. The child was quick to mimic actions, and in this case the noise simply followed by accident. Yet as Sam continued to vary the pitch of the toy plane's flight, Francis promptly followed Sam's lead, duplicating Sam's noises almost exactly.

Exactly... *Too* exactly.

Wait a minute. He couldn't hear, and yet...

"Look out! Look out! We're hit and leaking fuel! Brr...brr—" Sam choked out a vivid rendition of engine cough.

"Brr...brr—" came the high-pitched voice of the younger pilot in a nearly perfect counterpoint.

Kate swung around the corner into the living room, her heart suddenly racing. Sam was sitting cross-legged on the floor, and Francis, plane in hand, was running around him in circles. Kate's eyes were glued to Francis when Sam spoke.

"Hey, there, Katie. All finished upstairs?"

Kate's gaze flickered to him briefly. Then, seeing that Francis hadn't yet noticed her, she called loudly, "Francis!"

It was as if the child were attached to a rope and she'd jerked it. He nearly fell over trying to stop as he cast his startled, almost frightened gaze around the room. When he saw her, some of the confusion left his features, but he looked as if he might cry, and Kate forced herself to give him a reassuring grin and wave. He looked at her a moment longer, then his expression cleared, and he returned the smile and the wave before taking off with his airplane again.

Kate didn't believe it. Lifting her foot, she slipped off her flat, leather shoe, waiting until Francis's back was turned, then tossed it across the room. It hit the wall and landed with a clatter on the bare floor—and Francis whirled, his startled gaze shooting across the room, searching for the source of... *of the noise.*

Kate's first impulse was to yell for Cressie. Instead she drew a steadying breath and told herself to stay calm. She didn't want to frighten Francis with any more loud noises. The very thought that she *could* frighten him that way was staggering.

Slowly, her gaze shifted to Sam.

"He heard me," she said, her voice weak with shock.

Sam unfolded his lanky form from the floor and strolled toward her, his hands stuck in his back pockets. "We've been having a fine time," he said. "You're right about Francis being one smart kid. He doesn't miss a trick, and—"

"Sam, I said Francis *heard* me! He heard me call him, and he heard my shoe hit the wall! He heard your airplane noises, too, and he imitated them. But how could he?" She shook her head, glancing once more at Francis, who had abandoned the plane and was busy constructing block towers again.

"Well, so?" Sam shrugged. "I know you said he had some problems with his hearing, but—"

"I said he was deaf. Permanently, totally deaf."

"Well, you sure could have fooled me."

"This isn't possible," Kate insisted. "It just isn't!"

"Who says so?"

She shot him a quick look. "Some very good doctors and audiologists say so. There must be a mistake here."

Sam snorted in derision. "Right, and I bet it's the specialists who made it."

"No, you don't understand—"

"Katie, let me tell you something." Crossing his arms, he leaned a shoulder against the door frame and looked at her. "Four days after I crashed that plane, I woke up to find out the right side of my body was more or less wasted. Besides the burns and a concussion, I had a broken back, a crushed leg, a slew of cracked ribs, a punctured lung and a bunch of ripped-up inside parts that were being held together with sutures. They waited until my head was clear, then the neurologist and the orthopedist told me, *if* I made it, I probably wouldn't walk again." In the face of her shock, he smiled, noting calmly, "But they were wrong. So, I'm sorry if it offends you, Katie, but I don't put much stock in what doctors say. I'd be in a wheelchair, looking at life through a cloud of painkillers, if I'd listened to them."

No, she thought, if he'd listened to them, he'd be dead. The Sam Reese she was coming to know wouldn't tolerate such extensive disability. If he hadn't been able to will himself to walk, she suspected he simply would have willed himself to die. As her eyes skimmed over his tall, straight and obviously healthy form, it occurred to her to wonder how on earth he could have recovered, not only so well but so quickly. A year, he had said, and yet . . . Good Lord, yesterday he'd carried her a good quarter of a mile without even flinching!

It seemed impossible. Inconceivable. And yet everyone had heard at least one story of someone who'd defied a bad prognosis to prove the doctors wrong; made-for-TV movies and women's magazines articles about athletes were full of such inspirational tales. "They said he'd never walk again," the stories always began. So, Sam's story wasn't *impossible*. It was only extremely unlikely.

Hearing loss from nerve damage was a different matter.

Kate gave her head a quick shake. "Sam, it's almost too amazing to be true, and I'm really glad you had the persistence not to give up after hearing the worst. But this isn't the same thing. Nerve deafness is a medical fact—not something you can just overcome!"

"Is that so?" Sam looked at Francis. "Well, I guess somebody better check those facts again. But, listen—" his gaze dropped to his watch "—it's getting close to lunchtime, and I have to pick up the glass for that window. Why don't you go tell Cressie the good news, so she can get over being excited—and so you can see to it that Francis gets to hold his sister, which I know you're going to want to do—and we can get out of here sometime before dinner?"

Clearly, Kate thought, his own nearly miraculous recovery had jaded him. He must believe that if he could get better, so could everyone else. Regardless, why was she standing here arguing?

With another quick look at Francis, Kate turned and ran toward the stairs, calling for Cressie.

Chapter Five

A half hour later, when they started to town, Sam settled behind the wheel and let out a sigh. "That baby's a real doll, isn't she?"

With a smile flirting at the corners of her lips, Kate agreed. "She sure is."

"It's hard to believe people are ever that little."

"It is pretty amazing."

"You know, Katie—" he looked at her for a moment "—it was a pleasure seeing you with those kids this morning. You're really good with them."

"You're pretty good yourself," she said, eyeing him thoughtfully. With his jacket discarded, one arm draped over the steering wheel, the other resting loosely on the stick shift, and with a warm breeze whipping through the open Jeep to ruffle his sun-streaked hair, Sam looked young, almost carefree—not so tough and hard. A result of his time with Francis, she figured. It seemed the tough guy was a sucker for kids. And she was rapidly becoming a sucker for tough guys.

"I like kids," Sam told her. "But liking isn't the same as understanding. And you really seem to understand them, if you know what I mean."

"I think so," she replied. "But, heavens, don't compare yourself to me on this score. I've had a lot of practice."

"Yes, Ruth Davenport told me you're the oldest of six."

"That's right."

"Do any of them besides Cressie live around here?"

"No. Dad owns a marina in Ontonagon. My oldest brother, Kyle, is married with two kids, and he works with Dad. Wayne and his wife got transferred four years ago to Vermont by the lumber company he works for. My sister Linda and her husband and daughter live in Chicago. And Joshua is finishing his first year at Western in Kalamazoo."

"That's quite a lineup," Sam remarked. After pausing, he said, "Mrs. D. also told me your mom died when you were a teenager."

"I was twelve."

"And you took care of the crew after that?"

It must be paranoia, Kate thought. Had ten months of listening to Scott Gibson talk about himself made her that suspicious? She couldn't help wondering whether Sam was only filling the silence or if he was genuinely interested in her. It was hard to guess with this man. He could communicate volumes with a look. He could also be as unrevealing as a stone wall.

"You and Mrs. D. must have had quite a talk," she said.

Sam offered a sketchy shrug. "So, is it true? Did you take over when your mom died?"

"I wouldn't put it that way," Kate hedged. "Dad was there as much as he could be, and summers we spent a lot of time with our aunt and uncle in Grand Rapids. But the marina took up most of Dad's time. He couldn't afford to hire a manager. So, with Kyle helping him, it was natural that I'd take care of the house and the other kids."

Sam was silent for a moment. Then he said, "My mom died when I was two. But I didn't have any brothers or sisters. Seems to me yours were pretty damned lucky they had you. Still, it makes me wonder if having to raise them is the reason you haven't got any kids of your own."

Kate started to speak but couldn't. With a few succinct words, Sam had paid her a compliment that meant a great deal, because it came from someone who'd been there. Then, when she was about to tell him how much she appreciated it, he'd plunged a knife into her and twisted.

Sam didn't notice her stricken expression. "I know a guy, another pilot," he said, "who married a woman who was the oldest in a big family like yours, and she told him straight out, before they got married, that she didn't want kids. Said she never wanted to see another diaper. I always thought she was sort of cold anyway, but I could see her point. If you spent your childhood raising one family, why do it all over again?" Sam shook his head. "But you're nothing like her. You're anything but cold, and you like kids. Hell, you even deliver babies for a living. But you're the only one of six kids, besides the college freshman, who isn't married. And you're—what? Twenty-eight, twenty-nine?"

"Thirty-one."

"Yeah? So, I wondered if going through all that with your mom dying left you feeling like you've already done your share of diapering."

Kate couldn't blame Sam for his curiosity. Everybody else was curious, too, about her apparent lack of interest in marriage and a family. But for some reason, it was hard to offer Sam the standard response she offered others. *"Oh, I'm too busy delivering babies to think about having them, and besides, I haven't met a man I want to marry."* It was a lie—all of it. She thought about having babies a lot, especially when she delivered one. And she had wanted to marry Rick Sommers, regardless of how foolish it might have been.

Gazing out the side window of the Jeep, Kate watched the posts of a split-rail fence flash by, as she murmured "Just because I don't have a family doesn't mean I wouldn't like to have one."

Her eyes closed briefly to block out the pain of knowing what might have been. But they snapped open when she felt her hand, lying clenched in her lap, being covered by Sam's.

"Katie, I'm sorry," he said quietly. "I guess I'm the one being too nosy today. I should've kept my mouth shut."

Lowering her gaze to look at his hand resting familiarly on hers, Kate felt the strongest desire to tell Sam the truth. It wouldn't matter if he knew; he wouldn't be here long, and no one would be hurt by his knowing. And it had been so long, such a long time, that she'd carried the secret locked inside her.

Yet voicing it smacked of feeling sorry for herself and crying about something she couldn't change. So, with a flustered wave of her free hand, Kate said, "It's okay. You don't have to be sorry for asking. Everybody asks me the same thing. Maybe I'm a little sensitive about it because of that."

The woods had disappeared, and the houses of Bourner's Crossing greeted them. Sam gave her hand a little squeeze before letting go to pull the Jeep to a stop at Kate's front gate.

"Tell them all to go to hell," he said. "And you can tell me to go to hell, too. But first—" he shifted in his seat to face her "—I'd appreciate it if you'd tell me if there's a town within sixty miles that's got a decent restaurant."

Kate smiled, her good humor restored by his no-nonsense yet sensitive apology and his clever shift of topics. "Sure. This is tourist country, remember. But if you want fancy—" she grimaced "—well, then, you'll have to drive for it."

"It doesn't have to be fancy, as long as the food's good."

"Casey's, in Ontonagon, is my favorite when I want to stuff myself silly on seafood. It's about an hour's drive."

"So, go with me Friday night."

Kate's smile froze on her lips, and her heart jumped to her throat. All morning she'd sensed something like this was coming, but still, he'd caught her off guard. And she had a feeling Sam would always catch her off guard. Which was, after all, one of the things that made him both exciting and a little scary. Swallowing the lump in her throat, she determined that, before this went any further, there were a couple of things she needed to settle between them.

"Sam, I—" Kate looked away from the disturbing heat in his eyes and began again. "I meet a lot of men who come up here for hunting season or to camp or ski. I don't usually go out with them, because I'm not very good at, well, casual acquaintances. So before I answer you—" she lifted her chin slightly and met his gaze "—I guess I'd like to know what your intentions are."

His mouth twitched in amusement at her choice of words. But when he spoke, his tone was absolutely serious. "My intentions, huh? Katie, I'll be real honest. I spent a good part of last night and a lot of this morning thinking about going to bed with you." His eyes drifted downward, lingering over her breasts and thighs. "You are one sexy lady. And if you said, 'Sure, Sam, let's do it,' you can believe I damn well wouldn't argue."

Kate's skin tingled every place Sam's gaze touched, and she knew she was blushing. But she forced her gaze to remain steady as his eyes met hers once more.

"I know that's not about to happen," he continued. "You aren't the kind of woman who'd jump into bed with a man she hardly knew. And I guess I ought to tell you, I'm thirty-eight years old, I've never been married and, in fact, I've never had a relationship with a woman last more than maybe a year."

The news didn't surprise her, but Kate still felt compelled to ask, "Why not?"

The frown that appeared on his brow as he tilted his head was as puzzled as her question had been. "I'm not sure I know why not." Then, his expression clearing, he added, "I just haven't given settling down much thought. And even if I had, I've been working for a man who builds planes that don't look or behave like anybody else's, and my job's been to prove they're better than everybody else's. But most women aren't eager to get attached to a man who tests out the latest experiments of some modern-day Wright brother."

Experiments? As in *untried*? As in the plane in his pilot's fairy tale?

Alarmed curiosity had her murmuring, "I see what you mean." She also saw that flying had been more important to him than anything else that had come along—like a woman. But then, that had been the point of the fairy tale; the only thing that had mattered to the imaginary young pilot was flying. Down here, on the ground, he hadn't been able to make things work. And she began to wonder exactly how much of that fairy tale was indeed true.

"After the crash," Sam continued, "I spent seven months in the hospital. And since then I haven't—"

"You don't have to explain yourself, Sam."

"Well, hell, Katie! Yes, I do!"

Kate jumped at his frustrated outburst.

"You deserve answers to those questions you asked yesterday about what I'm doing here and how long I plan to stay. And all I can tell you is that I've got some things on my mind that I've got to work out, and this seemed like a good place to do it. I don't have any idea how long it's going to take."

They stared at each other, Sam scowling and Kate's brown eyes wide and serious. Then, quietly, Kate said, "I understand."

Gradually, the lines in Sam's forehead smoothed, and his look became strangely sad as he said, "Honey, *I* don't even understand."

Kate felt as if the door was opening a crack, but before she could think of a way to prod him into expanding on that cryptic remark, he sighed heavily.

"What I said yesterday about you being a home-and-family woman—partly what I meant is that you're the kind of woman a man feels he has to make promises to. And the fact is, I can't. I can only tell you that I'm not out to get you in the sack for a one-night stand." His eyes roamed her features. "I'm not out to hurt you, Katie. I want to see you. Anything else is up to you."

Kate tried to pretend she wasn't shocked by any of Sam's frank little speech. But it was hopeless. She knew she was

totally out of her league here, and Sam had as much as said
he, too, realized that. She was certain he was accustomed to
far more experienced—and far less cautious—women than
she. And probably there had been quite a few of them.
Common sense told her she should thank him for his invi-
tation and politely refuse.

Yet something stopped her. Something that looked very
much like uncertainty hiding in the deepest recesses of Sam's
gray eyes. Uncertainty in a man she doubted ever wavered
from his beliefs or goals. A man who scorned fear and
would never, even under the most dreadful circumstances,
admit to pain. Oh, yes, Sam's machismo was real enough.
Yet there was a hint of brittleness, a frayed-around-the-
edges quality, about him that came through the tough-guy
demeanor every so often. It had been there, in his voice, as
he'd talked of the boy who was mostly alone and felt best
when he was flying. It was there now, in his eyes, as he
waited for her answer. And Kate found that scrap of vulnerability immensely appealing. She also found it reassuring. He wasn't really so all-fired sure of himself. And maybe
she wasn't so far out of her league after all.

Besides, she wanted to know the man who talked about
jets racing down a runway like angels lifting off for heaven.

Meeting Sam's gaze directly, Kate said, "I can't go to
Ontonagon Friday night. That's Doc's night to play check-
ers with Cal Drinker in White Pine, and I'm on call. But if
you don't mind spending the evening at my house—" she
offered him a smile "—I'd be glad to fix dinner for us."

Sam's lips curved slowly upward. "That sounds fine."

"Six o'clock?" she suggested.

He nodded. Then, with a glance at his watch, he said,
"Now I've got to get over to the store and pick up the glass
Mr. D. ordered for me. He said it ought to be in by noon."

Kate pushed open the door of the Jeep. "And I've got to
see what Doc found out this morning about our back-
ordered supplies. If they don't come in soon . . . No, don't
bother getting out. I lug this pack around all the time."
Hauling her traveling medical kit out, she added, "Just give
me some ideas about what you'd like to eat on Friday."

When he didn't answer, Kate glanced at him, and it confused her to see him scowling as he stared at his hands, wrapped around the steering wheel. What on earth was wrong now?

"How about spaghetti?" he asked. "Or maybe something with cheese."

"*Something with cheese.*" He said it as though he expected prison rations.

She tried not to laugh. "Are you sure?"

His tone was anything but certain as he grumbled, "Yeah, well . . . I don't like too many kinds of meat, and I wouldn't want you to go to a lot of trouble to fix—"

"That's fine, Sam," Kate put in gently. "And it's no trouble. I'll see you at six on Friday. Now you should go before Mr. D. closes up for lunch."

Kate stood at her front gate, watching as Sam drove up Main Street. Slowly, a bemused smile formed on her lips. What was a woman to think, when a man she'd had pegged for steak and potatoes admitted, nearly blushing, that he'd rather have a spinach pie?

Sam stopped at Davenport's where he picked up two panes of glass, a can of window putty and the tools necessary to do the job, then headed out to the cabin. Since he hadn't felt like settling in the night before, after installing the new windowpanes he unpacked his few belongings and spent some time familiarizing himself with his temporary quarters.

The cabin was spotless and furnished to suit the needs of men who came to hunt the northern woods in the fall—inexpensive but comfortable furniture, braided rugs partially covering the pine floors, and a noticeable lack of fussiness. Overhead, the rough-hewn beams of the rafters were exposed; the walls were paneled in light pine and decorated with prints of Canada geese and loons. An antlered buck's head hung over the door, and a black bear rug separated the dining and sitting areas of the main room.

The tiny bedroom contained two twin beds, which didn't suit Sam's six-foot-two frame, so he moved the nightstand from between them, pushed them together and decided he could live with the makeshift king-size results. There was no phone, but the generator's heat, light and well-water system provided all the amenities he required. He didn't want to talk to anybody, anyway.

No, that wasn't true. He wanted to talk to Katie. He'd have liked it if she'd been there with him, helping put away the groceries he'd bought the night before and teaching him how to use the blasted gas stove, which wasn't anything like the electric one he was used to. She'd have found his efforts at making pancakes funny—though she'd have tried not to laugh.

But she might have smiled.

Oh, that smile. Those luscious, apple-pie dimples. He'd have happily burned the entire batch of pancakes for the pleasure of seeing them. He wanted to touch them—not with his finger, as Francis had done that morning, but with his mouth. Hell, he wanted to touch all of her, with his mouth and his hands and every other part of him. In fact, Sam thought as he slapped the last pancake on top of the six on his plate, Katie turned him on faster and harder than any woman had in a long while. Maybe because he knew he turned her on, too. It was tough not to want a woman who responded so obviously and with such melting honesty every time he looked at her. It was impossible not to wonder how she'd respond if he did more than look.

Sam drowned his pancakes in maple syrup and began digging his way through the stack. As he ate, he thought about how stupid it was to have asked Katie out—and how stupid it would be to spend an evening at her house. He was crazy for starting something with a woman when everything about his life was up in the air. Especially when the woman was the type he was sure would want a commitment, at least vows of love, before she'd even let him kiss her.

He didn't know anything about those kinds of commitments. He knew even less about love; it was an elusive thing other people always seemed to be in some stage of wanting or getting or having. But if he'd ever wanted it, it had been a long time ago, so long that he had no memory of missing it. And it sure wasn't something that had entered into the picture with the women he'd known over the years.

What was he used to, anyway? Women he'd met at Willy's Bar. Divorced friends of his buddies' wives. There had been that cute redhead who worked ground crew at Rutger. And maybe any one of those women could have turned out to be one he'd have stuck with if he'd given himself and them a chance. Some of them had sure dropped hints in that direction. But when a woman started acting like she might be thinking in permanent terms, that had always been his signal it was time to call it quits. He'd told himself it was because he wasn't ready to settle down. But now...well, like a lot of other things, he just didn't know.

He did know he couldn't bring himself even to consider having a hot but meaningless affair with Katie. And he knew why. In light of all the other changes he'd been going through, it fit right in that his taste in women had suddenly taken a drastic turn toward the conservative.

Sam cursed silently—and somewhat guiltily—at the quirk of fate that had ripped the rug out from under him. The day he'd crashed that damn plane, his entire frame of reference had been taken away from him. Maybe he could have handled that, if somebody had seen fit to replace it with something else. But no. He'd been squirming for five months, since he'd gotten out of the hospital and found out just how different things were going to be. He'd tried to go on with his life, but it seemed like, piece by piece, everything he'd been and done was being examined, then tossed out, having been declared worthless. Now it looked as if he was being told that if he wanted to end his long abstinence and get involved with a woman, he'd have to start from scratch.

And Katie Morgan was it. The bottom line. Exactly the kind of woman he didn't know a thing about and had spent all his adult life avoiding. Hell, she could even be a virgin. And wouldn't that just give his conscience something to chew on.

Sam didn't know what he'd do with Katie, how he'd ever fit her into his mixed-up life. But he knew the memories of his past relationships didn't satisfy him anymore. He didn't want another woman who wouldn't care when or if he came or went. He didn't want one who tried to use sex as a way to tie him to her. He didn't want one he had nothing to say to when the sex was over. He didn't want another woman who left him feeling empty.

He wanted Katie. And instinct told him he could have her. All he had to do was keep her from finding out that the man who turned her on was a freak. A medically, scientifically verified freak, who had already altered the course of dozens of people's lives—her own and Francis Fournier's included.

Chapter Six

What did you say that's called?"

"Russian vegetable pie." Kate set the bubbling, golden-crusted dish atop the stove and closed the oven door. Then, pot holders in hand, she picked up the pie and started toward the small dining room, where her grandmother's old pine table was set for two.

Sam, who was leaning casually in her kitchen doorway, didn't budge as he eyed his dinner. "And what exactly is *in* Russian vegetable pie?" he wanted to know.

"Well . . . cabbage and mushrooms and cream cheese and hard-boiled eggs and—"

"Stop." His eyes snapped up to meet hers. "It smells great. Let's leave it at that."

Kate tried—and failed—to hide a grin as she took another step toward the dining room, but when he didn't move to let her through the doorway, she stopped in front of him to give him an expectant look.

"Do that again," he said.

"Do what?"

Sam reached up and touched her cheek, and for an instant Kate couldn't breathe, though she was mortified for reacting so idiotically to such a simple gesture.

"Well?" he said.

"Well what?"

"Where is it?"

She stared at him, eyes wide, lips slightly parted, until suddenly it dawned on her what he was waiting for. Then she blushed a rosy pink. The smile she gave him was a little flustered and a little shy.

Sam's eyes held a look of satisfaction as his finger trailed over her dimple, then traced the line of her jaw. "That's better," he murmured. "Now I can stop feeling guilty."

"Guilty?"

"Yeah. For being jealous of a kid. I've been wanting to do this since I saw Francis do it Wednesday morning."

Well, Kate, here he is—a man who's more interested in you than he is in your cooking. So what are you going to do with him? With her eyes holding his, Kate whispered, "Sam, the dish . . ."

His gaze dropped to the casserole she held, and with a growled, "Sorry," he let his hand fall from her face and moved out of the way.

As they sat down and began to eat, Kate pondered what she might be in for when it came time for Sam to go home. More, she suspected, than a lukewarm peck on the cheek.

"Katie, you know, this is good." Sam's tone was amazed as he stuck another forkful of the steamy concoction into his mouth. "It sure tastes better than it sounds."

"Most food does," she said, chuckling. Then, looking at him from under her eyelashes, she asked, "Would it be too nosy to ask about your family?"

Sam helped himself to a biscuit as he replied. "No, but there's not much to tell. My dad works on an assembly line at the GM plant in Detroit. I've got an aunt—my mother's sister—I haven't seen in about fifteen years. And my father has a brother. I see Uncle Harvey and his wife and kids sometimes at Christmas."

Reaching for the blue Fiestaware pitcher to fill their water glasses, Kate said, "You told me your mother died when you were two. Who took care of you after that?"

"The Happy Days Day Care Center. It was close to the GM plant and cheap, which meant it was mostly full of kids whose parents worked at the factory." He frowned as he examined a piece of hard-boiled egg on his plate. "Katie, what are these little green specks?"

"Dill weed."

"Dill *weed*? Never heard of it. But, hell, you can't argue with success."

"Thanks. Remind me to give you some to take home— you put it on eggs and cucumbers. So, did you like this day-care center?"

"It was okay," he answered. "There was one older lady, Mrs. Montague—we called her Miz Monty. I liked her a lot. But she was only there part-time. Then, after a while, she left. I guess she retired." He tilted his head thoughtfully, remembering. Then, with a shrug, he dismissed the matter.

Kate thought that careless shrug said a lot about how Sam had learned to cope with the harder side of life. Everything was "no big deal." Except, of course, that wasn't true. The picture of the alone and surely the lonely fictitious young pilot had lingered in her mind since Wednesday morning. As Sam continued to relate the bare-bones facts of his life, the picture came into better focus.

He'd grown up in an old apartment building in a rough section of Detroit. His father, Carl Reese, was fair and honest but strict in an old-school sense; things were either right or wrong in Carl's book, and Sam learned early that it was easy to make a mistake—and that the consequences of making one were tough. He'd done okay in school but didn't really like academics, except for math and history, and he wouldn't have bothered with college, but he'd had to have a degree to get the Navy to teach him to fly. So he'd gone to Wayne State, graduating in three years with a degree in math, then straight into Aviation Officers Candidate School.

He'd been in the Navy for a little over seven years, much
of it spent overseas, nearly all of it spent racking up flight
time in fighter jets. And he'd probably have stayed in, he
said, if he hadn't gotten an offer for a job he couldn't turn
down. No, it wasn't the money that had tempted him—it
was the planes he'd be flying. So he'd traded the Navy and
F-14 Tomcats for the Mojave Desert and a strange list of
mostly unheard of experimental aircraft designed by a man
others in the aviation industry considered a renegade. And
it was clear he didn't regret the decision.

He didn't see much of his father; he wrote now and then
but didn't usually expect a reply—his father wasn't big on
communicating. Carl Reese had remarried eight years ago,
and Sam described his stepmother, Susan, as "a real spit-
fire." He smiled as he admitted he'd never have dreamed his
father would tolerate a woman who refused to iron shirts.
But Sam liked Susan and was glad to see his father enjoy-
ing himself; they even had a vacation to Florida planned for
the winter, which surprised Sam, since the farthest Carl had
ever been from Detroit was the U.P.

"Did he come up here to hunt?" Kate asked.

"No." Sam laid his knife and fork across the top edge of
his empty dinner plate with a satisfied sigh. "He brought me
on a couple of fishing trips when I was a kid. I remembered
the place being real pretty, especially in the fall."

"That's my favorite time." Resting her elbows on the table, Kate wrapped her hands around her coffee mug and
gazed wistfully over the top of it. "I had a friend in grade
school whose father ran a seaplane service. He flew people
all over Lake Superior—Isle Royale, Thunder Bay, even into
the Boundary Waters in Minnesota. Once, on my eleventh
birthday, he took Patsy and me for a ride. I'll never forget
it." She glanced at Sam and smiled. "My birthday's in
September, and the birch forests were at peak. All I could
think of, looking down on those trees, was that we were
flying over the Land of Oz, following the yellow brick
road."

Sam's mouth slanted in a crooked grin. "The yellow brick road, huh?"

"Well, it was beautiful."

"I know. I've seen it. I've seen aspen groves in the Rockies, too, from the air. And pine forests covered with snow...and whales migrating south along the Pacific coast..." He looked away, his grin slowly fading, and for an instant his eyes lost their focus, the gray irises turning clear as crystal. An instant later his countenance changed, quickly assuming its usual unrevealing lines.

Shifting his gaze to Kate, he asked, "So is that why you're still up here? You're bent on following the yellow brick road?"

Kate had to fight to swallow her disappointment. Sam had given her another peek at that side of him he kept so carefully guarded—but then he'd snatched it away.

"Well, maybe that's part of it," she said. "I really do love the U. P., no matter what time of year it is."

"You must have gone away to school."

She nodded. "When I was twenty, I went to Ann Arbor and did my bachelor's and first master's degree at the U. of M. Then I went to the School of Midwifery at Georgetown University in Washington, D.C. for my master's degree in nurse midwifery. I was away eight years, total."

"But you came back. Because of your family?"

"Yes," she answered, "and because I don't like living in big cities. And because they need good medical professionals here. I suppose I could have found another isolated spot where I'd be just as useful, but Cal Drinker—he was my family's doctor until he retired, and he helped me through school—he told me about Doc Cabot needing help, and..." She trailed off with a palms-up gesture.

Sam completed the thought for her. "You felt like you owed it to him."

"Partly. Cressie was here, and that made a difference. But I wanted to do it, too." Dropping her gaze, Kate added, "I wanted to...come home."

When she looked up, she found Sam studying her closely.

"In that conversation I had the other night with Mrs. D.," he began, "she said your mom died having a baby. Does that have something to do with your being a midwife?"

Kate drew a quiet, steady breath. "If you mean am I on some kind of crusade to improve obstetrics in the area because of what happened to Mom, no, I'm not. First of all, she didn't die from lack of medical care. She had heart failure during delivery, and there wasn't any reason to suspect ahead of time that it might happen. Besides, I don't really perform that many deliveries—only when there's no way the woman can get to the hospital. I just—" she tried to smile "—I just like babies, that's all. And I like taking care of women who are getting ready to have them. It's such a . . . a happy time."

Sam's gray eyes remained unblinking as he continued to search her features. "You spent a good part of your childhood taking care of people," he said. "And I think most people in your shoes would've been pretty damned resentful. But you're not. And when you were given a choice, you decided to be a nurse and go on taking care of people. You get real pleasure out of it, don't you?"

Kate's lips parted, and a bewildered frown appeared on her brow. "Of course, I do." Shaking her head a little, she added, "Oh, I guess maybe if the reason I had to help my family was somebody's fault, I'd feel resentful. But it wasn't. My mother's dying was just a horrible thing that happened. Dad loved us, and we loved him, and we all did what we could to make things better. As for my being a nurse—" She paused, looking for words that explained what she'd never really thought about consciously. "Sam, I like taking care of people. And I think I'm pretty good at it. And I truly believe a person ought to do what they're good at and what they like doing best."

Sam gave her the strangest look, one that reflected a great deal of respect; but there was something troubled, too, hiding in the depths of his eyes, something she had the most compelling desire to understand.

"Yeah," he said quietly. "A person ought to do what they like and do best. Can't argue with that."

Kate sensed she'd said something very important. Encouraged, she started to ask if that wasn't how he felt about flying. But before she could speak, she heard a noise that made her heart skip a beat.

Sam's head snapped up as she jumped from the table and hurried toward her bedroom. "What's that?" he called.

She tossed an answer over her shoulder. "The local version of an emergency beeper—my citizens' band radio. Sounds like Bob Bradley over at Wanagan Campgrounds."

By the time Kate grabbed the handset from its hook and sat at the small table in front of the CB radio, Sam stood in the doorway behind her, listening.

"Kate! Kate, are you there?"

"I'm here, Bob. What's wrong?" She already had a pencil in one hand poised over a pad of paper, ready to write.

"I've got a bad one for you." Bob's voice was raw as he rushed to explain. "A bear wandered in, and these two guys I've got staying down in section three tried to shoo him out. Well, you know all they did was rile him, and he attacked one of them."

"How bad?" Kate asked quickly.

"Oh, God, Kate—" Bob's voice broke. "He's bleeding like crazy—from his left leg, mostly. His friend's with him, but—"

"How far up the leg?"

"Just above the knee."

"Have you radioed for a medevac?"

"Yes, but I had a hell of a time getting it. They had a big truck wreck down on Route 51, and all the crews are out. Lord knows what they're sending us—or when. I don't know if this guy's going to—"

"Bob, do what you can to stop the bleeding. Keep him warm. Elevate his legs. I'll be there in ten." Kate dropped the radio mike, raced to snatch her jacket out of the closet, and rushed past Sam. "I'm sorry, Sam. I have to go. There's pie in the kitchen. You're welcome to stay and have some."

"You've got a chopper coming?" he asked, grabbing his jacket off the couch to follow her.

"I hope so."

"What's flight time to the trauma center?"

"About forty-five minutes, over to Marquette." Kate pulled her jacket on over her yellow blouse and linen skirt as she ran down her front steps; she'd dressed for Sam, not for work—a mistake, she realized now, but one she'd have to live with.

"Listen," she continued, "you don't have to rush off. It's fine if you—" She stopped with a hand on the door handle of the pickup to give Sam a confused look as he opened the passenger door. "Where are you going?"

"With you," he said, swinging into the front seat.

"But—"

"I'll stay out of your way. Let's go."

Kate wasn't about to waste time arguing. She hopped into the truck and turned the key waiting in the ignition. The wide truck tires sent gravel spraying in all directions as she made a U-turn in the middle of the street, hung a left at the intersection onto Bourner's Mill Road, and tore out of town, headed east. It was eight o'clock, and there was still light left in the sky, but when the road passed into the woods outside town, twilight deepened. In the shadowed interior of the pickup's cab, Kate cast Sam a quick glance.

"You know, this man's going to be in awful shape," she said.

"I got that idea," Sam replied.

"The chopper's probably coming from Ashland, Wisconsin, and isn't going to get there for a while. I'm going to be busy until it does."

"Katie, what's your point?"

She spared Sam another look to find him staring intently at the road ahead. What *was* her point? She remembered that seeing someone in pain bothered him. But she also remembered that he moved quickly and confidently when something needed doing fast. He might not know a thing about emergency medicine, but his training as a pilot would give him an edge over most people in controlling the urge to panic. The more she thought about it, the more she realized that, if she needed help, she couldn't think of anyone she'd rather have with her.

"I'm sorry the evening got ruined this way," she answered finally. "But I'm glad you came."

And she was. It felt strange, racing off on an emergency call with someone riding beside her, but it felt strange in a good way. The next few hours had the potential for being a nightmare come to life, and no matter how the story ended, it would be nice, for once, not to have to face it all alone.

Sam's heart was pounding, the adrenaline pumping through his veins at a furious pace, as he rode beside Kate. It was a jarring ride, and he had to keep one hand braced on the door and the other along the back of the seat. His respect for Kate's driving grew with each passing mile, though it never surpassed his respect for her composure.

He wondered what it would take for him to feel the way she looked. But then, if she had his problem, would she be so calm? She only had to worry about whether her training, time and luck would be enough to save the man's life. If they weren't enough, she'd feel terrible, but she wouldn't be called upon to violate the laws of nature to snatch the guy back from the grave.

He'd try to get through this without giving himself away. But if he couldn't, well . . . it wouldn't take long to pack his things and leave. But as Kate spun the pickup onto a rutted dirt road, where a wooden sign read WANAGAN CREEK CAMPGROUNDS, Sam had the craziest moment of wishing she *did* know the truth about him. He didn't have any choice in this business. No more than he'd had in California. But maybe, he thought briefly, just maybe it would be easier to live with that fact if he didn't always have to go into these situations feeling so damned alone.

Chapter Seven

Kate dropped to her knees in the blood-soaked dirt beside the unconscious man. He was covered by a blanket, his lower body elevated by a board, and in the light cast by the Coleman lantern someone had lit, she quickly observed her patient's cold, white skin and his shallow, rapid breathing. His pulse was barely palpable, and she didn't have to take his blood pressure to know it was dangerously low. He was in shock from loss of blood, and close to death.

Clenching her jaw in rebellion against the voice that said she was too late, Kate did a quick check of the man's upper body, noting abrasions and bruises, none of which were life-threatening, before turning to focus on the one wound that was. Across from her, Bob Bradley swore, his hands slipping on ragged flesh as he tried to staunch the flow of blood from the man's left thigh.

"He was on his face," Bob rasped. "I turned him over and tried to get the dirt out of his nose. But I can't stop the bleeding!"

"Lift his leg," Kate told him, her steady voice giving away none of her anxiety.

Bob complied as she snapped back the lid of her emergency kit and grabbed a bandage that would serve as a tourniquet. Slipping the strip of cloth under the injured man's thigh, she secured the tourniquet in seconds flat. Then, with a sinking feeling, she reached for the only bag of IV solution she had—250 cc of Ringer's lactate. It wouldn't be enough. Yet if she thought now about her frustrations over getting medical supplies, she'd go nuts. So she set up the IV, telling herself it would have to do.

The man's shirt, like his jeans, was in tatters, and it was easy to rip off the sleeve. But when she tried to find a vein for the IV needle, she was hindered by the growing darkness. She started to call for more light, when the sudden brightness of a high-power flashlight beam, focused directly on her patient's arm, made the request unnecessary.

Kate glanced up to find Sam, crouched next to Bob, holding the flashlight for her. Offering a quick thanks, she finished setting up the IV, then, with towel in hand, turned to have a closer look at the leg wound. What she saw, after she'd mopped up the pooled blood, made her stomach lurch.

"Lord Almighty," Bob muttered, then quickly turned away.

The chunk of flesh the bear had ripped from its victim's leg went down to the bone. He wasn't a big man—probably five foot seven or eight and less than a hundred and sixty pounds—and he'd already lost a tremendous amount of blood.

With a worried glance at her patient's pale face, Kate's eyes dropped to his chest as she picked up his wrist to check his pulse. There wasn't another thing she could do, and what she'd done wasn't working. He was getting worse.

"What's the ETA on the chopper?" she asked.

The man standing behind her answered. "Thirty minutes. I've got a CB in my truck, and I checked the time just before you got here."

"Are you this man's friend?"

"Yes."

"What's his name?"

"Ray Cooney. Mine's Jeff Lindstrom. We're up from Chicago on a fishing trip. Is he...? Well, should I call his wife?"

Kate held Cooney's wrist with one hand as her other moved in an unconsciously soothing gesture across the blanket that covered his chest. "You'll have to fly with him to Marquette," she replied. "You can call her from there." *And pray it isn't to tell her that her husband's dead.* But with every passing second, Kate grew more certain it would be.

Time. She needed more time. She needed an emergency room ten minutes away. She needed an ambulance that didn't take an hour to arrive on the scene. She needed more Ringer's solution, because the 250 cc was almost gone. And what she needed most was a miracle.

"Kate, I've got to set up flares in the meadow for the chopper."

Kate acknowledged Bob's statement with a nod, then, with a glance at Lindstrom, said, "Could you try to get me an update on the chopper? Maybe you could hurry them along."

Looking grateful for something to do, Lindstrom took off toward the pickup parked on the far side of the clearing. That left Kate and Sam, kneeling across from one another, with the dying man between them.

Sam's voice was low and rough. "Katie, is this guy going to make it?"

"Not if the chopper doesn't get here in the next five minutes," she muttered. "He's in severe shock and—"

"Move your hand a little."

"He's barely—What?"

She broke off when Sam reached out to nudge the hand holding the blood-drenched towel away from the tourniquet. Flicking the towel aside, he placed his own hand directly over the gaping leg wound, while his other hand rested on the unconscious man's chest. Then, with a long, shuddering sigh, he closed his eyes, and his head dropped forward.

At first, Sam's actions merely baffled Kate. Then she wondered, somewhat doubtfully, if he could be praying. But when he lifted his head and she saw the expression on his face, her thought was not that he was praying but that he was fighting the devil himself. He was covered with sweat, and the sharp angles of his features were drawn in lines of pain.

Casting a quick glance around to see that Lindstrom was still in his truck, fifty yards away, and that no one was witnessing this bizarre scene, Kate whispered, "What on earth are you doing?"

"Watch," Sam whispered. "Just keep acting busy and...and watch."

Kate's mouth dropped open. "Sam, what are you talking about? You can't—"

"Shh. Quiet."

She might have gotten angry then, but at that moment Sam's face contorted in pure agony and he threw his head back, his breath rushing out in a hoarse groan.

"Katie, it's okay," he rasped. "You'll see...I can't—I've got to—"

"I'll see *what*?" she demanded, her voice breaking with panic. It was bad enough that she was facing the loss of a patient. It was more than she could handle to discover that Sam had lost his mind.

Reaching out, she grabbed Sam's hand to pull it off the wound, but the instant she touched him, she jerked back, gasping. His skin was hot. Burning hot.

"Katie..." Sam's whisper was barely audible. "Trust me. It's going to be all right now..."

His words didn't register. Her mind was in a state of terrible confusion as she stared, speechless, at his blood-drenched hand. Telling herself she must be wrong, she reached out to touch him again, but before she could, something happened that drove all other thoughts from her mind.

Her fingers, pressed to the chilled flesh of Cooney's wrist, had been keeping tabs on the deteriorating pulse. And it suddenly penetrated her awareness that it wasn't deteriorating anymore. In fact, it was a little stronger than it had been a few moments ago.

Her gaze fell to the injured man's chest, and she was stunned to see it rising and falling as he drew deeper and deeper breaths; they were ragged breaths, to be sure, but far stronger than any she'd expected him ever to draw again. A glance at his face made her eyes widen, she dropped his wrist in order to lay her palm against his cheek, unable to account for his improving color—or the fact that he was no longer so cold.

"Sam . . ." she said brokenly.

"Shh."

"Sam, he's breathing better, but what—"

"Shh," he repeated softly.

Her gaze flickered upward to see that his eyes were still tightly closed. But as she watched, his countenance underwent a dramatic transformation. The marks of pain and suffering began to fade. His jaw relaxed, and his lips, which had been pressed together, slowly assumed their sensual contours. His brow smoothed, and a few seconds later his eyes opened.

When he met her gaze, Kate uttered a soft, startled cry. Compassion. Tenderness. And a kind of vulnerability that took her breath away. Not the defenselessness that comes from innocence, but the fearlessness the comes from having faced the worst and won. His very soul lay open for her to see in the almost ethereal light shining from his eyes. *This* was what she'd glimpsed all those other times. *This* was the thing he tried so hard to hide from her. But even as Kate realized Sam was hiding nothing at that moment, she balked at naming what she saw.

"Loosen the tourniquet," Sam said quietly, urging her with a nod when she merely continued to stare at him.

Kate's heart was pounding as she let her gaze drop to the blood-soaked bandage. Rationally, she knew what would happen if she loosened it; there hadn't been enough time for the torn veins and arteries to close off. And yet... She reached for the bandage hesitantly but then pulled back, filled with an unaccountable fear—not that the man would bleed to death but, absurdly enough, that he wouldn't.

"Go on," Sam coaxed. "It's okay. I promise."

He sounded so certain. And so calm. But Kate's insides churned as she reached for the tourniquet.

Her cold fingers shook, making her clumsy, and she let the pressure off in slow increments, not trusting her intuition. Finally, though, the ends of the cloth were untied, and Kate dropped them, pressing a clenched fist to her middle as she whimpered in shock.

The bleeding had stopped—completely. And for several long seconds, Kate stared at the open wound in Ray Cooney's leg, her common sense trying to account for what her eyes beheld, while a quiet voice inside her insisted that she accept the impossible.

"Katie, don't be scared. It's all right."

Sam's gentle reassurance sank in slowly, and Kate's eyes rose to his. He met her numbed look unwaveringly, his stark features awash with tenderness and concern. She couldn't help being afraid—afraid of what she didn't rationally understand or accept. Yet she couldn't deny what she had seen or the conviction growing within her that, somehow, against all odds and biological laws, Sam had saved Ray Cooney's life.

Kate tried to speak but couldn't, and an instant later Bob came racing toward them along the path that ran through the woods. Following him were two state troopers, carrying a stretcher. Kate hadn't even heard the helicopter arrive.

Abruptly, Sam pulled his hands off Cooney's unconscious body and shoved himself to his feet, taking a couple of steps backward. His eyes continued to hold hers, but before Kate could think of anything to say, the others were there.

"They sent a police chopper," Bob announced breathlessly. "No medics."

"Sorry, Miss...?"

"Morgan." Kate offered her name tonelessly.

As the men went into action, strapping Cooney to the stretcher, the trooper told her about the interstate accident that had tied up all the medevac crews. Kate didn't hear a word he said. Her eyes were glued to Sam's as he gave her a long, piercing look; she knew he was asking her not to tell anyone what had happened.

How could she? She didn't know!

At that moment, though, it didn't matter whether or not the past twenty minutes made a scrap of sense. It only mattered that a man Kate had expected to be dead by now wasn't. And she wasn't responsible for his being alive. Sam was. She didn't know how, but she knew it was true, just as she knew that, should it become necessary, he could do whatever he'd done again.

With a strange sense of calm stealing through her, Kate turned her attention to helping the others get the patient ready for air travel.

In less than a minute the rescue crew was hurrying through the woods, the troopers carrying the stretcher, Kate trotting beside it, and Sam, carrying the emergency kit, following with the other men. The helicopter awaited them in a meadow, inside a ring of glowing flares. The wind created by its whirling blades hit Kate full force, and she ducked, gathering her hair in her fist to keep it from blinding her. There was no protection from the deafening noise. She ran with the others under the blades, grabbing for a hold to step aboard as Bob and the state troopers loaded the stretcher. With an instant's hesitation, Jeff Lindstrom climbed in after her.

Then, crouching in the doorway, Kate pivoted on her toes to take her emergency kit from Sam. He slid it in beside her, and she pushed it out of the way to make room for him in the confined space. When he hung back, making no move to climb aboard, Kate blinked in confusion. He must not understand, she thought, that it was okay for him to come. It wasn't really, but she would make it okay if anybody said anything. She held out a hand, beckoning him to get in.

Instead, Sam hesitated, looking at her, then casting his gaze over the length of the helicopter. When he took a step back and shook his head, Kate's eyes widened and her heart thudded into high gear.

"You're coming, too!" she shouted over the noise.

He took another step in the wrong direction as he yelled, "He'll be all right! You don't need me!"

But she *did* need him! He'd become indispensable to her. Didn't he realize that? What if Cooney started bleeding again? What if he wasn't really as improved as her mere clinical assessment indicated? Would Sam save a man's life, then let him go on to the hospital without him?

Would he let *her* go on to the hospital without him?

Sam gave Kate her answer with another backward step. And when one of the state troopers closed one of the double doors, he turned and ran out of the way. The other door closed as the chopper prepared to take off, and Kate was left staring at solid metal. It made no more sense than anything else that had transpired in the past half hour, but she felt, in that instant, as if she'd been abandoned.

It was a bleak and wretchedly familiar feeling.

Sam trudged across the dark field and through the woods to Kate's pickup, fighting nausea every step of the way. He had a knot in his stomach the size of a football, and it didn't go away as he drove Kate's pickup to Bourner's Crossing or during the ride to his cabin. When he stripped off his bloodied clothes and climbed into the shower, it was still there. And it kept him awake long into the night, as he sprawled naked across the bed, staring through the darkness at the beams above him.

There was no avoiding it. No way to deny or rationalize it. He'd been lying to himself long enough, passing off the couple of minor incidents since the crash as residual effects of a bad experience. He'd been sure they were no big deal. Only a temporary thing that would take care of itself. But he couldn't pass this one off. It had hit him smack in the face, standing there next to that chopper, when he'd wanted to climb in and go with Katie—and couldn't.

He had a problem. A bad problem. Far worse than anything he'd imagined. Sure, the other things he'd had to put up with lately were annoying and a little embarrassing. He didn't like not being able to eat a steak, or to drink a cold beer on a hot afternoon. And he missed the smell of brewing coffee and the rush that first cup in the morning gave him. He missed smoking, too, as bad a habit as it might be. But in the long run, those things weren't all that important, and he could accept having to give them up.

But this? No. He'd never be able to accept it.

And he'd never forgive himself, either.

For the first time in his life, Sam felt as if he'd truly let a woman down. And she was, maybe, the only woman he'd ever been consciously aware of not wanting to disappoint. But he'd seen the look of confused panic on Katie's face when she'd realized he wasn't going with her to the hospital. And if that look hadn't been enough to make him grit his teeth and climb into that damned chopper, he wasn't sure anything ever would be.

Sam rolled over in bed, exhausted but unable to sleep, and he thought about the woman he'd deserted that night, and about the way she'd handled herself in the face of imminent tragedy. He thought about the wholehearted manner in which she'd given herself to an unconscious stranger, who would have died on her, and he thought about the others to whom she gave so much.

He'd healed a man tonight who'd been more dead than alive—something he'd have done whether or not Katie had been there. And he had a gut-level knowledge, however recently he'd acquired it, of the things that went through a person's mind when faced with another human being's suffering. He knew how Katie had felt, kneeling there, watching that guy die. And he wondered how she stood it—the pain of knowing that, sometimes, what she gave wouldn't be enough, the fear that there would never be enough of her to go around to all the people in need.

Which was why he felt so godawful about deserting her. He knew how she felt. He'd wanted to help her. But it would have meant flying with her to Marquette. And that he hadn't been able to do.

Staring out the window at the three-quarter moon rising above the trees, Sam let out a ragged sigh. Face it, Reese, you're not a man anymore. You're a coward. And the last thing Katie needs is a gutless bastard like you to add to her list of burdens.

Chapter Eight

In the light of day, things didn't look much different. If anything, the slate-gray sky heightened Kate's sense that she'd been snatched out of the real world and plunged into a world of illusion. All night long she'd managed to behave as though everything were normal, following the hospital routines, filling out forms for the chopper crew. But a voice inside her kept asking, *Don't they know? Don't they realize something strange is going on here? Why aren't we talking about that instead of filling out these silly forms?*

If she could have believed that what she'd seen Sam do was an illusion—merely a misunderstanding on her part— it would have been easier. But the facts refused to allow it: Ray Cooney was alive and in astonishingly good condition, and she'd had a heck of a time explaining his condition to the head of the trauma unit surgical team. The doctor simply couldn't understand how Cooney had survived so long, and so well, with so little body fluids. Well, Kate didn't understand it, either.

Something incredible had happened. Something she couldn't describe or name. Something that made her insides tremble. And she desperately needed to know what it was.

A state trooper brought Kate home at 8:00 A.M., and she went straight to her bedroom, shed her blood-caked clothes and got into the shower. Then, giving her long hair a lick and a promise with the dryer, she left it unbraided to finish drying on its own and pulled on a pair of jeans and an oversize shirt of soft, dark green chamois. She was dead tired, but she couldn't have slept if her life had depended on it. So at 8:45 A.M., she headed out the front door.

The air was warm, in spite of the promise of rain, and as the pickup bounced over the old lake road toward Sam's cabin, Kate rolled down the window, thinking the fresh air might clear her head so she could figure out what to say to Sam.

She knew what she wasn't going to say. He couldn't have realized how upset she'd been that he hadn't gone with her to Marquette, and there was no reason to tell him. Ray Cooney hadn't needed him, and, therefore, neither had she—not really. She shouldn't have felt Sam had abandoned her; it was foolish to have taken his refusal to go personally. Yet, after pulling to a halt in front of the cabin, Kate approached the door hesitantly, afraid of discovering her feelings weren't foolish at all but an accurate measure of the way things stood between them.

The door was slightly ajar, and Kate knocked as she called, "Sam? It's Kate." The grumbling response she heard was not encouraging, but she ventured to ask, "Can I come in?"

Several seconds later he called something vaguely positive, and she pushed the door open.

At the far end of the big room, dressed in jeans and a white T-shirt, Sam was standing, absolutely still, staring out the window over the kitchen sink. She walked toward him, her wariness increasing when he didn't turn to acknowledge her presence. Stopping beside him, she took in his worse-for-wear appearance—the rumpled hair and a day's growth of beard darkening his jaw.

"Good morning." She greeted him on a questioning note.

"Morning," came his gruff reply.

Still he didn't look at her, and Kate wondered if she ought to leave. For a moment her need to talk to him warred with her suspicion that he didn't want to talk to her. The decision between the two was postponed, though, when she caught a whiff of a familiar odor, and her eyes dropped to the sink.

"I see you've been fishing this morning," she remarked with forced cheerfulness. "Those are beauties. Four pounds apiece, I'll bet, even after you've cleaned them."

"Do you eat fish?"

"I love them," Kate answered, lifting her gaze from the two walleye pike to Sam's oddly still face. "I like to fish, too, but I don't get much chance these—"

"Take them."

Kate broke off, blinked at him, then began a protest. "Oh, Sam, that's really nice of you, but you'll want—"

"Take them. Please. Just..." He swallowed hard, squeezing his eyes shut.

Kate's eyes widened as she noted his growing pallor. Her gaze dropped from his face...to the knife in his hand...to the fish.

"Katie, I hate to tell you this, but—"

"Leave the room, Sam." Taking his arm, she spun him around and pushed him gently away from the sink. "Go wash your hands and change your clothes. I'll take care of this."

Sam muttered something crude under his breath, but he followed her directions, striding across the cabin to disappear into the bedroom.

Kate rolled up her shirt sleeves and set about disposing of the problem. Wrapping the fish in a brown paper bag, she put them in her truck. Then she opened two cabin windows for ventilation and gave the sink and countertop a thorough scrubbing with a bleach cleanser. When the cabin was rid of all traces of fishy smell, she dried her hands and went to check on Sam.

She stopped in the bedroom doorway, taking in the scene. The unmade bed, its twisted blankets evidence of a restless night. A dresser drawer hanging open, clean underwear and socks stacked in the front of it. And, in a pile near the bathroom door, the clothes Sam had worn last night, jeans and shirt both stiff with dried blood. Sam was standing by the open window, one bare shoulder against the frame, a fresh pair of jeans slung low on his hips without a belt, his hands shoved deep in their pockets. He'd removed his T-shirt but hadn't replaced it, and in the pearl-gray light coming through the window, he looked lean and strong and every inch a man.

At the moment, though, the man was vulnerable—a rare occurrence and one Kate knew she must handle with care.

Approaching slowly, she stopped several feet away to study him. The color had returned to his face, and the lines of strain had relaxed. Yet he looked terribly unhappy. And as he gazed out at the forest, the low, gravelly words he spoke were edged in bitterness.

"My dad taught me to fish. It's the only thing we ever really did together."

His sadness was an ache Kate felt in her own heart, even if she didn't understand its cause. Cautiously, she moved to stand beside him, and he shifted a little to make room for her in front of the window.

"On weekends, in California," he continued, "one of the other pilots, Sid Golden, and I used to go up to the mountains and fish, six, sometimes eight, hours a day. And once in a while a bunch of us would drive down to the coast, hire a boat and go deep-sea fishing. I like to fish. It's relaxing and easy and... Hell." He uttered a soft, self-deprecating sound. "I don't know why I expected it'd still be that way. Nothing else is the same as it used to be."

Questions. So many questions ran through Kate's mind as her eyes searched the stoic line of Sam's unshaven jaw, then ran quickly over the scars on the right side of his body.

She didn't know where to start, which question to pick. So she simply reached out to lay a hand on his arm.

"Sam, talk to me," she said softly. "Tell me what's wrong."

His head turned slightly, but he didn't meet her gaze. And after a moment, he looked away.

Kate let her hand fall from his arm, and she turned her gaze out the window, too, drawing the curtain aside a bit farther with her finger. They stood that way for a long time, side by side, listening to the eerie cry of a loon on a nearby lake and the faint rustling of the wind through tender new leaves.

After several minutes Sam straightened slowly, pulling his hands from his pockets to fold his arms across his bare chest. Lifting his head a notch, he squared his shoulders, and Kate realized with dismay that, if he spoke now, it would be the tough guy talking. His pride had taken all the beating it could stand for one morning, so to salvage what was left of it, he was putting on his armor. Except the armor had cracks in it. And through them she caught glimpses of the man within.

"Remember the first day we were here at the cabin?" he said.

She gave him a single nod. "Yes."

"Remember when you said it was a miracle I survived the plane crash—and I said that maybe I didn't? You got disgusted, thinking I was being a smart ass."

She hesitated. "I remember."

"I meant it. I died on the operating table after the crash. For fifteen minutes, they told me later, I was dead—no heartbeat, no respiration, nothing."

"Dear Lord," Kate whispered. "Fifteen minutes is—"

His jaw tightened, his expression becoming even more closed, and Kate cut herself off.

"Have you ever heard of a near-death experience?" he asked.

She replied slowly. "I'm not sure what you mean. I've read about cases where a trauma team has resuscitated someone whose vital functions have stopped."

Sam shook his head. "I wasn't resuscitated. They did all the stuff doctors do to bring people back, but after five minutes of trying, they gave up. The head surgeon had already signed the death certificate."

"Then how—"

"I found out it wasn't time for me to die. So I...came back—let's say, with some strong encouragement."

For several seconds Kate could only stare at him, her lips parted in disbelief. Finally, she swallowed and started to ask, "Encouragement from—"

He stopped her again. "It isn't something I like to talk about, okay? Half the time nobody believes me anyway. I'm not saying you wouldn't but right now, I'd rather not go into it. The point I'm trying to make is, when I died, I didn't just lie there on the operating table. My body was dead, but my mind or...soul or whatever you want to call it *went* somewhere."

Kate's look went from skeptical to utterly astonished. "You— You remember being dead? I mean, how could you know—"

"Because I was there," he cut in, a muscle twitching in his cheek as an emotion Kate couldn't begin to name passed swiftly across his features.

A moment later, his head turned, and he looked at her with eyes so startlingly clear Kate felt as though she were looking through the window to infinity. *He knows,* she thought. *He knows things I can't begin to imagine.*

More gently, Sam told her, "It isn't a bad place, Katie. I don't want you to think that. In fact, it's...beautiful. I've got some books written by people who've either had experiences like mine or who've studied them. I'll lend them to you if you're interested. And sometime, maybe, I'll tell you about it, but—" He hesitated, then glanced away. "But not now."

But now was when she needed to know. Kate wondered how long she could wait for what she was sure must be the key to understanding him. His effect on her, from the beginning, had been astounding; it was more powerful than ever now. There was an aura about him that shimmered like

heat rising from a fire. On the surface, it appeared as a brazen sexual energy, the potency of which sent tendrils of
arousal curling through her. But there was more to it than
that. And she was drawn to know the source of his magne-
tism. She was drawn to know the man.

"The thing last night was close," Sam went on. "And
when it's that close, I need some time afterward to get settled. Remind myself I'm here—not there. Otherwise, I walk
around with a replay running in my head of the things that
went on when I was there, not here. It makes it hard to go
on acting like . . . like a regular person."

Well, that made sense. Didn't it? As much as anything
else in the past twelve hours.

"Sam, I think I understand," Kate began. "I won't ask
you about . . . dying. But please, tell me—"

With a muttered curse, he turned and took a couple of
strides away from the window to stand at the foot of the
pushed-together beds. Then, rubbing a hand over the back
of his neck, he drew a ragged breath.

"Katie . . ." He whirled to face her. "I know what you
want to hear. You want me to give you a reason that guy you
took to the hospital is still alive. All I can tell you is that he
was going to die, and I couldn't let it happen. So I put my
hands on him and made the bleeding stop. I made his
heartbeat get faster and his breathing get deeper. I knew it
would work because I've done it—or things like it—dozens
of times now. But honest to God, I don't know *why* it
works."

The look he gave her was an odd mixture of defiance that
she might dare not to believe him and hope that she would.
Kate didn't know what to think.

"Are you trying to tell me—" she began.

He waved her off with an arm flung wide. "Something
happened to me," he said urgently. "When I was dead, I
mean. The experience . . . changed me—though I didn't find
out until months later, after I got out of the hospital."

"How could you not—" Kate stopped herself this time,
realizing she was asking the wrong question. He couldn't
give her reasons. But perhaps he'd give her facts.

Choosing her words, she asked, "How did you find out?"

Sam stared at her for an instant, then turned and paced toward the door. Kate thought the conversation had ended, but he stopped in the doorway, standing in silence for several moments. Then, with a heavy sigh, he hooked both hands on the door frame above his head, assuming a negligent pose, as he spoke in a flat, matter-of-fact tone.

"There was an accident," he said. "It was a few weeks after I got out of the hospital. My friend Sid and I were helping a friend put a deck on the back of his house. Actually, I was mostly watching, since I wasn't walking too well. Sid was working with a power saw, and his hand slipped, and the blade hit him. It cut his leg open at the groin. I was standing maybe five feet away, and in the couple of seconds it took me to get my hands on him, the ground was covered with blood. When the medics got there, they shoved me out of the way and started working on him. One of them said something about it being the femoral artery that was cut, and he said it like that meant Sid was already dead. But then the other one realized the bleeding had stopped. Sid had passed out, but he was alive. They took him to the hospital, and I . . . I went home."

"*. . . and I went home.*" That was it?

The starkness of Sam's speech sent chills up Kate's spine. The understatement with which he described what must have been a horrifying event was unbelievable, as was the complete absence of description as to what he'd actually *done* in those moments before the medics arrived. Where was the emotion she'd seen in his expression last night when he'd put his hands on Ray Cooney?

Kate had her answer when Sam turned to look at her from across the room; the lines on his desert-bronzed face were deep with strain and exhaustion, and she knew the words he'd left out, the details of the scene, were as vivid in his mind as if it were happening at that very moment. It was costing him a great deal to tell her this story.

"Go on," she urged softly. "That was the first time you . . . you healed someone?"

"Yes," Sam replied in the same emotionless tone. Then, with a brooding frown, he added, "But I'd been feeling...different...for a while."

"Different?"

He lifted a shoulder. "It started in the hospital, with the TV. I couldn't watch anything where people were killing or hurting each other. And I hated being around other sick people. Then, after I got out of there, I'd be in a place like, say, the grocery store, and I'd see some person with a handicap—a crippled leg, maybe—and I'd get this urge to fix it."

Kate gave him a bewildered look. "Fix it?"

"Make it go away," he explained succinctly. "The thing with Sid triggered it, though. After that, it got so I *had* to try to fix it. Then, one day, when I was driving home from visiting Sid at the hospital, I passed an accident. Except—" His breath caught for an instant. "Except I couldn't pass it. There was a kid. He'd been riding a bike, and a car had hit him. He had a cracked skull, and I don't think there were two breaths left in him. But I put my hands on his head, and..." He gave Kate a quick glance, then finished. "I understand he's still got some problems with his eyesight, but otherwise he's okay."

Kate shook her head, trying to translate images from the previous night into the scene Sam described. "Weren't there other people there?" she asked. "Had the ambulance come?"

"Lots of people. No ambulance yet. But there was a cop."

"And how did you get him to let you near the child?"

Sam hesitated a moment. "I told him I was a doctor. It didn't matter. I would have said anything it took to get my hands on the boy."

"And what did the hospital say? Dear heavens, Sam! How did you get away with such a thing?"

He snorted softly. "I didn't."

Kate struggled to control the rush of thoughts and emotions coursing through her as she watched Sam push off from the door frame to wander restlessly around the room.

"The next morning a neurosurgeon named Martin Anderson called and asked if I'd come to the hospital to tell him about my role in saving the kid's life. I went because—" He stopped, bending to snatch last night's bloody clothes off the floor. Staring at the clothes in his hands, he continued. "I knew what had happened to me when I died was related to what I'd done with the boy and with Sid. I hadn't been able to get anybody to listen when I tried to tell them about the near-death experience. The nurses and doctors at the hospital thought I was hallucinating. I knew I wasn't, but I shut up about it because I didn't want them putting it in my medical records that I was crazy. But when Marty Anderson called, something about him made me think he might listen. I went to talk to him, because...because I had to know what was happening to me."

"I should think so," Kate murmured. Then, seeing his confusion over what to do with the ruined garments, she crossed the room and gently took them from him. Turning to walk in the direction of the kitchen, she spoke over her shoulder. "So, what did this Dr. Anderson have to say?"

"He asked questions, mostly," Sam replied, following her slowly. "But when I told him about the crash and the near-death experience, he went wild."

"You mean, he didn't believe you?"

"Oh, he believed me, all right. He gave me a book and sent me home to read it. The next day I was back there, looking for him. The descriptions in the book of what people said it had been like to die sounded just like what had happened to me." Watching as Kate ran cold water over his clothes in the kitchen sink, he added, "It was good to find out I wasn't the only one. But I still didn't understand what the near-death experience had to do with this crazy thing with Sid and the boy."

Swishing the clothes with a squirt of dishwashing detergent, Kate turned off the water. "And Dr. Anderson told you?"

"Hell, no," Sam grated, wandering around the kitchen. "Marty didn't have answers—only suspicions. He took me to see a couple of his patients in the hospital, and he didn't have to ask for me to want to help them. Every time I even glanced at a sick person, I . . . well, this thing happens to me where I . . . want to make them well.''

The hint of embarrassment in Sam's tone made Kate frown in puzzlement, and she watched the interplay of emotions flickering across his features as he picked up a box of cereal off the table, stared at it, then tossed it down again to move on.

''The business with my hands only worked on two out of five of Marty's patients,'' he admitted. ''But that was enough for Marty, and the next thing I knew, he was on the phone with some friend of his at a hospital in New England. A couple of days later I was headed back east to this place where they study people who have what they call paranormal abilities.''

''What sort of place was it?'' she asked.

Sam caught the note of suspicion in her tone. ''A research center,'' he answered. And when he named the major university to which the center was connected, Kate's eyes widened. ''Yeah, it's legitimate. No hocus-pocus. It's run by scientists with M.D.s and Ph.D.s in everything under the sun. For three weeks I filled out questionnaires and sat through hours of interviews and let them hook me up to machines that measure brain waves and dreams and electromagnetic fields and God only knows what else. They tested my blood cells and my skin cells and every other cell they could put on a slide or in a test tube to look at. And I've got to say, after putting up with seven months of the same kind of stuff in the hospital, I wasn't the most cooperative subject they ever had.''

And I'll bet that's putting it mildly. Kate watched with growing concern as Sam made his third trip around the kitchen table, each time pulling out and pushing in the end chair as he passed. ''Would you like to go for a walk?'' she asked.

He gave her a quick, relieved look. ''God, yes. Let's get out of here.'' And with that, he headed for the front door.

Biting her tongue against the urge to tell him that he might get cold without a shirt, Kate followed.

Outside, Sam started down the cleared track that led to the old lake road. He'd gotten about ten yards when his steps slowed and he glanced over his shoulder, watching as Kate hurried to catch up. When she reached him, he mumbled an apology, shoving his hands into his pockets as he continued at a slower pace.

They walked for a few minutes in silence, Kate looking at the spring beauty and bloodroot that had bloomed that week, Sam staring at the track in front of him.

Finally, when she thought he seemed a little more relaxed, Kate asked, "So, what did all that testing tell you?"

Lifting his gaze to stare ahead, Sam let out a sigh. "Not much, really. The only thing they had me do that seemed worthwhile was to work on patients from the university hospital. They'd tell me what was wrong with the person, and I'd try to cure him...or her. It turns out this weird thing I've got is selective. It doesn't work on birth defects or disease, which is why I'd had such bad luck with Marty's patients. Once in a while—about five percent of the time—I can slow down a progressive illness. But so far, at least, I haven't been able to cure one."

Leaning to snatch a small pebble off the ground, he flicked it into the woods. "On the other hand, about ninety-seven percent of the time, I can stop bleeding. And I do almost that well with problems left by an injury or an illness—like bad circulation from diabetes or arthritis that develops from a break. Once I worked on a woman who'd had polio. Afterward she could lift her arms above her head, where she couldn't before, and not long after that her leg muscles had developed to where she could walk without braces."

Kate's eyes grew wide. "Sam, that's wonderful!"

He passed off her praise with a shrug. "Yeah, I was pleased."

Pleased? Not elated or wild with excitement? He was just *pleased*? Kate didn't believe it. Not for a minute. He might talk about this amazing power he'd acquired as though it were so mundane as to be boring—"this weird thing I've got," he'd called it—but she knew he couldn't possibly feel that way about it.

But how did he feel? He certainly seemed less than thrilled, but for the life of her, Kate didn't understand why. She herself had barely begun to accept what he was telling her, but still, she was in awe. It was astonishing enough to learn someone she knew had the kind of gift Sam was describing; it was incomprehensible to think he might not want it.

"So, what happened?" she asked. "Did the center just . . . send you home?"

Sam shook his head. "I left. I couldn't take being looked at through a microscope anymore. Besides, they were getting all their questions answered, but nobody was answering mine."

"What questions were those?"

"Well, dammit, Katie! What do you think?" He erupted suddenly, all pretense of indifference wiped from his features. "I hadn't asked for this thing. I wanted to know when it was going to go away. And all those brilliant doctors and scientists would tell me was that my body's energy field had been altered, apparently as a result of the near-death experience. Well, hell, I already *knew* that. I even knew why!"

Kate's brow creased. "You did?"

"Sure," he declared. "If you think about it, it makes a crazy kind of sense. To come back from being dead, it was like I *made* my body stop bleeding and . . . well, turned it back on. And whatever the hell I did over *there* to get back *here*, stayed with me. All they did at the center was put a label on it. In their lingo, I'm what's known as a bona fide healer. I finally figured out that meant I'm stuck with this thing." Gruffly, with that odd, half-embarrassed catch in his voice, he conceded, "So, okay. I can handle that. As long as I've got it, maybe I can do some good with it. But does that mean every time I see someone who's sick or hurt I'm supposed to try to cure them?"

"Of course not," Kate replied instantly. "Even if you could heal all different kinds of things, you can't possibly cure every sick person in the world. And nobody could expect you to."

He shot her a cynical look. "Yeah? Tell that to the hundred or so people who knocked on my door between the time I got back to California and the time I left, four weeks later."

Kate stared at him in shock. "Dear heavens, Sam. Where did they come from?"

"Everywhere." His arm swept the air in an all-encompassing gesture. "Just . . . everywhere."

They'd reached a place where the track bent to the left. Straight ahead, a few yards into the woods, Kate noted a casualty of Tuesday's storm—a huge red maple uprooted and stretched across the forest floor, its new leaves withered. When Sam left the track, headed for a look at the damage, Kate followed him, picking her way through the low-lying brush.

He stopped beside the fallen giant to lay a hand on the three-foot-thick trunk. She came up beside him, tilting her head to look at the cloudy sky through the break in the green canopy the tree's demise had·caused. A minute passed in silence before Sam continued.

"Word got around about me," he said. "And before I knew it, I had parents bringing children with leukemia. Blind people who hadn't seen the light of day in forty years. Vietnam vets, paralyzed from the waist down. You name it, I saw it. Some of them were rich, some not so rich. Some wanted to pay me. They all wanted me to take away their pain and make their lives bearable. Well, God, Katie—" His control slipped, and a shudder went through him. "It was awful. Some of them I helped, but there were a lot I couldn't help. And they had a hard time understanding that... Hell, so did I."

He turned his head away slightly as he murmured, "It's not so easy to see somebody hurting and not be able to help them."

"Yes, I know," Kate said quietly. *Like it's not so easy to see you hurting, when I don't know if there's anything I can say or do that will make one scrap of difference.*

As her gaze searched his profile, Kate had to fight to keep from reaching out to touch him. She wanted to let him know she understood at least some small part of his torment. But something told her he wouldn't accept any such gesture. Sam was an incredibly strong-willed man. He'd had the guts and persistence to overcome pain and disability that would have crushed a lesser man's spirit. Granted, the circumstances he'd described were fantastic beyond her wildest imaginings. But that made it even more ridiculous to think about patting his shoulder and telling him she sympathized with his predicament.

But what could she do for him? Was there anything?

Turning sideways to lean a hip against the broad maple trunk, Sam crossed his arms over his chest. "Still," he said, "I helped enough of the people who came to me that more kept coming. And Marty Anderson had me at the hospital two days a week, working on patients. Then he started calling me, sometimes in the middle of the night, for emergencies. I didn't mind doing it for him—he'd done a lot for me. And I had the time, since I couldn't . . . well, I had the time, but . . ."

He trailed off. Then, shifting his weight uncomfortably, he ran a hand through the hair that had fallen over his forehead. "This thing can be pretty exhausting. Seems crazy, I guess, since all it looks like I'm doing is putting my hands on somebody, but it can wipe me out to work on somebody who's in really bad shape or on a lot of people in the same day."

"That's not crazy at all." Kate boosted herself up to sit on the tree trunk. "Energy is measurable, Sam. When it's gone, it's gone."

"I'm only one man. And I'm not God."

"Of course not."

"That was the worst—when people would come, not to ask me to cure them, but to ask for my advice. Like I was some kind of preacher or guru or something." He uttered a short laugh. "But the last straw was the guy from one of the local TV talk shows who started badgering me to be on the show. Hell, if it wasn't so pathetic, it would almost be funny.''

An instant later, he bit out a violent curse. "But it isn't funny! There's nothing funny about any of this. It's terrible to see people suffering and to suffer for them—and never be able to turn it off." Shaking his head, he finished, "Everybody else who knows calls this thing a gift. But from where I stand, most of the time it looks more like a curse."

"Sam, no," Kate whispered. "You don't mean that."

He gave her a scowling glance, then looked away. Several seconds went by in silence until, gradually, the set of his jaw relaxed. When he returned his gaze to hers, the scowl was gone.

"No," he said. "I don't mean it. I'm not sorry I could help those people. And if this hadn't happened to me, the doctors who said I'd never walk again would've had the last word. I got back on my feet under my own steam, but just barely, and I doubt I'd have made it more than ten years before I ended up where they said I'd be—in a wheelchair—living on drugs. I can't pretend I wasn't damned glad when I figured out I could cure myself, too. It was harder working on myself—it didn't happen on the first try, all at once—but bit by bit everything got to be right again. All I've got left now to show for the crash are the scars."

And a wonderful gift that he looked upon as a curse. The thought ran through Kate's mind as she asked, "Doesn't the good you've done for others—and for yourself—make the trouble you've put up with worth it?"

He shook his head. "Katie, since I found out about this thing, I haven't had time to figure out what's worth it and what isn't. The last week in California, I was living with the blinds pulled down, the lights out, and the phone off the hook. I'd lived in that house for ten years, and I had some pretty good friends in Mojave. I was trying to...well, to get back to work. But I couldn't stay there. I had to find a place where people would leave me alone. A place I could get some peace to work things out in my own head.''

"So," Kate noted quietly, "you came up here to get away from sick people, and, instead, you found one bleeding to death.

"How about that," Sam murmured. Then, with a deep sigh, he hooked his heel in the bark of the tree trunk and levered himself up to sit beside her. "Except I wasn't really trying to get away from sick people. I just wanted to go somewhere they wouldn't know it was me helping them. I'm not trying to...to hold out on anybody, Katie. I just need some peace." Grunting softly, he added, "And the first place I went looking for it was worse than what I'd left."

"You didn't come straight here from California?" Kate asked.

"No, I went to Detroit to stay with my father and Susan." He shook his head. "There's lots of sick people in a big city. More than I could ever cure. I'd planned to stay in Detroit, but I wasn't there a week when I started reading the classifieds, looking for a place up here."

He paused, staring sightlessly into the woods, with a look of something that might have been sadness tightening his features. "It wouldn't have worked, anyway, staying with Dad. He was glad to see me healthy—he'd come once to the hospital, after the crash, and I think it about killed him to see me so messed up. But he's...narrow in his outlook, I guess you'd say. I couldn't have told him about this healing business. It wouldn't fit into anything he'd be able to accept."

Or anything you can accept.

Slowly, the pieces were coming together. In trying to envision Sam and his father having this same talk...well, she couldn't imagine it, given what Sam had said about the older man. And she thought that might account for at least part of Sam's discomfort with his awesome gift. The man who'd raised him was steeped in traditional notions about the things that made a man a man, and Carl Reese had passed those notions on to his son. Men didn't cry. Men didn't admit to pain. And a *real* man was never afraid—or, if he was, he'd didn't say so. What experience, in that motherless household, had Sam had with being nurtured, or with gentleness? Very little, Kate imagined. And yet the gift he'd been given was inherently a nurturing one.

It was a little like dumping oil and water into the same glass and expecting them to mix. Sam was struggling to reconcile his healing gift with his macho image of manhood, trying to remain tough in spite of the torrent of intense emotion that poured from him every time he was compelled to touch and heal another human being. Emotions such as tenderness and compassion—those things she'd seen carved into his face last night. Emotions she was certain had always been there, inside him, but that he'd learned to deny. Well, he'd denied them so successfully that he didn't know how to cope with them when they refused to go away. They made him angry, embarrassed; they caused him pain. And he didn't like it. So he was handling the battle inside him— the one between the real man and the healer—by trying to relegate the latter to nuisance status. But it wasn't working.

"Anyway," Sam went on, "I'm planning to stay here until I've got some control over this thing. Which basically means learning how to make choices about who, when, where and how often I help people. I know that must sound cold to you, but—"

"It doesn't sound cold at all."

When his head turned and his startled gaze met hers, Kate added, "I can't begin to imagine how I'd feel in your position, but I know any medical professional—or, for that matter, anybody in the business of helping people—makes choices all the time. If they don't, they get burned out pretty fast. You couldn't have kept going the way things were in California."

Kate paused. "You made a choice last night, you know. You waited until I'd done everything I could do. Then you asked me if Ray Cooney was going to die."

Yes, he'd realized it. But the quick flash of wariness that touched his features said he wasn't sure of her reaction.

"Actually," she continued, "If I'd had enough IV solution, you might not have had to do anything."

"But you didn't," Sam growled.

"No. And if you hadn't been there, he'd be dead this morning." Holding his gaze, she added softly, "I'm glad you were there, Sam."

He didn't look away. And he didn't shrug off her gratitude.

"So am I," he said quietly. "I was glad *you* were there, too. Knowing you were doing all the right medical things gave me a chance to feel like the choice between life and death wasn't all on me."

"Is that how it feels?"

"Sometimes." He studied her closely. "It felt that way standing in your living room the other night."

"Last night, you mean. When you decided to go with me."

"No. Tuesday night, when I brought you home after the storm, with your ankle busted."

Chapter Nine

It was you," Kate breathed, her mind flooding with the memory of Sam standing at the foot of her bed, removing the ice pack from her ankle to replace it with his hand. The image was blurry—she couldn't remember what either of them had actually said—yet she remembered his tenderness. And she remembered the incredible lightness, the floating sense of well-being, that had filled her. Until that moment, though, even after seeing him heal Ray Cooney and listening to his story, she hadn't made the connection between Sam and her injured ankle's recovery.

"I was on my way out the door," Sam admitted. "But then I thought about all the people who depend on you. And I couldn't handle wondering what might happen if you couldn't do your job."

"You looked so... I thought you were mad at me. I see now. But, Sam—" Kate shook her head a little "—it might only have been a sprain. I'd hate to think you felt you had to—"

"It was broken."

She stopped short, her lips parted. "You could tell?"

He nodded, his gaze holding hers. "But it wouldn't have mattered. I'd have done the same thing. You do a lot for other people, Katie, and I wanted to do something for you. Mostly, though, I think I did it for me. I didn't want you laid up with a broken ankle." His eyes made a slow trip over her features. "I wanted you here, like you are right now, with me."

When his eyes fastened on hers once more, Kate felt a slow flush of heat coloring her cheeks. She wished she'd been fully awake and aware of what was happening that night, for, although his hands had touched her ankle, the look in his gray-crystal eyes said he'd known her, in those few moments, very well indeed. And she felt as if they'd shared something very special and very intimate—more intimate than any other experience she'd ever shared with a man.

Lowering her gaze, Kate twisted her fingers together in her lap as she tried to imagine saying thank you for something that... Well, somehow it didn't seem like the thing to say.

A second later, though, another thought occurred to her, and her eyes snapped up at Sam's. "Francis..." she whispered. "Sam, did you..."

His eyebrow arched in a dry look. "What do you think?"

"Dear Lord," she breathed, the chill of shock racing over her skin. "And you were able to heal him because his deafness was the result of the virus. If it'd been congenital—"

"It's a sure bet he'd still be deaf." Sam glanced away, grumbling a little as he admitted, "But I'd probably have tried anyway. I mean, how could you turn your back on a kid with a smile like that?"

"Oh, Sam..." Kate blinked at the tears stinging her eyes.

"I hope you won't think you've got to tell your sister."

She shook her head. "No, of course I won't tell Cressie or Steve. I won't tell *anybody* anything you've told me. I promise I won't. Oh, Sam, I could—"

Kate hesitated all of about two seconds. Then, with the tears brimming in her eyes, she threw her arms around his neck and kissed his cheek, saying, "This is for Francis...and this is for Cressie and Steve...and this is for me...."

But when she pulled back from the third kiss, Sam's arm clamped around her, his eyes holding hers fast.

"And this is for me," he said. "For listening." Then his head angled and dipped, and his lips caught hers in a kiss that spoke of things far more potent than gratitude.

Kate trembled as Sam's mouth moved across hers, his lips shaping hers with a firm, persuasive pressure. Her hand resting on his forearm tightened its hold, fingers digging in as her senses filled with the sound of his breathing, the scent of his skin, the warmth of his breath on her cheek. The first easy touch of his tongue skimming the seam of her lips made the butterflies wild inside her. But it also sent warning signals shooting through every nerve in her body.

She tried to pull back. "Sam..."

"Hush, now." He shifted forward on the fallen tree far enough to plant his feet on the ground. Then, tugging her off her perch, he drew her around in front of him, nestling her thighs between his. Their faces were level, and he reached up to thread his fingers through her hair, gathering a handful of the long waves. "No more talking," he said as he pulled her close, his lips grazing her temple, her cheek, the line of her jaw. "We've both been wanting this. You know that."

Yes, she knew it. But she also knew she'd been afraid of it. And the instant his mouth slid, open and seeking, onto hers, she knew why. In less than a heartbeat she was quivering with excitement, and her safe world, her passionless world, was in danger of being set to flames. Not even if she had pushed him away in that instant would she be able to settle for passionless again. Which was reason enough, since it was too late, anyway, simply to give in.

On a moan of yearning, Kate's hands rode up Sam's arms to cling to his shoulders, her lips parted to match the shape of his, and her body leaned into his with a lush, giving softness that made him suck in a quick breath, then swear, then fold her into a kiss that quickly taught her she'd never really been kissed before.

Kisses as she'd known them were perfunctory things, a preliminary that led to something else. Sometimes they were pleasant. Sometimes merely okay. But they were rarely genuinely exciting. And they were never anything at all like *this*.

Sam's mouth took hers in deep, voluptuous strokes that grew more provocative with each pounding heartbeat. The low, throaty sounds he made told Kate he was as staggered and as aroused by the erotic intensity of the kiss as she was. He left no doubt about his arousal when his arm moved low around her hips and he pulled her tight against the front of his jeans. He was hard, rubbing against her, so hard, and so close to the aching place between her thighs he was made to fill. Their clothing kept them from consummating the act, but his mouth said open up to me, give yourself to me, come with me. And Kate felt no other joining could have been more intimate than that hot, lusty mating of their lips and teeth and tongues.

Oh, but hadn't she known it would be this way? Yes, just as she'd known she wasn't ready for it. Yet now that she knew what she'd been missing, she didn't want to stop. Not yet.

And Sam clearly wasn't thinking of stopping. With one arm still holding her to him, his other hand began to sweep over her thighs and hips, up over her waist and ribs, then down again. Each pass he made grew more thorough in its exploration, until finally his fingers slipped under the bottom edge of her oversize shirt to splay against the warm skin of her back. Kate arched into him, her breasts crushing softly against the ridges and contours of his bare chest. When he slanted his mouth to take even deeper possession of hers, she honestly wondered if she might faint—but she gave him what he wanted because it was what she wanted, too.

His hand roamed over her, fingers trailing down the curve of her spine to dip below the waistband of her jeans. But as his hand rode up again to her shoulders, unhindered, and he finally realized that the only fabric that lay between them was her shirt, he went utterly still. An instant later, with a harsh, guttural sound and an almost violent shudder of his body, he slid his palm around to cover the side of her bare breast.

His action stole Kate's breath away. She knew she should stop him, but her heart raced at the thought of him touching her, and she couldn't resist letting him push them a little closer to the limit. He did it in slow degrees, his fingers sinking into the pillowy softness of her, tracing the upper curve, dipping into the warmth and satiny smoothness beneath. Then, shifting his chest away from hers slightly, he took the full weight of her breast into his palm, cradling it, stroking it, groaning at the discovery that the firm mound spilled beyond the boundaries of his large, long-fingered hand.

Lifting his mouth so their lips barely touched, Sam muttered something that made Kate burn deep inside with a liquid, quivering need. She knew she had to stop before she couldn't anymore, before he couldn't anymore, before they wound up making love in the middle of the woods with the earth beneath them. But as she tried to draw a gasping breath to speak, his mouth claimed hers again, and his fingers captured the swollen tip of her breast.

Feeling. Shards of electrifying pleasure racing through her, controlled with exquisite finesse by the tugging, rolling movement of his fingertips. Slicing downward from her taut nipple, the current of pleasure centered in the hot, yearning place between her thighs, setting her hips into unconscious motion against Sam's steely hardness. When he shifted his denim-clad thigh between hers and pressed upward, she tore her mouth away from his and let out a moan.

Her head fell back, her eyes drifting closed to block out the sky above her. His mouth trailed to the base of her throat, and for a moment she was lost, panting and shaking, in a cloud of sensual pleasure. But when the cloud began to split apart and she felt the first tiny tremors of fulfillment ripple through her, her eyes flew open in shocked awareness.

"Sam. Sam, stop." Kate's fingers fluttered against his jaw, sifted through his hair as she tried to lift his head. But he didn't seem to hear her hoarse utterance. His mouth slid downward over the fabric of her shirt, and Kate realized with alarm that his goal was her breast. She hadn't even been aware that he'd raised her shirt to bare it.

"Oh, no... Wait." Her hands moved frantically to nudge at his shoulders, and this time he got the message.

But it was clear he didn't like it. Pausing, his lips brushing the upper curve of her breast, his breath caught on a ragged note.

"Sam, please...don't," she breathed, knowing what she was asking of him—what she was asking of herself.

He hesitated an instant longer, then, almost desperately, his arms went around her, crushing her to him, as his mouth came back to hers for a quick, hard kiss. With his lips still on hers, he spoke in a rasping whisper.

"Katie, honey, what's wrong?"

"Nothing," she panted. "Nothing's...wrong. It feels wonderful...."

"But?"

Her breath came out in a quick rush. "But I'm not ready for this. It's...Sam, you're going too fast for me. Please."

A couple of seconds passed without either of them breathing. Then his eyelids lifted halfway, and, at a distance of mere inches, he met her hazy brown gaze. When he realized she meant it, he let out a long, resigned sigh, and, catching her lower lip between his for a last sensual tug, he ended the kiss.

Still, when Kate started to pull away, he said, "No," and levered himself away from the tree trunk to stand. Keeping his arms around her, one hand rose to hold her head against his chest. "Stay here for a minute," he urged, his voice raw. "Just be still and let me hold you."

She wasn't ready to let go, either. With a tiny sound, Kate rested her head against Sam's scarred chest, her body relaxing as she listened to the racing of his heart.

Gradually, his heartbeat slowed. Eventually, her body ceased to tremble. One by one, tiny distractions began to seep into her awareness—the wind stirring the withered leaves of the fallen maple, the lyrical call of a thrush some distance off in the woods.

Kate squeezed her eyes shut even tighter, wishing the sounds would go away. Wishing she could stay where she was forever. But wishing wouldn't make it so. In all likelihood, the amount of time she might have with Sam could be counted in days. She shouldn't let herself feel too good, or too cared for, as she stood wrapped in his embrace. Still, when she opened her eyes to face the real world, it was with a pang of regret that she didn't have the kind of nerve it took to live for the moment, for she was very sure she'd just passed up the best chance she might ever have to experience the pleasures of being a woman.

The words she spoke were a reflection of her ambivalence. "I'm sorry."

There was a split second's hesitation, then came Sam's gruff reply.

"Sorry? What in God's name do you think you have to be sorry for?"

"I'm just not, well, used to...to..." She closed her eyes, unable to tolerate hearing herself stammer.

Sam finished for her, and to his credit, there wasn't a trace of amusement in his tone. "You aren't used to being kissed like that?"

She nodded, her head moving against his chest.

"Katie, are you a virgin?"

Her eyes blinked open. "What?"

"You heard me."

Yes, she'd heard him, and before she could give him a mature, sane response, her stomach knotted and she went all-over cold at the sudden, painful memories his question evoked.

"Now, don't go taking that the wrong way," he said when she stiffened in his arms.

"How should I take it?" she asked on a brittle note.

"Plain and simple. A point of fact." Locking her to him with one unyielding arm, his other hand lifted her face upward to meet his gaze. "I wasn't insulting the way you kiss.

You know damned well what that kiss did to me, and if it makes you feel any better, I haven't been that close to coming with my clothes on since I was, maybe, fourteen.''

Well, if she hadn't been pink with embarrassment before, she was now. Trying to look away, she murmured, ''I'm sorry. I'm not reacting very well.''

''Honey, if you were reacting any better, I'd be the one apologizing and feeling embarrassed as hell.'' Sam's hand smoothed the length of her hair, stopping to rest at the small of her back. ''Katie, it's all right. I'd say we're both pretty strung out. But I would like an answer to my question.'' His arm tightened when she started to pull away. ''Because I think the chances of my kissing you again are about a hundred percent.''

Kate hesitated.

''And I think the chances are good,'' he continued, ''that, sooner or later, we're going to finish what we started. And I've got to tell you, my experience with virgins is pretty limited. Like zero. So I guess you'd better tell me what I've got to know, so I don't get my signals crossed again.''

Her voice was barely audible. ''You didn't get any signals crossed.''

''You said I was going too fast for you.''

''*I* was going too fast for me, too.'' And because he'd been honest with her, she added, ''You weren't the only one who...came close.''

''I guessed that,'' he murmured, his lips buried in her hair. ''But you acted like it was an awful big surprise. So, are you or aren't you?''

She shook her head. And her eyes shut briefly as she steeled herself to say, ''No, Sam, I'm not a virgin. But it's been...a long time and...and it didn't—'' She broke off, her breath catching a little. ''It didn't end very well.''

''How long is a long time?''

''Six years.''

A moment passed, then Sam growled, ''He must have been one hell of a bastard if you still can't talk about him without shivering.''

It wasn't so much that, Kate thought, as it was that, in six years, she'd *never* talked about Rick Sommers. Not to anyone. Not because she wouldn't have liked to. But there was no one to tell who wouldn't have been horrified or deeply hurt and disappointed in her. And so, rather than disillusion any of those she loved, she'd allowed the feelings to become frozen inside her, along with the story of how they'd gotten there. And for every day she'd had to live with the devastating consequences of her one disastrous attempt to find love and intimacy with a man, a new layer of pain had been added to the wall encasing her heart.

But the knowing look in Sam's eyes told her he'd found the crack in *her* armor.

"I'm sorry he hurt you, Katie," he said.

She lowered her gaze, and this time when she pulled away, he let her go. She didn't go far, though. Only a couple of steps.

With her back to him, she managed to say, "He didn't hurt me so much as I let myself be hurt. But for pity's sake, it happened years ago, and if there's one thing I can't stand it's people who complain over spilt milk. I think you're right. I'm just a little strung out."

When she turned to look at him, it was immediately obvious that he didn't believe her. She didn't blame him. But he let her get away with the act, even if it was woefully frayed around the edges.

Carefully, Sam asked, "Is this person the reason you're nervous about starting something with me?"

Yes, she thought. Because you know even less about commitments than he did. And because I'm afraid to trust a man who might leave me when I need him most—like you left me last night. Like you'll probably leave me to go back to flying planes like the one that . . . killed you.

"Maybe," she replied. Then, gathering her wits a little, she added, "But, Sam, it's not just that. I meant it when I said it's happening too fast for me. I can't . . . have an affair with someone I just met a week ago. I know it seems like much longer, and so much has happened, but—"

"But it has only been a week."

"Not even a whole one. And I know you're probably used to things happening fast that way, but I'm not. My friends in college all thought I was just about the most unliberated, prudish female—"

"Prudish!"

"—ever to come down out of the woods, but I can't help it. That's the way I was raised, and we aren't in a city where nobody gives a hoot what you do with your life. I already had three neighbors ask me who that man was who carried me up my front walk, then stayed until ten o'clock Tuesday night, and if I—"

"If you sleep with me, everybody's going to know it."

"Yes. And I'd better be darned sure I'm ready to take what the grapevine dishes out. Because after you're gone, *I'll* have to live with it, and—"

"And that's the problem, isn't it?"

His question stopped her.

"You're scared of getting into something, then having me take off next week."

"Well, Sam," Kate began in sensible tones, "I understand about—"

"I told you, I can't make you any promises, Katie. And by now you ought to see why."

"I do. I'm not asking you to. It's just that—" She stopped, half turning away and wrapping an arm around her waist as a stab of anticipated pain shot through her.

"It's just that you need a little more reassurance than I've given you," he finished.

Pressing her lips together, she nodded. "Something like that. I guess."

Sam let out a sigh. "I started to tell you the other day, since the crash, I haven't been involved with anyone. And I didn't come up here looking for a woman. I ought to be telling you to get the devil out of here, because getting involved with me can't do you a bit of good, but . . . dammit, Katie—"

When he didn't continue, she turned her head to see him struggling for control. Their eyes met, and a moment later he said, "I don't want you to go."

The admission, uttered in a hoarse whisper, cost him more, she thought, than anything else he'd said that morning.

Kate searched Sam's features, torn between the need to protect herself and the almost overwhelming desire to give him what he wanted—what he needed—which, she was beginning to believe, was more than he'd ever allowed any woman to give him. His next words only strengthened her belief.

Dropping his gaze from hers, he said roughly, "I'm not good at this—talking about relationships. I'm used to things being casual and loose-ended. No pressure. No strings. But that's not going to work for you...and, to tell you the truth—" he passed a hand over his face and through his rumpled hair "—I'm not sure it'll work for me anymore, either."

With a soft, disparaging noise, he muttered, "Dying has a way of making you think about what's important, or whether all you've been doing is...wasting time."

Cautiously, Kate asked, "Is that what you think you've been doing? Wasting time?"

He waited a long time before he answered. "In some ways, yes. In others...."

He trailed off. Then, with a frustrated sound, he began to pace. "I do know one thing, though. Friends are in damned short supply these days. Most of the people I know were completely freaked out that their old friend Sam, of all unlikely people, woke up one day and discovered he could cure the sick and dying. Even Sid doesn't know what to say to me anymore. And I sure as hell wouldn't want to think I'd found a woman who could watch me do it, then listen to all the things I said to you this morning—without getting freaked out—then have her run away because she's afraid I'm only interested in getting her into bed."

He came to a halt by the dying tree, turned his head and met her gaze as he finished, "I'm not, Katie. I want more from you than that."

It was as close as he could come to a promise, and it wasn't enough. Yet it was more than she'd expected to get. He was asking for her friendship. And that, Kate couldn't refuse him. Not after all he'd done for her. Not after they'd come this far.

Holding his gaze, she spoke clearly. "If I haven't run away from you yet, Sam, I don't guess I'm going to."

A moment of silence passed between them, and finally Kate had to look away. She stared, unseeing, at the forest floor, until he walked slowly toward her. Stopping in front of her, he slid his hands under the curtain of hair that had fallen to hide her features and, bracketing her face, lifted her gaze to his.

"Katie Morgan, you're a pretty amazing woman," he said.

Kate returned his look steadily. "It's occurred to me that you're a pretty amazing man."

A corner of Sam's mouth quirked upward. "So, does that mean you're willing to take a chance on hanging out with me some more, even if it means we end up like we did last night?"

"You're the one taking the risk." A tiny smile formed on her lips. "Hanging out with me means you'll be exposed to more sick people than if you stayed put here, in the woods, like you planned to do in the first place."

"Yeah." Sam grimaced, a spark of humor lighting his eyes. "It's kind of a pain that you're a nurse. But, hell, Katie, we've all got our faults. You keep kissing me like you did a while ago, and I think I can forget about you being a nurse—or just about anything else."

Kate felt herself blushing, but she enjoyed the sound of his deep, earthy chuckle.

"Besides," he went on, casting his gaze around at the dense forest, "I've had about all I can take of talking to these damned trees. It felt good being alone this past week, but enough is enough.''

Kate grinned. ''Getting a little stir-crazy, huh?''

''A little ... Well, make that a lot. I've never been good at sitting still. And I've done enough of it the past year for another two or three lifetimes.''

''There aren't too many accidents on the streets of Bourner's Crossing,'' she suggested. ''I don't think a trip into town now and then would be too risky. And you could always—'' Her breath caught at a sudden thought. A second later her expression brightened, and she went on to say, ''Sam, I'm going to Cressie and Steve's on Sunday, for dinner. Dad and Kyle and his wife and kids will be there. And Steve's going to fly Josh up for the weekend from Kalamazoo. I know you'd be welcome to come, and goodness knows, you'd have plenty of people to talk to.''

It had seemed like a good idea, but when Kate saw a frown appear on Sam's brow, she started to brush aside her suggestion. ''Of course, it'll probably be chaotic. And I can't promise they wouldn't ask you a bunch of questions you might not want to—''

''I'd like to go with you.''

She hesitated. ''Are you sure?''

''If you think it's okay to invite a stranger for a family dinner.''

''You're not a stranger to me,'' she said simply.

Sam held her gaze for a moment, then let his eyes fall to her lips. Brushing them with the pad of his thumb, he asked, ''What time should I pick you up?''

''About one. Dinner's at four, and I want to get there early to help Cressie get ready.''

''Sounds fine.''

''Sam, I hate to say it, but I really ought to get back to town. I'm on call all weekend, and I can't even hear the CB in my truck from here.''

He gave her a single nod, but his hands slid from her face only to lock around the back of her neck. When his gaze remained fixed on her mouth, she started to tell him she really couldn't handle another kiss—definitely not.

"Sam, I—"

"Not yet."

"But—"

"One more, Katie." His head lowered, his lips parting hers on a whisper. "Just a kiss. I promise. . . ."

He kept his word and didn't attempt to push her further—although the actual number of kisses was closer to three or four, not counting the one he gave her through the open window of her pickup once she was safely inside. By the time Kate was on her way to town, her hands were trembling, her knees were rubbery, and certain parts of her were throbbing with the liquid heat of pure sexual excitement. She felt as if she were floating along in a sensual fog. And she wanted to relish the feeling.

But she couldn't. Not when her heart was at such risk. She was very close to being in love with Sam—a realization that came as no great surprise but terrified her all the same. In the first place, it was a little shocking to think she even *knew* somebody with the kind of healing powers Sam possessed; the idea of being in love with him was . . . well, it was sobering.

Most of all, though, how could she allow herself to fall in love with a man who, by his own admission, had never had a relationship with a woman that lasted more than a year? She wondered if he even knew the meaning of the word *love*, much less what it meant to be *in* love with someone. He wanted her, but he talked about it in terms of going to bed together, not of making love. And if he couldn't even say it, then she couldn't do it.

With every tender instinct in her, Kate wanted to give Sam the warmth, the shelter, the love she suspected he'd never had and that she knew he needed. But she also knew in her heart that he had the power to hurt her in ways Rick Sommers never had. If he wanted her, he'd have to prove he had the emotional honesty—and the staying power—that Rick had lacked.

She was asking a lot of a man whose entire life had so recently been turned upside down.

Then again, maybe she wasn't. Sam was a strong man, one who possessed a powerful and very special gift. And his awesome ability to heal other human beings had tapped into a well of emotion inside him, the depths of which left her breathless. The feelings frightened him, embarrassed him. But if he could accept that compassion and tenderness were part of his essential humanity, not weaknesses to fight against, she thought he might discover something else that, thus far, life hadn't taught him: that being able to understand and feel for others left a person's heart open to the possibility of love. And when Sam found out just how deeply and fiercely he could love...

She wanted to be there.

He hadn't wanted to let her go.

Sam stood watching as Kate's truck disappeared down the track, wishing he could have kept her there a little longer. Like maybe all day. Or all week. Or forever.

He felt alive. Good. Happier than he'd been in a long, long time. His body ached in all the right places. And he didn't even mind that it might go on aching. The thick, heavy throbbing in his loins was real. Something familiar and normal that he understood. In fact, it was damned reassuring. And his only qualm about it was that he was hot for a woman his conscience said he ought to leave alone.

She'd been hurt bad. It had made him ache to see the pain in Katie's eyes—the kind of pain he couldn't touch and make better. She did a good job of hiding it, but under her sweet, cheerful surface, Katie was about as defenseless as a woman could get. And if he hurt her again, Sam thought, he'd be no better than the jerk whose face he'd had ideas of rearranging a little while ago.

He *could* hurt her, too. It stunned him to realize how easy it would be. He'd known from the start Katie was the kind of woman who needed security. The kind who expected marriage. And the idea of spending the next eighty years or so with her struck a faint but strangely resonant note somewhere deep inside him.

The note was drowned out, though, by what he saw as the realities of his life. How the hell could he think about the next eighty years when he couldn't even plan for tomorrow? Katie needed a man who was ready to settle down and have a home and kids and the whole nine yards. And it was stupid for him even to consider whether he might want those same things. It was stupid to be thinking about leading a normal existence, when there was nothing about him anymore—except the hard bulge in his jeans—that reminded him he was a normal, ordinary man who had a right to expect a normal, ordinary life.

Hell! Forget the chaos he knew would ensue if anyone found out there was a healer living in Fournier's cabin. He didn't even know how he was going to earn a living. And he wasn't about to tell Katie why he couldn't go back to Chris Rutger—or anyone else—and tell them he wanted to fly their planes.

She'd handled it real well this morning when she'd found him turning green over the fish, hadn't uttered a word to make him feel any worse than he already had. But how would she react if she knew he'd been throw-up-and-pass-out scared last night just looking at the chopper? He didn't want to know. The fish had been humiliating enough.

No, there were too many problems he had to work out for him to go making promises to Katie or any other woman. Which led Sam to wonder why he was standing there wishing Katie hadn't gone, when he ought to be packing his Jeep and leaving himself before things between them went any further.

But the answer was pretty simple. She hadn't treated him like a freak. She'd listened to his story. God knows, she'd seen him at his worst. Then she'd turned around and given him the sweetest, hottest, most honest passion he'd ever had in his life. She'd made him feel starved for something he couldn't even name. And when she was still shaking from it—and from hearing him say he couldn't make her any promises—she'd looked at him with those big brown serious eyes and said, if she hadn't run from him yet, she didn't guess she would.

No, he wasn't going anywhere—except to Katie's sister's for dinner next weekend. After that...well, he didn't know. But for the first time ever, Sam began to see there might be rewards in sitting still that he'd never considered.

Up until a year ago he'd been hurtling through life at multiples of the speed of sound, his only goal being to punch bigger and better holes in the sky. But all he had to show for it was a bank account he rarely touched, the things he could pack into his Jeep, and a bunch of scars. In the long run, the only place it had gotten him was dead.

So this was supposed to be his second chance. And he'd gotten the message loud and clear that a big part of it was going to be spent doing things for other people. Last night he'd also gotten the message that he wasn't going to be punching any more holes in the sky. He didn't know how he was going to face that; the thought of not being able to fly was ... God, he couldn't think about it without wanting to scream.

But if he *had* to sit still, maybe there was something else he could have that would help fill that empty place inside him that flying had always taken care of. Because sitting still, taking things slow and easy, might get him Katie. And it occurred to him that having her—even if it was just for a little while—might give him something worth as much...and maybe more ... than anything he'd ever had.

Chapter Ten

Kate began the week thinking she'd see Sam again before Sunday. But a broken arm, a sawmill accident, the arrival of the overdue medical supplies, a day spent in Matchwood talking to Alison Lenox's science classes about prenatal development, and two days of office appointments prevented her from sneaking in even a short visit to the cabin. Everywhere she went, though, gossip about Sam's trips into town aroused her curiosity and made it harder to wait to see him.

Bert Andrews at the post office said Sam had come in on Monday to mail a letter to Detroit. Floyd Gibson, Scott's father, reported that Sam had brought his Jeep into the shop for work, and Ed Davenport said he'd been in the store on Tuesday for groceries and again on Wednesday for bait.

Bait? As in *fish*? Was Ed sure of that? Absolutely.

On her way to baby-sit for Cressie and Steve on Thursday evening, Kate tried not to worry about Sam forcing himself to catch fish that made him sick, only to prove he still could. It seemed he'd not only caught fish, though, but had taken them to Cressie's the previous evening.

Was there a problem at the cabin that had brought him out? Kate wondered. No, Cressie said, it had been a social call. The instant Sam had walked in the door, Francis had corralled him into building block towers and playing airplanes—and the fact that Sam had seemed happy to oblige a two-year-old impressed Cressie no end.

Sam had impressed the daylights out of Steve, too. The man knew his planes, Steve said. They'd talked aviation history from World War One to the present, until Cressie had begged them to stop. Had they flown Steve's plane together? Kate asked. No, it'd been too dark. Come to think of it, Steve hadn't heard Sam say whether he actually had a pilot's license. Kate bit her tongue, wondering how much Sam wanted people to know.

In any event, Steve said he'd make certain Sam got up with him in the Mentor on Sunday. He and Cressie both were glad Kate had invited Sam to join their family gathering—a "new baby" party that had expanded to include a surprise celebration of Francis's recovery. Kate was glad, too, that she'd invited Sam, since he was responsible for half her family's good fortune.

By Friday afternoon she was sure she wouldn't make it until Sunday without seeing him. Then her last office visit of the day—an hour spent with Lynn Nielsen—ruined her half-formed plans to take dinner out to Sam's cabin that evening.

"Lynn, why didn't you call me yesterday, or have Erik come get me?" Kate handed Lynn a Kleenex and waited for her to blow her nose.

The pregnant young woman had come without an appointment and had been a bundle of anxiety as she told Kate she'd woken up the previous morning bleeding. Terrified that something was wrong with her baby, Lynn had started crying the instant Kate had located the baby's healthy heartbeat with her electronic fetoscope that put intrauterine sounds on speaker. Now, with the exam over and her tears winding down, Lynn was feeling reassured.

Kate, however, wasn't.

"I know I should have come in or called." Lynn wiped her nose and wadded the tissue in her fist. "But the radio's broken, and Erik didn't finish installing the stove in the lodge kitchen until ten last night. Then he fell asleep on the couch. Besides, it wasn't much bleeding, and it stopped after a couple of hours. And I figured if—" the tears welled up again in her blue eyes "—if something was wrong with the baby, it was . . . too late. So, I . . . I . . ."

"So you worried all night and waited until Erik got home with the truck this afternoon so you could bring yourself in."

Lynn nodded. "Kate, nothing's wrong with the baby, is it?" she pleaded, her hand spreading over her rounded belly.

"Not that I can tell," Kate replied, opening the Rolodex on a corner of the desk. "But you're going to need a sonogram. And if I can get Dr. Logan at the hospital, I'd like to send you down there now."

"You mean, tonight?"

"Hmm." Locating the number, Kate picked up the phone and started to dial. "You go home and get Erik to drive you, though. And it might be a good idea to take an overnight case, in case Dr. Logan wants to keep you."

Lynn's mouth dropped open. "At the hospital?"

Tucking the phone under her chin, listening as it rang in Adrian Logan's office, Kate looked at the distraught young woman sitting in the chair alongside the desk. If Lynn went into labor at thirty-three weeks, her baby might survive—*if* the infant received excellent and immediate neonatal care. And *if* the conditions that might have caused the bleeding didn't become acute when Lynn was an hour from the hospital.

When Adrian Logan's answering service picked up, Kate left a message, then hung up to turn to Lynn. Seeing her young patient's anxious look, she reached across the desk and took her hand.

"Lynn, bleeding this late in a pregnancy isn't good. Maybe it'll turn out to be something minor. Maybe you can stay with your parents in Ironwood." She raised her eyebrows in warning. "But if Adrian Logan thinks you should be in the hospital, you're going to have to listen to him."

Lynn's mouth tightened perceptibly. "So you really think this could be serious?"

"Yes, it really could be." And Kate explained the basics of several conditions that might have caused the bleeding.

Lynn thought a moment. Then her lips thinned in a determined look. "All right. I appreciate your calling Dr. Logan for me. But I can't go down there until Tuesday."

Kate frowned. "I don't think you should wait that long."

Hesitating, Lynn chewed on her bottom lip, but an instant later she shook her head. "I can't do it sooner. I have to talk to Erik. If I'm going to have to be in the hospital, it'll mean... Well, there are some things we'll have to work out."

Kate tried to change Lynn's mind but soon realized she was arguing with a brick wall. Finally giving up, she insisted, "At least promise me you'll go home and go straight to bed. And stay there. I don't want you to get up except to use the bathroom."

"I promise," said Lynn promptly. "And if the bleeding starts again, I'll... I'll send Erik in if the radio's still not working or... well, I'll do *something*."

Kate wasn't satisfied with the compromise, but later, when she talked to Doc about her day's appointments, he assured her he'd check in on Lynn over the weekend. That helped a little.

It was nine o'clock when Kate got home, and she was too exhausted to do more than eat a bowl of cottage cheese and go to bed. When the phone rang at 3:00 A.M she groaned but woke up quickly as a frantic David Graff told her Laura was in labor and didn't think she'd make it to the hospital. Laura was right. Kate got to the Graffs' twenty minutes before Issac was born. His father was proud. Laura was elated, if a little staggered at how quickly the whole thing had happened.

Kate left their house smiling, at 5:30 A.M.—and went home to cry herself to sleep.

Would it ever end? she wondered. Would she ever have any peace from the conflicting emotions that plagued her

every time she delivered another woman's baby? She was
thrilled for Laura and David; it always made her a little eu-
phoric to participate in what she thought of as the core experience of life. But it also hurt. She'd thought it would get
better, that being a midwife would help satisfy her unfulfilled needs. But with every baby she delivered, she realized, it was only getting worse.

Kate spent all day Saturday cooking for Sunday dinner.
It solved the problem of what Sam would do when faced
with Cressie's baked ham. It was also good therapy. Seeing
Sam might have been better therapy, but she was in rotten
shape, and she didn't want their next meeting to occur when
either one of them was an emotional wreck. She wanted
them both to be at their best—and for the day to be normal.

Actually, she wanted everything to be perfect. And when
Sunday finally came, it gave every sign—at first, at least—
of living up to her wishes.

Standing at her front door on Sunday afternoon, Sam
looked lean and tall and sinfully sexy, dressed in khaki
slacks and a dark brown shirt, with his sun-streaked hair
swept back in careless disarray. Kate was certain her
expression conveyed her thoughts when his mouth sloped
into that assured, wicked grin. His eyes traveled downward, taking in the luxurious mass of shining waves falling
around her shoulders, the creamy skin exposed by the deep
lace collar of her white blouse, the curve of her hips beneath the soft, clinging folds of her flowered skirt. When his
gaze rose to caress her features, his grin had softened to a
warm smile and his eyes spoke of shared intimacies.

"I missed seeing you this week," he said.

"I missed seeing you, too," she returned.

"You look pretty. All soft and sexy."

Kate blushed, as she was sure he wanted her to, and murmured a nervous thank you.

His smile took on a hint of teasing. "I hear you've been
busy."

"I hear the same about you."

"So, let's swap local gossip while we ride. Otherwise, I'm going to kiss you. Then it'll be a while before we leave, and I want to get you out of here before the phone rings or that radio crackles and we end up losing the day."

Kate's dimples appeared as her lips curved upward. "That won't happen. Doc's on call until tomorrow."

"Don't give me that stuff," Sam replied. "After what I've heard this week, I think you've got a bigger problem than I do knowing your own limits."

She didn't like to admit it, but given her emotional state the day before, she was afraid he might be right.

It was a gorgeous day, full of warm sunshine and yellow daffodils and the clean smell of spring. With the Jeep's windows open, Kate relished the breeze whipping against her skin as they rode. And when they passed the old McCarron place—an abandoned farmhouse Kate had always loved—she got a rush of spring fever seeing the pink dogwoods blooming among the weeds on the lawn of the rambling house.

"So how did you make out with Aaron Spencer and his broken arm?" Sam asked. "I hear he fell out of the barn loft."

"He's lucky he didn't break his neck," Kate muttered. "I think his mother is hoping the cast will slow him down, but I wouldn't bet on it. He was quite a handful at the hospital."

"You went with him?"

"Yes. And don't look at me like that. Doc already yelled at me for it, but Nancy's two months pregnant and feeling crummy, so I drove them down. But how did you hear about Aaron?"

"From Mark White, who apparently works with Aaron's dad at the sawmill. I was in Davenport's when Mark came in with his hand all bandaged up. He said he lost a little skin out of his middle finger on a saw blade."

"Actually, he lost the end of his finger," Kate corrected. When Sam shot her a stunned look, she added, "It could have been a lot worse. It's always amazed me that we have as few serious accidents as we do at the mill.''

The lines on Sam's forehead came together in a familiar scowl. "Like the one at Sadler's logging camp last fall?''

"My, my, you did get an earful at Davenport's, didn't you?''

"Mr. D. said a tree fell on top of some guy, but that he died because the medevac chopper was delayed.''

"That's not exactly true. The helicopter got here in record time—forty minutes—but that wasn't fast enough.''

Sam was silent for a moment, then growled, "This town ought to have its own chopper.''

Kate laughed at the impossible notion. "Yes, wouldn't that be nice? But the whole county put together couldn't afford it.'' She understood now why Sam was so concerned with the health of the people around him, but she knew from personal experience that obsessing over all the things that might go wrong did no good.

When his scowl deepened, she said, "I hear you were at Cressie and Steve's on Wednesday.''

"What? Oh...yes.'' Sam's reply was reluctant, but he let her divert him, and gradually his expression cleared. "I met Steve at Gibson's Garage, and he invited me out.''

"He said the two of you talked planes.''

Sam lifted one shoulder in a negligent shrug.

"I think Steve enjoyed talking to somebody who appreciates flying," she said. "All he gets from Cressie about it is fretting.''

"Yeah.'' Sam chuckled. "She keeps him hopping. But after this week she'll have to find something else to fret about. Some guy from Pittsburgh is buying the Mentor, and Steve's flying it down to him on Tuesday.''

"That's a shame. He's worked so hard on it." Kate sighed, then asked, "Why didn't you tell him you're a pilot?''

Sam's gaze flashed to hers. "Did you?''

"No. I figured if you'd wanted him to know you'd have told him.'' When he looked away, she continued, "Do you *not* want people to know?''

"It doesn't matter."

His reply was almost curt, and it was clear that it did matter. Kate gave him a puzzled look. His eyes were focused on the road, his features set in a stony expression she recognized all too well.

"Listen—" he slowed the Jeep to make the turn into Steve and Cressie's driveway "—Cressie said they were taking Francis to see the audiologist on Thursday. Do you know how they made out?"

Kate knew he was deliberately changing the subject, but this was not the time to press him.

"I hear it was . . . um, an interesting visit," she replied, smiling. "The doctor spent three hours trying to prove that Francis's nerve damage hadn't completely repaired itself. But he finally had to admit that it looks like it has."

One corner of Sam's mouth quirked upward. "Must have been frustrating as hell. Did he give them an excuse?"

"No. And they don't care." Kate tilted her head, studying him as they pulled to a halt in the side yard. "That pleases you, doesn't it? Them not knowing."

"It pleases me that they don't care. They're not looking for explanations. They're just willing to accept the . . ."

"The gift?" she finished for him.

Sam frowned, one hand resting on the steering wheel, the other on the stick shift. "I wish I thought it could always be that easy."

Then, giving his head a quick shake, he said, "But I don't want to talk about anything weird today. I just want to enjoy the sunshine—" his eyes skimmed over her "—and looking at you."

Without giving her time to respond, he opened the door of the Jeep and got out. She watched him walk around the front to her side, thinking she was going to enjoy looking at him, too. But she also thought about what he'd said—that he wished it could always be that easy.

Was it unreasonable for him to want to remain anonymous to those he healed? Given what his life had been like recently, it seemed not only reasonable but essential. Sam was right in thinking he needed time to get used to being a bona fide healer—time away from the demands people were bound to make of him, however understandable they might be.

How long, though, would he be able to keep his awe-some gift a secret? Not forever, that was certain. But while he was learning his limits and growing accustomed to his new powers, what would the burden of keeping the secret be like for those he trusted to know? Those, for instance, like her. She'd be more than willing to protect him from discovery in whatever way she could. But would he let her? Or would he look at any protection she might offer him as a slur against his manhood?

She had a suspicion she knew the answer.

Similar protective thoughts were running through Sam's mind several hours later as he sat next to Kate at the dinner table in Steve and Cressie's big farmhouse dining room.

The Morgans were basically good people. They laughed a lot and teased each other with affection, and they made him feel welcome without a lot of fuss. He'd gotten considerable pleasure out of seeing their happiness over Francis and was glad Steve and Cressie had saved the announcement for today, so he could share the excitement. Yes, generally speaking, he liked the Morgans just fine. Except for one thing: He was having a hard time keeping his mouth shut about the way they treated Katie.

Oh, they cared about her. In fact, they practically worshiped her. And that was the problem. It was a toss up, who competed hardest for her attention—Cressie, Kyle, Josh, Kyle's two kids, or Francis. Sam had a feeling if Katie's other siblings had been there, they'd have wanted their nickel's worth, too. On subjects ranging from the advantages of buying a bigger house to the best way to can tomatoes, Katie was the last word.

Watching her, Sam had to give her credit for the way she handled the situation. She never criticized. She praised every success to the hilt. And she never outright told them what she thought they should do; she just listened, which made them feel important. And that was fine, except that while they were feeling satisfied with themselves, none of them stopped to think about what Katie was getting out of this—which didn't look like a hell of a lot, since they didn't think to ask her how *she* was or what *she'd* been up to lately.

Katie's dad wasn't any help, either. John Morgan was an amiable man, in his late fifties, Sam guessed, robust and healthy-looking in spite of the weathered lines in his face. He didn't say much, but he showed Katie a certain deference, a quiet, adult respect that didn't extend to his other children. She was his daughter, yet he treated her like a peer. Which only made matters worse.

The in-laws were better. Steve and Kyle's wife, Judy, acted as if they were used to the routine and had learned to tolerate it. They didn't solve the problem, but at least they didn't contribute to it.

In all fairness, Sam realized nobody was being deliberately inconsiderate. They just didn't think. Katie was the predictable influence in their lives, the one who came through for them every time. The one they turned to for approval and all that good stuff. And she was incapable of refusing them.

Well, hell. He knew what that was like, didn't he? Yes, and he wanted to say, "All right, gang, that's enough. You've had your piece of her. Now, I'm going to take her home and..." And what?

Keep her safe. Somehow protect her from her own inability to say no, and from poor needy bastards who couldn't solve their own problems and wanted her to hold their hands.

Sam had never in his life asked anybody to solve his problems. His father had expected him to handle things on his own, and there hadn't been anybody else to ask. Maybe, a long time ago, when he was very young, he'd wished he had somebody to give him what Katie had given her siblings. He hadn't had a mother when he'd needed her, and that was too bad. But it was too late; he didn't need one anymore. And he didn't know what to make of the tableful of adults acting as though they wouldn't know what to do if Katie weren't there to tell them. Especially since it wasn't true—they were all doing fine, as far as he could see.

It made him want to laugh when he looked across the table at Kyle, Katie's oldest brother, and caught the territorial challenge in the younger man's eyes—a look that had appeared when Katie introduced them. Sam understood what was going on. Kyle's suspicious gaze flickered to Katie, then back to him, and the message in Kyle's eyes couldn't have been clearer: *"You better watch yourself, buddy, if you're thinking about messing with my sister."*

Sam's expression remained impassive. Okay, so maybe he did want to mess with Kyle Morgan's sister. But in the last few hours, his guilt that he wasn't doing Katie any good and should stay away from her had undergone a surprising transformation. At least, he thought, he wasn't asking her to solve his problems. And he sure as hell expected to give her back something for what he was asking her to give him. In fact, Katie's pleasure was getting to be more important to him than his own.

Holding Kyle's dark gaze, his face giving away nothing, Sam blinked lazily. Under the table, though, he reached to find Katie's hand, lying in her lap. She was talking to Judy, sitting to her left, and he heard her breath catch when he touched her. But she didn't pull away. And, without missing a beat of her conversation, she gave him a quick smile and turned her hand over so he could entwine his fingers with hers.

A corner of his mouth twitched as he let his gaze slide away from Kyle's. *You better watch it yourself, buddy,* he thought. *You might think the lady belongs exclusively to all of you, but I think she's got other ideas.*

When it came time to do the dishes, Sam wasn't surprised that Katie got up and quietly began clearing the table, and that no one else followed suit. He looked across her empty chair and saw Judy biting her lower lip, her eyes darting over the table, laden with twelve people's dirty dishes. Cressie was telling her something about a bell choir concert in Wakefield, but she interrupted Cressie to speak.

"Kate, I'll be there in a minute to help."

"Oh, I'm just going to pick up a little," Kate replied as she started toward the kitchen with a stack of plates. "Sit still."

"Don't bother with the dishes," Cressie called after her. "I'll do them tonight after everybody's gone."

Right, Sam thought. He could just picture Katie leaving Cressie with this mess. But if they all sat here long enough, Katie would have the dishes done and put away.

Enough was enough. Sam had never offered to wash dishes in front of other men in this life, and he didn't offer then. He simply got up, picked up his plate and one of the serving dishes, and followed Kate to the kitchen.

He found her clipping her hair back out of the way; she already had a ruffled apron tied around her waist. When she saw him enter the big kitchen, her expression was startled.

"Oh, Sam, you don't have to help!"

"Yes, I do," he said, setting the dishes on the counter. "Because I couldn't wait anymore to do...this." He bent to cover her parted lips with his, kissing her just long enough to let her know she was being kissed—but not so long that he'd have to wait for the effects to wear off before he could walk back into the dining room. When he straightened to look down at her, her brown eyes were soft with surprise and arousal.

"You wash. I'll clear," he said. Then, before he gave in to the urge to kiss her again, he headed to the dining room.

As he gathered up serving dishes sitting on one corner of the table, Steve asked him if he wanted to watch the Tigers' game. He said no, he didn't think so. It gratified him to see Judy get up and make motions toward helping. An instant later, Cressie followed Judy's lead. By the time he'd made two more passes back and forth to the kitchen, the only ones not helping were Mr. Morgan, who'd been sent to the living room to sit with the sleeping baby and keep tabs on the ballgame, and Kyle, who'd gone outside with the other children.

Judy and Cressie scraped plates and put away leftovers. Josh, at eighteen the adolescent of the crew, perched on the counter with a dish towel to dry glasses and stick them in the cupboard behind him. Before someone could usurp him, Sam parked himself next to Katie to dry the plates she put in the drainer, stacking them on the table behind him for Steve to put away. It got to be as noisy a scene as the dinner table had been, and Sam was feeling relaxed and pleased with himself for having engineered it. Until Steve ruined it.

"What do you say, Sam? How about taking the Mentor up with me for a little exercise?"

Sam's fingers, gripping a flowered dinner plate, tightened. In two seconds flat his heart was pounding, and he felt the cold dampness of fear chilling him inside and out.

"You can help me run through the checklists," Steve continued. "By the time this KP duty is finished, we'll be ready to take off."

"Do you know about planes, too, Sam?"

Sam's gaze snapped up to meet Josh's. Then, with a lift of one shoulder, he muttered an affirmative response.

"Hey, come on." Steve gave him a companionable slap on the back. "In case you haven't noticed, this family doesn't stand on modesty. Except Kate. We have to twist her arm to get her to own up to anything." Then, speaking to Josh, who was suddenly all ears, he said, "You're always asking me about planes. Well, this man can tell you about every aircraft the Air Force and Navy have used since the beginning of World War One. And you should hear him talk about jets."

"Supersonics?" Josh wanted to know.

"Yes, *and* drawing-board ideas for planes most of us don't even think could exist."

"Gosh."

Sam went on doggedly wiping the same plate he'd been drying for the last two minutes, thinking he should have kept his mouth shut on Wednesday. But it had been too long since he'd talked shop with another flying addict, and he hadn't been able to resist talking to Steve. He knew Katie was casting him sideways looks; he could feel her concern, the same way he felt everyone else's eyes on him. Panic was a tight knot in his gut. But he reminded himself that, as long as he was standing there, drying dishes, he was safe. Nobody was going to drag him into the yard and throw him in the damned plane.

"You know, Sam—" Judy nudged him aside and reached around Kate for a garbage bag from under the sink "—I don't think I remember hearing you say what you do for a living."

For a moment during which his eyes bored holes in the plate he was drying, he considered lying. But finally, he admitted, "I work for a company called Rutger."

"Rutger... Say!" Josh waved a hand in an excited gesture. "Aren't they the ones making that wild-looking flying wing I saw a picture of in the paper two weeks ago? There was a big article."

"The Pegasus," Steve supplied. "Howard Industries gave Chris Rutger a contract to build it years ago, and the aviation mags have been speculating about it ever since."

"It looks like a monster sea gull," Josh continued. "The article said it's supposed to be *real* fast, too. Sam, have you seen it? In person, I mean."

Sam twisted to set the over-dry plate on the stack behind him, then picked up another. "Yeah. I've seen it."

"Jeez, you haven't *flown* it, have you?"

"Joshua," Kate broke in quickly, "I think you should—"

"It's all right, Katie." Sam met her worried brown gaze. No matter what, he wasn't going to let her cover up for him. That would put him in the same league with her brothers and sisters—the last place he wanted to be.

Letting his eyes slide from hers, he told Josh, "Yes, I've flown it."

"Really?" Josh's voice was full of enthusiasm. "You're a pilot? A *test* pilot?"

Sam nodded once.

Behind him, Steve uttered a short laugh. "No wonder I got the feeling you could take the Mentor apart and put it back together in your sleep."

"What's the Pegasus like?" Josh asked.

Sam added another dry plate to the stack as he replied. "Like every other plane Chris Rutger has built—like no other aircraft ever made."

"The article said it's an executive jet, but it sure doesn't look like anything that...well, boring." Josh's face scrunched in a disgusted grimace.

Sam's mouth twitched at the corners. "That's what Howard Industries asked for—a big, fast executive jet—and that's what they're getting. But they're also getting a radically different kind of aircraft. The Pegasus is lightweight and highly maneuverable, and it'll give you more speed than you'll ever need if you don't care about the fuel costs. If you do, then what you've got is a plane that'll go halfway around the world without refueling."

"You make it sound like a dream." Steve came to lean against the counter next to Josh, his kitchen duties forgotten. "But I hear they had a lot of problems with it. In fact—" he frowned thoughtfully "—I remember reading an article about a crash. It happened around the same time I bought the Mentor—about a year ago—because I remember wondering what the devil kind of nerve it must take to fly a plane that everybody else in the industry says won't fly."

Sam's lips tightened into a bloodless line. "Oh, it flies."

"When was the last time you flew it?"

"About a year ago."

An instant of confused silence passed. Then Steve burst out, "Sam, you aren't the pilot who—" He broke off, his expression changing rapidly from disbelief to shock. "My God, you are, aren't you?"

Behind him, Sam heard Cressie's horrified, "Oh, my Lord," and the sound of a chair scraping the floor as she plunked down with a whimper.

Tonelessly he explained, "The nosewheel got hung up on landing, but the computer didn't indicate there was a problem. So I hit the runway with the wheel partially extended, one wing tip caught the ground, and the plane cartwheeled. That was the original test plane. The front end's been modified since then."

"Lord almighty," Steve whispered.

"But how come—" Judy began, then hesitated, her eyes running over him as she stood at the counter on Katie's far side. "You *must* have been hurt," she said.

Sam shrugged. "It kept me down for a while." Then, because he couldn't tolerate doing nothing while they all stared at him, he reached for another plate. But there weren't any more. Katie had stopped washing and was gripping the edge of the counter with white knuckles as she stared out the window over the sink.

Josh wanted to know, "Are you still with Rutger?"

Sam uttered a harsh laugh. "Chris doesn't believe in taking anybody off the payroll unless they're dead and buried." *And I get a letter from him about every other week asking me how long it's going to be before I'm ready to get the hell back to work.* "Officially, I'm on disability leave."

"Jeez, but . . . you're okay, aren't you?"

The boy seemed younger at eighteen than Sam ever remembered being, and his stoic expression softened a little as he said, "Yeah, Josh, I'm okay."

They were all silent for a minute.

Finally, Steve shook his head. "Well, that's one heck of a story, Sam. Flying a Pegasus . . . Lord! I'd give my eye-teeth—" He cut himself off, then added, "I guess I see why you don't want to bother with my old T-34."

Steve was offering him an excuse. All he had to do was shrug and say something like, *"Yeah, well, you know how it is. . . ."* But he couldn't do it. He might be a coward, but, dammit, he hadn't lost his integrity.

Glancing briefly at Josh, Sam asked, "Has Steve ever told you about his plane?"

"Well, not a lot," the boy admitted, shooting Cressie a look, where she sat behind Sam at the table. "We, uh, don't talk about it much."

"Then you're missing a piece of history." Flattening his hands on the counter to control their trembling, Sam spoke roughly. "The Beech Craft T-34 Mentor isn't famous, and it isn't rare. But it was put into service in the Air Force and Navy in 1949, and it's been turning kids into pilots ever since—including me. In fact, the T-34's got one of the longest service records of any plane in military aviation history, and I don't know a pilot who won't say it's one of the best-handling aircraft he's ever flown. Besides that, it's fully acrobatic, which means it's just plain fun to fly.''

Josh was obviously impressed, yet he still gave Sam a dubious look. ''But it isn't like what *you're* used to.''

''No, it sure isn't,'' Sam agreed. ''Since I left the Navy, the planes I've flown don't have any history, and they haven't proven much of anything to anybody yet. They're just expensive pieces of hardware with possibilities and good intentions.''

''All right, all right,'' Steve said, chuckling. ''I get the message. So how about we take the old war bird up for a spin?''

This was it. With his vision blurring and his insides shaking, Sam didn't know what to do. It seemed his only choice was to tell the truth. Which meant looking like a fool in front of Katie...

''Steve, please, do you have to do it *now*?''

Staring at the empty dish drainer, Sam was so caught up in his own inner turmoil, he almost missed Cressie's anxious question.

Steve's tone was exasperated. ''Cressie, I told you I had to—''

''But the kids will want you to put on a show for them.''

''Well, what's wrong with that? It'll be gone by Tuesday. This'll be the last chance they get to see it.''

''But it makes me so nervous!''

Josh groaned. ''Everything makes you nervous, Cressie.''

''Oh, go stick your head in a bucket,'' she retorted. ''I know you all think I'm just being a nagging fishwife, but I don't care. Flying scares me, and that's the way it is.''

''Aw, Cressie, for crying out loud—''

''It scares me, too.''

Kate's quiet announcement brought the argument to a dead halt. Sam's eyes flashed to her, but she was looking at the others and didn't meet his gaze. With her hands twisting together at her waist, she looked as anxious as Cressie.

"Kate, you've never been scared of planes," Steve noted, clearly confused.

"I know," she said. "But all this talk about crashing is enough to make anybody nervous. I'm not doubting your judgment, Steve, but if something went wrong and Dad and the kids were watching...well, I don't think any of us want to stand there and see it happen. Besides, it's getting late. So let's stop this business and talk about something else. Can we?"

You bet they could. For Katie, they'd jump through any hoop. They might have ignored Cressie's objections, but all Katie had to do was let them know, in the gentlest possible way, that she didn't exactly approve, and that was the end of it. No one breathed a word about planes for the remainder of the day.

Yet Sam had to wonder. Did Katie know? He didn't see how she could—unless she'd heard his heart pounding. But the possibility that she might have figured it out bothered him almost as much as the idea of flying itself. It would be like having her find out he was crippled. Flying hadn't been just a way of making a living. It had been his life, his identity. Take it all away, and ... well, he didn't know what was left, but he knew it wouldn't be enough. Not enough for Katie.

She needed somebody she could rely on, somebody who'd take care of her. She needed a man. And he didn't want her to find out that he wasn't exactly up to standards anymore.

Chapter Eleven

Sam, are you going back to Rutger when you leave here?"

Riding home in semidarkness, Kate glanced at the man beside her, and in the Jeep's dim interior, she saw his mouth twist in a dry smile.

"Are you worrying again about me leaving next week?"

"That's not why I asked. I wondered if the idea of going back to California might make you look someplace else."

Sam was silent a moment, then admitted, "It might. There are other companies that build planes. And there are foreign countries, too, looking for test pilots."

Kate looked at him sharply, but the only hint she got of his mood was the grim defiance of his tone. "You'd consider that?"

"Why not?" he replied.

Why not, indeed.

Kate's fingers toyed with the scalloped edge of the crocheted shawl she had draped over her shoulders. "You know, with all the talk today about planes and your crashing that Pegasus thing . . . I was thinking that, with the time you spent in the hospital, and the uproar since you found out about your—'' she paused ''—your special talents, I guess you haven't . . . had much chance to fly.''

"Katie, I'd just as soon not talk about this if it's all the same to you.''

His quiet warning had an edge to it, and Kate figured the smart thing would be to back off.

"I'm sorry,'' she began. "I was just thinking how hard it would be if I had to be away from nursing for so long. I'd be awful anxious to get back to it again.'' She waited for him to answer, and when he didn't, she sighed. "Of course, I suppose if you don't *have* to think about it, you might as well relax. A lot of people would love to be able to take a long vacation from their jobs.''

There was the barest trace of humor in Sam's tone as he asked, "Are you afraid I'm going to starve to death?''

That hadn't been her main concern, but . . .

"Sooner or later I'd imagine that would get to be a problem. Wouldn't it?''

"Honey, they pay test pilots a pretty outrageous amount of money to take the risks they take, and I haven't spent much of it. It'll be a good while before I have to think about money.''

There wasn't enough money in the world to make Kate think it was worth the risks, but she was glad to hear he didn't have financial problems to add to his troubles. Especially if her suspicions turned out to be true.

When they arrived at Kate's house, Sam got out of the Jeep, opened her door and walked with her up the front steps without another word being spoken. But when she reached to open the door, Kate paused, staring at her hand wrapped around the metal handle of the screen door.

"Sam, last Friday night . . . why didn't you go with me to Marquette?''

When she looked up, she caught a brief glimpse of his shock at her question. He recovered quickly, but his tone was clearly defensive as he replied.

"What for? The guy was okay.''

"True, but—'' she hesitated ''—but I didn't know that.''

"I told you he would be."

"Yes, you did, but—"

"Katie, are we going inside? Or do I have to kiss you out here, with Sarah Winfield taking notes?"

Kate's eyes flew up to meet Sam's, and when a corner of his mouth curved in that familiar, half-teasing, half-seductive smile, she grimaced. "You heard about that, huh?"

He nodded slowly. "I carried a box of groceries over there for Mr. D. on Tuesday, and that nice old lady spent a good half hour giving me the details on the men you've dated in the past three years. All one of them. So unless you're out to liven up her evening..." His gaze fell to her lips.

Kate groaned, pulling the screen door wide. "You'll give Sarah vertigo."

"What?"

"Never mind. Just come on inside. Anyway, I baked a cherry pie for you to take home, and I want to give it to you."

The living room was bathed in a soft amber glow from the Victorian lamp on the table beside the front window, and Kate didn't bother to turn on any others. As she tossed her shawl and purse over the back of an armchair, she was aware that she and Sam had different ideas about what would happen next. But if he couldn't be honest with her...well, then, neither of them was going to get what they wanted.

"Can I fix you a cup of coffee?" she asked.

Sam ambled into the small living room, stopping in front of the mantel to examine a photograph. "No thanks," he replied.

"A piece of pie?"

"I'm still full from dinner. Who're these people? Your grandparents?"

"Yes. My mom's mother and father. Would you like to sit?"

He gave her a glance over his shoulder, let his eyes drop to the sofa facing the fireplace, then turned back to his examination of her picture gallery. "In a minute, maybe."

He moved on to look at a picture of her parents while Kate stood gripping the back of the sofa. She felt as if she had a stick of dynamite in one hand and a lit match in the other. Only a fool would light the fuse. Or a woman set on loving a man who wasn't sure that he wanted—or knew how—to let her.

"Sam, were you afraid?"

His back stiffened, and he went very still for a moment. Then he moved to look at the anniversary clock in the center of the mantel. "Afraid of what?" he replied.

Kate took a shallow breath. "Last Friday. Were you afraid to ride in the police helicopter?"

He laughed, a short, rasping sound. "What kind of crazy question is that?"

"It doesn't seem crazy to me."

The seconds ticked by, and when Sam didn't say a word, didn't look at her, simply stood there, unmoving, she asked again.

"Were you afraid? I'd really like to know."

"Dammit, Katie, what is this?" The words burst out of him as he whirled to stride away from the mantel. "Haven't you had enough of playing mother hen for one day? You think you need to turn me into another one of your permanent infants?"

Kate's lips tightened when his shot struck home. He pivoted in front of the window to face her, and she prepared herself for an attack. But when he met her gaze across the room, his breath caught, held for an instant, then came out in a groan.

"Katie..." Sam's eyes slid from hers. "I'm sorry. That was stupid talk. I say things I don't mean sometimes, because—" He shook his head, turning to face the curtained window. "Hell, I don't know why I say them. You shouldn't put up with it."

Kate's answer was quiet and clear. "Why don't you let me decide what I want to put up with."

"You put up with too much," he murmured, his voice soft like the muted light from the lamp in front of him. Staring at the lamp, he added, "You're probably the most generous, unselfish person I've ever met. And I wouldn't want you to be any different. But I'm not used to having somebody worry about me, and it... Well, I'm not comfortable with it.''

Kate smiled. "I know." *But I'm going to do it, anyway.*

Pausing, her eyes fastened on his angular profile, she asked the question one more time. "Sam, did the crash make you afraid of flying?"

His jaw tightened, and he spoke through clenched teeth. "You don't give up, do you? I told you I don't want to talk about it." Then, without a glance in her direction, he headed for the door. "And maybe I'd better get out of here before I say something else I don't want to say."

He stopped with the door half open, one hand on the knob, the other braced on the frame. For a long moment he simply stared through the screen door into the shadowed darkness, his shoulders rising and falling with his rapid breathing. Kate closed her eyes, clamping her mouth shut against the urge to beg him not to go, to give himself—and her—a chance. Just one chance—that's all she wanted—to show him that he didn't have to handle everything alone.

When the door clicked shut, her eyes flew open, and she nearly cried to see he hadn't left.

With his hands still on the door, Sam bit out an explicit four-letter word. Then he growled, "Who the hell am I kidding?"

Drawing a shuddering breath, he spoke over his shoulder. "Katie, you don't want to hear this."

"Sam..." She spoke very softly. "I... I care about you. I do want to hear it."

Still he hesitated. "I don't want you looking at me like you do your brothers and sisters."

"Believe me, I don't feel even vaguely the same about you as I do about them."

That made him turn around. Kate was not surprised to see him struggling to put his armor in place. But he wasn't going to be able to do it this time, and she didn't know whether the tears that kept lodging in her throat were ones of heartbreak for him or of tentative hope that she might be more important to him than his pride, after all.

The first words he spoke threw her.

"I got grounded."

Kate frowned. "You mean, you lost your pilot's license?"

Sam shook his head. "The final medical report I got from the hospital said the nerve damage in my spine would screw up my reflexes, and that my body couldn't take the stress of high speeds or altitudes. The FAA medical examiner wouldn't give me a medical certificate. And without a certificate, you don't fly."

Her frown went from puzzled to worried. "But you told me you're all right now."

"I am."

"So—"

"I fought for three months to get the certificate back, but I wasn't about to tell them why the hospital report was worthless—too many people already knew about the healing thing. Then I told Marty Anderson about the trouble I was having. I didn't know he was doing it, but he started talking to the FAA, and somehow, about a week before I left California, he got them to issue me a clean certificate."

"Then you *could*—" She bit her lower lip. He could—but he couldn't.

"Yeah, how about that," Sam muttered, moving away from the door. He only went a couple of steps to the lamp table, though, as if to say he still might decide to leave. With his gaze directed once more at the opaque glass lamp, he asked, "How did you figure it out?"

Her voice quavered a little as she answered. "Your face. After dinner, when Steve asked you to go up with him. You were... You looked like you did last week—over the fish."

"You mean I was green." Having been backed into the corner, he wasn't about to show himself any mercy. "So your whole family knows."

"I doubt it. You're not an easy man to read, Sam."

"You seem to be doing a pretty good job of it."

"I've had a chance to practice." *But I'd rather you told me what you're feeling.*

He was silent for a minute, reaching out to bat at the fringe that hung from the lampshade. Then, he said, "Up until now, I've had excuses I could give myself. I didn't have a medical certificate. I don't like flying commercial. I wanted to have my Jeep so I'd have transportation."

He hesitated, stuffing both hands into his pockets. "Last Friday night...that was the first time since the crash I really had to face it—where I've been in a situation I couldn't rationalize my way out of. Katie, I knew you were scared. I wanted to go with you, but..."

"It's all right," Kate said quietly. "It's enough to know you wanted to."

His reply was hard and grim. "It's not enough for me."

"But, Sam..." Taking a few steps, she stopped at the end of the sofa, her hand reaching toward him. "A lot of people are afraid of flying—people who've never been near a plane and don't have a single real reason to be scared of one. And you have the best reason in the world!"

"Come on," Sam grated. "'A lot of people' are not jet pilots with thousands and thousands of hours of logged flight time. Being scared of what you don't know anything about isn't the same as wanting to vomit and pass out just at the *idea* of doing what you've been doing for over seventeen years."

No, it wasn't, Kate had to admit. Still...

"For heaven's sake, Sam," she reasoned, "whether you're a pilot or not, you're human! You died in that crash! Anybody has a right to be scared of something that *killed* them!"

For a fraction of a second, Kate thought she saw his harsh mask waver, his face lose a trace of color, his jaw slacken.

She spoke in gentle tones. "Please, don't be so tough on yourself. It's a normal reaction. You *must* know you'll get over it."

His countenance hardened instantly. "I'm not being too tough on myself...and I'm not going to get over it."

"How can you say that? Sam, it's only been a year since you crashed that plane, and you spent most of it in the hospital. At least give it some time before you decide it's hopeless."

"Time isn't going to make any difference. And it's not a matter of deciding." His voice dropped to a low rumble. "It's just part of the price."

Kate's eyes widened. "The price for what? Your life? That's . . . Sam, that's ridiculous."

He shook his head slowly. "No, it's fair. I got a second chance. But it's not free. There are things—lots of them— I've had to give up."

She stared at him for a moment. Then, suddenly, as the strange logic of his reasoning began to make sense, she whispered, "Meat."

"And coffee and any kind of alcohol, and cigarettes," Sam added. "I can't put anything in me that slows me down or speeds me up or feels . . . dead."

"And the fish," she concluded.

He shrugged. "Catching them was fine. It was trying to clean them that did it. I couldn't cut up living, breathing flesh and watch it bleed."

Kate's eyes remained fixed on him as she moved around the sofa and sank onto a corner of it. It was finally hitting her that the man she was falling in love with was truly, fundamentally different than he had been prior to a year ago.

She couldn't quite see why Sam would miss the things he'd given up, or why he would resent the heightened awareness—the enlightened conscience—he'd acquired. But then, the changes in his life weren't the result of some spiritual discipline or radical social beliefs. They'd come as a total shock, the result of one profound, devastating experience. And unlike someone who might decide one day to "try out" a new lifestyle and the next day give it up, the changes in Sam—and in his life—were irrevocable. They had been thrust upon him, and he couldn't set them aside, not even for a little while. He had to learn to live with them. All of them . . .

"And you think flying's been added to the list," she concluded. "Like a . . . a sacrifice."

"That's not what I'd call it," he murmured. "It's just a payment, plain and simple."

A payment. And he thought it was a fair payment, at that.

Kate couldn't accept it. There was something very wrong here. The other things he'd given up made a kind of sense. It seemed right that a person who had the power to heal would find it hard to take a life, any life, or to do harmful things to his own body. But to be *afraid* of something—to be afraid of *flying* . . . No, it wasn't the same thing at all. She didn't believe he had to pay for the second chance he'd been given. Nor did she think there was anything fair about a man forfeiting the thing he loved most in the world. In fact, it seemed more like punishment. But for what? And who was doing the punishing?

Calculating her words, Kate turned on the couch to face forward, pulling a throw pillow onto her lap and placing her hands flat upon it. "Well," she sighed, "I've seen a lot of men lose their jobs—farms go under, mines close. They've found other things to do. You can too, I guess. I mean—" she lifted a shoulder "—there are other things in life besides flying."

When Sam didn't respond, Kate turned to see him staring at her, and the expression on his face said she might have suggested there were other things besides breathing.

"Would you quit nursing?" he asked.

Her eyes dropped to watch as she fingered the tatted lace edge of the pillow. "Well, no, but—"

"No buts," he retorted. "You wouldn't. Period. Not as long as you had your hands and all your faculties. Well, I've got the same kind of one-track mind. Flying's the only thing I've ever cared about. And you said yourself a person ought to do what they like and do best. Remember?"

Yes, she remembered, and she didn't mind his using her own words as an argument. But she couldn't help saying, "You know, there's at least one other thing you do very well."

Sam understood immediately what she meant, and he reacted exactly as she'd expected.

"Forget it." Taking a few long strides to stand at the mantel in front of her, he gave her a warning scowl. "Don't you start getting ideas. Because I'm not about to make a career out of curing people. In the first place, I'd never take money for it. And in the second place, I don't *like* being a healer. Most of the time, I downright *dis*like it."

"But you did tell me you were glad you could help people."

"But I didn't say I liked doing it."

"You don't?"

"Hell, no, I don't! You saw me with that man, Cooney. Did it look like I was having fun?"

Turning sharply, he set to pacing in front of the hearth. "Katie, you help people all the time. And it's obvious you get a lot of pleasure out of it. But you've been doing it all your life—you're used to it. And I'm not. It's like—" his hand searched the air "—like waking up one day and finding out you've turned into a sponge. It seems like the only purpose I've got in life anymore is to absorb pain." He shot her a dubious look. "And you think I ought to make a career of it? Lady, you're out of your mind. I'm looking for a way to make this thing livable. Not to make it worse."

Kate's eyes followed as Sam continued to pace in brooding silence. She was about to tell him she hadn't really been suggesting he make a career of healing, when he came to a halt, leaning an arm on the mantel as he let out a frustrated curse.

"Ah, hell," he muttered. "I don't know why I expect you to understand this when I don't understand it myself."

"But I think you do," Kate replied.

He was rubbing the bridge of his nose, but as she spoke he stopped rubbing to listen.

"It must be horribly disorienting to have your whole life turned inside out, and if it were me, I'd resent it like mad—for a while, at least. But underneath all the confusion—the day-to-day things that keep cropping up to upset you—I think you do know what's going on. I think you understand it very well.''

Sam turned his head to give her a sharp look. But after a few seconds, the lines of his face and the set of his shoulders slowly relaxed, and it seemed as if the defensiveness and the frustration drained out of him.

''Maybe I do understand it,'' he said quietly. ''Maybe I understand why having this...gift changes everything. And maybe I even see that what I do with it is more important than whether I fly a plane. But so far, understanding it hasn't made living with it any easier. Sometimes, it just makes it harder.''

Their eyes held across the short distance that separated them, and for a moment, he studied her. Then, with a purposeful look, he walked slowly toward her.

Kate drew back as he approached, a little frightened by the tension radiating from him. He sat on the edge of the sofa, turning sideways to face her, and when he reached for her hands, she was filled with a strange reluctance. Yet she let him draw her hands into his, feeling both the strength and the gentleness of his grasp. She started to speak, looking to relieve her uneasiness, but an instant later she forgot what she was going to say.

It was happening. Her gaze fell to his hands, wrapped around hers, as she realized they were growing warm. Not hot, like they'd been the night he'd healed Ray Cooney, but warm. A shimmering, electric warmth. And it seeped slowly into her own skin, the reluctance she'd been feeling drained out of her. There was nothing to be afraid of, nothing in this that would ever hurt her....

''Do you see what I'm saying, Katie?'' he asked. ''Do you feel it? Feel it *here*—'' his hands squeezed hers a little ''—feel what I'm trying to tell you.''

Oh, yes, she felt it. And she realized that until that moment, she hadn't begun to understand it. How had she thought it happened? She'd seen him lay these hands upon a dying man, and it had seemed like magic that the man lived. Yet the hands that held hers were flesh and blood. Strong and big and tanned, the backs dusted lightly with fine hair, the fingers long and tapered. They were wonderful hands—but a man's hands, nevertheless. And it was impossible to grasp that they could have become the vehicle for such a powerful force, the essence of life itself. The force wasn't the man, yet he somehow could contain it in his body. But how could he? And how could he go on, knowing...? But then, that was the problem, wasn't it?

In a voice filled with wonder, Kate breathed, "It doesn't hurt. It's so hot, and yet..."

"No, Katie," Sam said. "It doesn't hurt. It heals."

He released her then, and Kate stared at her hands, feeling the warmth he'd imprinted upon her skin fade until at last it was gone. Then slowly, she lifted her gaze to meet his.

His clear gray eyes were less guarded than she'd ever seen them, and they revealed that incredible strength of spirit she'd always sensed was there but had never seen in such full measure. Yet his eyes also spoke of things not so wonderful, things Kate could better understand, and the sum of it was a wrenching ambivalence.

"Katie..." Sam searched her features for a moment, then turned away. "I'm not trying to scare you or prove something to you. I'm trying to tell you I don't recognize myself anymore. Since the day I put my hands on Sid and stopped that artery from pumping blood, I wake up every day wondering what I'm going to find different about me. And often enough some new thing hits me off guard—like the fish last week. But it's more than a matter of changing habits or the way I live."

Kate's eyes followed as Sam rose to move restlessly around the confined space between the sofa and hearth.

"I spend all kinds of time thinking," he said. "Thinking about things and asking myself questions that never would have occurred to me before. And it's all tied up with knowing... knowing what comes after this. Knowing that being dead isn't an end to life. It's a continuation of it. Except it's... Oh, Lord..." Coming to a stop by the fireplace, his eyes closed on a long, ragged sigh. "Katie, there aren't any words to talk about that place. I could call it heaven, but that wouldn't tell you anything. There isn't any...any *language* to describe it. But in my mind it's got color and shape and size. I can remember how it feels. How...peaceful it was."

Sam's eyes opened slowly, and in a voice that held all the bitterness of a lonely lifetime, he said, "But I had to come back here. And now I'm supposed to go on living in a body that looks like mine—mostly—and feels like mine and has all my memories. But it's a body that feels things mine never felt—and that can do things *I* never knew how to do. And I ask myself, Are you really who you think you are? Do you even *know* who—or what—you are? And honest to God, some days..." He shook his head. "Some days I have to wonder."

Giving Kate a brief look, Sam's mouth twisted in self-mockery. "Katie, I didn't leave California to get away from sick people. I left to get away from the stares. I couldn't take being treated like a freak in a sideshow. I couldn't stand listening to people talk about me like I was either a washed-up pilot or a laboratory rat or some religious nut's latest idea of the Messiah." With an angry gesture, he insisted, "I'm just a man, dammit!" But in the flash of silence that followed his emphatic statement, he turned away, muttering, "Not that I'm even sure I know what the hell that means anymore."

And that, Kate thought, said it all.

She could no more have kept from going to him then than she could have stopped spring from coming. So many times she'd wanted to touch him, to reach for him, but hadn't for fear of...of what? Of making him angry? Of being rejected? Of falling in love with him? Well, it was too late for that. Still, as she rose from the sofa and walked slowly toward him, her heart was racing, and she was frighteningly aware that she was taking the biggest risk she'd ever taken in her life.

Chapter Twelve

Sam watched Kate approach, his body tensing. He didn't want her near him. He didn't want anyone near him. He wasn't even sure why he hadn't left in the first place, when he'd realized what was coming, except that it would have been like lying. To have walked out, when it was so clear Katie knew the truth, would have looked worse than simply admitting it.

Well, so, he had. He'd told her more about himself than he'd ever told another human being. And, honest to God, he didn't know where people ever got the idea that talking about their problems made them feel better. As far as he was concerned, they could have it. He felt awful. Raw. Like in the hospital, when the doctor had scraped the burned skin off his face every day so he wouldn't scar, and he'd had to lie there and not scream and act like he wasn't just horrified at the whole idea. They'd wanted to scrape the rest of him, too, and he'd told them to forget it. He'd take the scars.

So, when Katie stopped in front of him and raised her brown eyes to his, he felt like she must be seeing him without any skin. And he felt like screaming, then, too. He almost did, when she lifted her hand and placed it on the spot just below his heart, where, under his shirt, the long surgical scar began its arc around the right side of his body. But then she did something that knocked the wind out of him and made the muscles in his belly tighten, so he couldn't scream; instead, all he could do was stand there, holding his breath, watching as she let her gaze drop from his and began tracing the scar beneath the cloth with her fingertips.

It was as if she'd memorized it, for she followed the line unerringly. Her look was intent, her movements slow. When she reached the halfway point of the scar, she retraced the path to where she'd started, finally letting her hand rest lightly on his shirtfront as she lifted her gaze to his once more. This was no sympathetic pat on the hand but a deliberate attempt to shred the last of his control, and Sam knew the look he returned was suspicious and about as receptive as a brick wall.

"Sam," she said, in a voice that was low and kind of shaky. "I don't know what sort of man you were before, and it doesn't matter to me, because I know what kind of man you are now. I can tell you, you're more of a man than most men ever get to be. And it doesn't have a single thing to do with whether you can clean a fish or whether you can heal a person or fly an airplane. In fact, you're—"

She broke off, her lashes lowering in a way that made it sink into Sam's confused, wary mind that this wasn't at all what he'd expected—and that she was really nervous. But about what? Why should *she* be nervous? When her hand moved, fingers trembling as they slid up his chest, and a hint of pink crept into her cheeks, it hit him: This wasn't sympathy. It was seduction. And, damn . . . it was working.

Her eyes were warm and heavy-lidded as she raised them once more to his, and she continued on that same trembling note to tell him, "You're more of a man than any man I've ever known. You're enough of a man that all I have to do is look at you, and . . . Oh, Sam—" her eyes drifted closed

"—when you look at me or touch me, when you kiss me, you make me feel things no man has ever made me feel. You make me feel exactly the way a woman's supposed to feel. And it . . . it feels wonderful."

"Ah, Katie . . ." His hand lifted, his fingertips brushing her flushed cheek as he tilted her face up to his. How she'd done it, he didn't know, but in less than a minute flat she'd given him back every scrap of pride he'd spent the past hour wasting. He ran his thumb over her full lower lip. "Honey, when I look at you—when you look at me like you are right now—you make me feel exactly like a man is supposed to feel. And it feels good, Katie . . . so damned good."

"Does it?"

"You know it does."

"Kiss me, Sam. Please."

Her body was straining upward, toward him, and Sam felt himself bending, toward her. Their lips were only inches apart, and he could feel the current of anticipation running between them. But before he kissed her, he had to tell her. . . .

"Katie, we're not going to stop this time. I want . . ." He drew a quick breath, his eyes searching her pretty face, skimming over her shiny hair, finally locking with her deep brown eyes, sinking into them, drowning in them. "I want to make love to you," he said.

Her breath rushed out on a little sob, and her eyes closed briefly. When she opened them, they were hazy with desire. "That is what people do, isn't it," she whispered, "when they make each other feel this way?"

"Is it? I don't know." His lips touched hers once. "I've never felt this way before."

Nor had he ever pulled a woman into his arms, settled his mouth over hers, and kissed her as if doing it meant more to him than anything else in the world. But it did. Somehow, at that moment, it meant everything. And he tried to tell her that. He tried to tell her that she was special, different from any other, and that he was different, too. And, for once, he was glad of that, because making love with her was going to be different from anything he'd ever known.

Slow, he said to her silently. *Ah, Katie, we're going to take this so slow. Slow, like my mouth and yours blending this way, so we feel everything, taste everything, so I know your mouth the way I know my own, and you know mine. Slow, so when we get where we're going, we'll know exactly where we've been. Because getting there...Ah, Katie, getting there is going to be such a pleasure....*

He tried to tell her everything in that kiss—everything about needs and wants he hadn't known he had, and about wanting to give her things he'd never thought of giving anyone. And he told her until she was liquid in his arms. Until she was breathless and trembling, her face flushed and her lips wet and swollen. When he raised his head far enough to look down at her, her lashes fluttered, and she whispered his name. He kissed her again, briefly, then lifted her in his arms. He wouldn't have let her go for anything.

The bedroom was bathed in moonlight filtering through lacy curtains, and the moon provided all the light Sam needed to find the bed—and to see the look on Katie's face when he stood her beside it. The slight lowering of her lashes, the hint of uncertainty, reminded him of how long it had been for her and that she was probably feeling shy and maybe a little scared. And so, when he pulled her into his arms, he tried to tell her it was all right.

Some of it, he told her in words.

"Katie, honey, it's going to be good between us."

"It already is...Oh...Oh, Sam, when you touch me..."

"You're so soft. All-over soft, like I've never felt soft before. And your hair..."

"If it gets in the way, I can—"

"It's not in the way. I want to wrap us up in it and...Katie, don't ever call your hair, or anything else about you, plain and ordinary again."

"I've always thought I was."

"Well, honey, you're about to find out you're not."

He undressed her in a way meant to arouse, not to startle, and in a way meant to stretch it out and make it last a long, long time. His hands learned her through the fabric of her clothing, using the filmy lace of her blouse to shape the lush fullness of her breasts, and the soft folds of her skirt to mold the curve of his hips, to test the rounded swell of her bottom, and to caress for the first time the heated warmth between her thighs. An accidental brush, a deliberate stroke. A fingertip here, the palm of his hand there. Long before her blouse or skirt were even unbuttoned, the clothing under them was gone or undone, and he'd touched almost every inch of silky skin beneath them.

His own clothing came off in a slightly different way.

"Katie, if you're thinking about undoing the rest of the buttons on this shirt, or maybe taking something else off—"

"I've got plans along those lines."

"I was hoping you did, but I've got to tell you, I'm kind of nervous about it."

"Nervous? Sam, I don't believe you."

"You haven't seen all the scars yet."

"Oh, Sam. You don't really think these scars matter to me, do you?"

"Well, besides a bunch of burns... Oh, yes, touch it like you did in the living room. Yes, with your mouth... Ah, Katie, you've got the sweetest, hottest mouth."

"Help me with the buckle, Sam. I want to see you."

"There's burns, like the ones you've already seen. And they did... Here—let me get my shoes... They did some pretty serious cutting on my leg."

"I promise, I won't stare like I did the first time.'

"Katie, you can stare all you want."

"Not at the scars, though. Oh, Sam, you're...Oh, my..."

With soft, brief kisses, with the unmistakable trembling of his hands, with approving murmurs and deep, shuddering sighs, he let her know what she did to him every time she touched him. And he made it seem as if their touching each other was the most natural thing in the world. When the last of their clothing eventually fell to the floor, there wasn't a hint of nervousness or uncertainty in the way she pulled back the quilt, sat on the bed, and opened her arms to him.

Placing a knee on the mattress beside her, he wrapped a hand around the back of her head and bent to kiss her,

172   *MIRACLES*

feeling as he did so as if this was the beginning. The *real* beginning of the life he'd been given a year ago. So far, he'd only been surviving, watching the empty space inside him grow larger, until that's all there was. But in making love with Katie, it was as if he were taking the initial step toward filling that empty space. And he was choosing something— some*one*—to put into it who meant more to him than anyone ever had.

He came down to her knowing this was the most completely right thing he'd ever done in his life. And as he wrapped her body against his in the first, breathless, flesh-to-flesh embrace, he thought about how it would be to go on filling up the days and nights with the same rightness he felt at that moment, kissing, touching, coming to know this woman in his arms.

There was no doubt in his mind that she would last a man a lifetime. Warm and tender and full of an honest, almost innocent passion, she was everything he'd known she'd be. But he hadn't really known, because there'd been no woman like this for him. There hadn't been a woman whose lips molded this softly to his or whose mouth tasted this good. None whose passionate responses matched his so exactly and with such ease. No woman who felt so perfectly shaped for him, or whose body, entwined with his, gave him such pleasure.

And, oh, it was a pleasure to touch her. To touch her face and her soft, soft skin. To get lost in those long, silky ropes of hair. To hold her beautiful breasts, to shape them and suck on them and bury his face between them, and to hear her moan and feel her hips move against him, and to know the pleasure was not his alone. To feel the giving crush of her belly against the throbbing demand of his erection, to sink his fingers into her hot, creamy folds and watch her body arch as she gasped his name. Then, to have her reach for him, to feel her mouth and hands all over him. To hear her sighs and murmurs and sultry sounds of arousal as she learned his body... To lie trembling under the erotic perfection of her selfless loving and watch the last remnants of the jaded life he'd led slip away.

If he lived another hundred lifetimes, he would never forget the moment he slid inside her. The look in her eyes. The catch in her voice as she whispered his name. The clutch of her fingers on his back. The satin of her thighs embracing his hips. The tightness and slick heat of her stretching to sheath him. He'd never forget the way her eyes held his and the world seemed to fade away, everything important coming together in the wordless look that passed between them.

The look held them as surely as any lock as their bodies fell effortlessly into an easy, timeless rhythm. A rhythm that built the pleasure slowly. Slow enough to savor every fraction of each smooth thrust. Slow enough to notice every subtle shift in pressure, and to appreciate every change in each other's expression. Slow enough to forget how long they'd been joined this way and nearly enough to forget where they were going, because the getting there was such an everlasting pleasure.

They came together as naturally as the sun rising in the sky—the pearly blush appearing on the horizon, the first glimmering ray darting over the edge. Then the burst, the radiant beams, shimmering through the heavens. The steady, pulsing heat of it. The fiery brilliance as it rose higher and higher. And the light. The bright, unearthly light that poured into the mind and filled the senses with the wonder and beauty and power of it.

It wasn't heaven. But it was a piece of it. And all he'd had to do to have it was let himself die in Katie's arms.

Spent and shaking, his sweat-slicked body still atop hers, Sam dragged his head around on the pillow to brush Katie's cheek with his lips. When he tasted the salty wetness of tears, he spoke in a rasping whisper.

"Katie...?"

"Oh, Sam..." Her head turned toward him, her lips seeking his, kissing him over and over, soft, trembling kisses that told him her tears weren't anything he needed to worry about. They were only her way of saying what he couldn't have put into words, either. Hell, he almost could have cried himself.

But even if he could have let himself cry, he didn't have the energy left for it. He was too tired, and too bone-deep satisfied, to do anything but roll to his back, taking Katie with him to hold her close. Only a small, unwelcome voice in a corner of his mind kept him from drifting off.

What are you going to do now? the voice nagged. *What about the plan? Remember that? The one where you hid out for a while, got yourself together, than left to go back to work?*

Yeah, he remembered. But it didn't look like he was going back to work. He didn't want to go anywhere any time soon.

Fine, the voice returned. *And it's real smart, isn't it, getting stuck on this woman, when all it's going to take is one person with a big mouth witnessing one of your handy little tricks, and it's California all over again? Face it. This is nice, and maybe it's the best thing you've ever had, but it can't last. It never does. And the more stuck on her you get, the worse it's going to feel when you've got to leave. You're going to lose it, you fool. You're going to lose her. So don't go getting any ideas.*

But he couldn't help getting ideas. And he couldn't imagine walking away from Katie. Not yet. Not after they'd just . . .

Sam's eyes flew open at the sudden, unbidden thought. "Damn," he muttered, his breath hissing out slowly.

Katie was lying with her head on his shoulder, and he felt her stiffen slightly. He hadn't realized she was still awake.

"What's wrong?" she whispered.

Sam hesitated, reluctant to bring it up when it was too late anyway. But there'd be the same question in the morning, so . . .

Sliding his hand up her arm to her shoulder, he said, "Honey, I know it's a little late to be asking, but you're not using any birth control, are you?"

The silence that followed his question worried him. Either she hadn't thought of it either and was as rattled as he was, being reminded, or maybe she *had* thought of it, after their close call last week, but was shy about telling him she'd taken the precautions. Strangely enough, Sam didn't know which possibility worried him more. The idea of making Katie pregnant gave him an odd kind of satisfaction that he'd never felt, but the idea of having to leave her that way panicked him.

"Katie?"

He shifted a little, trying to get her to look at him, but she kept her face turned against his chest and her arm snugged tight around his waist as she spoke.

"It's all right, Sam. I won't get pregnant."

"Are you sure? Because—"

"It's all right. I promise."

He relaxed, assuming she meant it was a safe time in her cycle. He'd never liked taking chances like that, but, hell, in her line of business, she ought to know what she was doing. For now, anyway, it wasn't a problem. Later, they could talk about it. Later, they could talk about a lot of things. Talking things out with Katie was . . . Well, somehow, it didn't seem so bad anymore. . . .

Kate lay still and silent in Sam's arms, listening to the steady beat of his heart and the slow, even sounds of his breathing as he fell asleep. She'd nearly been asleep herself when he'd spoken. Now, though, her thoughts were in turmoil, and sleep was a long way off.

How could she sleep? She was lying in the arms of a man who, it was almost a hundred percent certain, could make her whole again. In all her life she'd never know why it hadn't occurred to her before; probably it had something to do with six years of being convinced it was hopeless. But of all the horrible moments she could have realized it might *not* be so hopeless, this was the worst. Because nothing on earth was worth the risk of losing him—and she was terribly afraid asking him to help her would accomplish exactly that.

Lying there in the semidarkness of her room, Kate looked down at the hand Sam had curled over her arm. His grasp was relaxed in sleep, his fingers twitching every so often. How would she say it to him?

Heal me, Sam. Put your hands on me and make it so I can have babies. Erase the mistake I made six years ago, be-

*cause, after all, haven't I suffered for it long enough? And,
by the way, I love you. And if you fix this problem for me,
I'll give you some babies, and we'll have a good life... Why,
I'll bet after a while you won't even miss flying anymore.*

Sure, he'd say. *We'll have a great life. When we run
through the money I made doing what I like to do, I'll get
some job that pays the bills. And maybe you'd like it if, on
the side, I cured people for you, too. You know, like I cured
your nephew and that man you couldn't keep from dying.
And like I cured you so you could have the babies you've
always wanted more than anything in the world.*

But she wouldn't have what she wanted. She wouldn't
have him.

Kate had no doubt that if she asked Sam to heal her, he
would try. But would he still feel safe and trusting enough
to bare his soul to her as he had a while ago, or to make love
with her as he had, or to lie here with her like this? Or would
he feel used? And would she become to him just like all the
others? The ones in California who'd wanted him for what
he could give them. The ones who'd made him feel like a
freak. The ones who'd nearly broken him before he'd finally had to leave.

She didn't want him to leave. She wanted him to give her
his heart. She wanted him to let her love him for the rest of
their lives. She wanted them both to have what they needed
and wanted most in the world. But neither of them would
have anything if she did or said something that made him
think she had become part of his biggest problem.

Chapter Thirteen

Getting to work the next day took Kate a little longer than usual. She discovered Sam was hungry in the mornings. Ravenous, actually. And brazen about it, too.

"Katie, you have the most incredible breasts."

"And you have the most . . . incredible mouth."

"You like the way my mouth feels on you?"

"Oh, yes, it's—"

"Lift up a little . . . that's it . . . so I can . . ."

"Mmm. Oh, Sam, that's good. It's . . . What are you doing?"

"Giving you more of what you like."

"But you— Oh . . . oh, my . . ."

"Open up these pretty thighs for me, Katie."

"Sam, I . . . Oh, Lord, that's . . . But Sam, you *can't*—"

"I sure as hell can. God, honey, you're soft. So soft and . . . hot."

"But it's not . . . I'm not . . ."

"And you taste . . . like us."

She groaned as her will to argue and her inhibitions about such intimacy were deftly shattered; her fingers clutched at his hair, holding him to her, and in what she thought must be a disgracefully short time, he showed her how silly her objections were. But it was more than sensual pleasure, she thought, that he gave her. It was her womanhood—or rather, the right to enjoy the full measure of it. A right she'd never truly understood and that no other man had been man enough to allow her to claim.

She'd barely stopped shaking from that first, breath-stealing climax when Sam sent her soaring again with the deep thrusts of his aroused body. But when she opened her eyes from the second time to see him gazing down at her, she knew by the look in his glittering crystal eyes—and by the pulsing hardness of his flesh still filling her—that they weren't finished yet.

With a moan of surrender, she begged, "Oh, Sam, I can't—"

"I think you will."

"But I should get . . . up and . . ."

"Honey, you come so easy."

And he was having a wonderful time proving it.

"Sam, you're— How can you . . . Oh, Lord . . ."

"Watching you is beautiful, you know that? You just don't hold back anything. Do it one more time for me, Katie. Once more. Then we'll take a shower."

It wasn't until they were in the shower, though, and he'd made a torrid production out of washing her hair, that he found his own release. Leaning against the tiled wall, with her legs wrapped around his hips and his body buried deep inside hers, Kate felt the shudders ripple through him as he growled against her neck. The low, rumbling sound of profound satisfaction made her own body as fluid as the water sluicing over them, and she instantly spiraled off with him a final time.

Yet again, the physical pleasure was only part of it. *This* was the man she'd wanted so badly to know—the one who wanted to fulfill her until her bones turned to water and she could do little more than moan. The one who, last night, had wanted to "make love"—and whose lovemaking had moved her to tears. And Kate knew that nothing, nothing on the face of the earth, could have given her more pleasure than seeing him this way. The way he'd been this morning. Confident. Bold. A little arrogant. Relaxed. And so obviously happy.

She intended to do everything in her power to see to it that he stayed that way. And, after all, making him happy was making her happier than she'd ever been in her life.

At ten, Kate sent Sam home with a promise to stop at the cabin after she saw Lynn Nielsen that afternoon. Then she went to the office, where she met Doc for their regular postweekend consultation.

"So, except for a trip out to see the Nielsen girl, I spent the weekend putting in spinach and broccoli and watching the ball game." Doc sat back in the squeaky leather desk chair to lace his fingers together over his belly. "I did get two or three phone calls, though, that I wanted to talk to you about."

Sitting in the chair next to his cluttered desk, Kate was looking over his notes on Lynn. "Who were they from?" she asked.

"Well, there was one Saturday morning from Evan Resnick, the audiologist who saw that nephew of yours last week."

"Oh?"

"Said he'd never seen anything like it. Not so much as a decibel of hearing loss evident, and no trace of nerve damage."

"It certainly is amazing, isn't it?" With her attention still directed on the medical chart, Kate smiled to herself.

"Resnick thought it was more than that. He called it a miracle." Pausing, Doc added, "Which is the same word the vascular surgeon at Marquette used to explain why that man Cooney is still alive."

Kate's eyes flashed to his briefly, held for a second, then dropped once more to the chart. "Dr. Straun called?"

"About an hour after I'd hung up with Resnick," Doc confirmed, his tone far too intent for Kate's comfort. "Said he was sorry it'd taken him so long to get to me—he was off on vacation last week. But he had to call, he said, to tell me what a fine associate I have. He can't figure out how you kept that man alive on a piddling 250 cc of Ringer's. Given the amount of time before you got to him, and the number of arteries and veins that had chunks out of them, and the fact that he was in severe shock—" Doc shook his head "—it does seem miraculous."

Kate closed Lynn's chart and laid it on the desk. She wasn't a good liar, and she loathed the idea of lying to Doc, or even of keeping something from him that was clearly his concern. But as she rose and walked over to open her knapsack, lying on the table beside the supply cabinet, she knew that was what she had to do.

"Oh, I think that's putting it too strongly," she said.

"I don't know. There seems to be a lot of it going around."

"A lot of what?"

"Miracles. Ray Cooney. Francis." Doc's chair creaked as he swiveled around to watch her. "And you."

Kate stopped with the supply cabinet door half open. "Me?"

"Mmm. Your ankle last week. I admit, I didn't think much about it, because it looked normal to me. And I figured you'd made a mistake. But that was foolishness on my part, because you don't make mistakes very often. And I've never once heard you exaggerate about anything, least of all your own problems. So if your ankle was as bad as you said it was, well then, doesn't it seem like a miracle that it got better overnight?"

Tossing a laugh over her shoulder, she pulled the cabinet door open and reached for a pack of surgical gloves. "Of course, I was wrong about my ankle. Heavens, everything that day seemed ten times worse than it probably was. I mean, I was scared to death, sitting there in that storm, and I was soaking wet by the time Sam found me, and—" she shook her head, sticking the gloves into her knapsack "—well, it was just an awful day."

Several long moments passed in silence as she continued to stock her traveling medical kit. Through the open window of the office came the sound of Laura Graff calling her three-year-old to come put her shoes on. A truck, loaded with lumber from the mill, drove by on its way out of town. Finally Doc broke the silence.

"Kate, is there something you ought to tell me?"

His simple question made Kate's hands tremble as she buckled the knapsack closed. "About what?" she asked. When he didn't answer, she glanced over to see him studying her.

"Maybe you could start," he said, "with what you think I should say when a Hopkins-trained vascular surgeon tells me my associate is a miracle worker."

"Oh, Doc, really!" Kate glanced at her watch, picked up her knapsack and looped it over her shoulders. "You tell him thank you very much, and forget it."

"I might have been able to forget Cooney," he replied. "Maybe I could have chalked up his recovery to luck and the man's own constitution, though Straun says he's got an ulcer and some other things that don't support it. But let's let that one go. Then there's your ankle, and maybe I could forget that, too, if I believed you were so upset you could have misjudged how bad it was. But when I get to Francis—" he shook his head "—I can't forget that one, Kate. And in the long run, I can't forget three separate *miraculous* recoveries in the same week."

Rolling her eyes, Kate started toward the door. "This is really getting silly."

"Is it? Then tell me how to explain these things, so I can forget them. I thought if anybody could, it would be you, since one of them was your own injury, and you were there the other two times."

"Doc, you're asking me to explain the impossible, and—"

He waved her off with an impatient gesture. "Kate, I'm an old man, and I've been doctoring for a lot of years—in

Korea, and here in the U.P. ever since. I've *seen* miracles. I don't need you or anybody else to tell me what they look like. And I've learned not to make excuses for them, because miracles don't need excusing." He looked at her from under his furrowed brow. "But when they start happening too often, and when they seem to happen when one particular person has been in the vicinity, well, it makes me wonder if that person *has* something. Something special. I think you know what I mean, Kate, and I was hoping you'd do me the courtesy of giving me a straight answer."

Kate let go of the doorknob, her eyes widening in genuine horror as she thought she understood the direction of his thoughts. "Oh, now wait just a minute here! You think *I* cured Francis and fixed my ankle and—" Her breath caught for an instant, then, abruptly, she turned to the door. "This is crazy. You're talking nonsense, and I've got other things—"

"What you've got is three hours of appointments scheduled, starting in half an hour. So I don't know where you think you're going."

Kate froze, her hand on the doorknob. Behind her, she heard his chair squeak as he rose.

"Relax," he said. "I'm leaving. Besides, I don't think there's much you could say I haven't already figured out."

What was *that* supposed to mean?

Kate stood staring at the door, frantically looking for an answer to the question, while, behind her, Doc made preparations to leave.

"By the way," he said. "I was going to tell you about the other phone call I got—one from a doctor out in California named Martin Anderson. Does that name ring a bell with you?"

Kate whirled to face him, her heart pounding at a rate that made it impossible to keep the anxiety out of her voice. "What did he want?"

Doc was sorting papers on his desk, and as she stood watching him, her hands clutching the straps of her pack, he gave her a glance before turning to his housekeeping.

"He wanted to talk to Sam. And when I said Sam didn't have a phone, he asked for an address. I gave him mine and said I'd forward the letter for him."

"How did he know where Sam was?"

"Called his father in Detroit. Apparently Sam sent his folks a letter last week—didn't tell them where he was, but there was the postmark, of course. Anderson looked up the post office, then got the name of the local doctor, rather than call the state police to track Sam down. Interesting that he would have done it that way, don't you think?"

"Is he—" Kate broke off, hearing the panic in her tone. Drawing a shallow breath, she tried again. "Is that all he wanted? An address?"

"Well, that would have been the end of it," Doc said, "except he started asking me about my practice, about the area... Seemed a mite long-winded for prime-time long distance. But he's a pleasant sort of fellow—a little excitable, but bright—and Earl Carver was late for his appointment, so I chatted with Anderson until Earl came in. Then, when I said I had a patient waiting, Anderson got nervous. He hemmed and hawed for a minute, then he said..." Doc paused, a medical chart in his hand, to turn his head slightly toward her. "Then he said he'd appreciate it if I didn't mention to Sam that he'd called."

Kate's eyes followed as Doc crossed the room to stick the chart in the file cabinet. "What did you tell him?" she asked.

Closing the cabinet drawer, Doc shot her a somewhat indignant look. "Well, I asked him why, of course. And he said to forget he'd asked, but that, if I was going to tell Sam about the call, would I give him a message? He didn't want Sam to know he'd called without knowing why, because it might worry him. Well, then, *I* started worrying about whether there was some medical reason Anderson needed to talk to Sam." Mumbling a little as he headed toward his desk, Doc explained, "The man's a neurologist, and I began having visions of untreated epilepsy and malignant brain tumors. But Anderson said Sam was fine. Absolutely healthy. And besides, he wasn't Sam's doctor, he was his friend—so he said."

Reaching for his black bag on the desk, Doc paused to look at her. "Is that right, Kate? Is Martin Anderson Sam's friend?"

Kate nodded. "Yes, he's... Yes." Taking a step away from the door, she asked, "But what was the message?"

Doc picked up his medical bag in one hand and hooked a thumb in his suspenders. "He said he was trying to find out if Sam was all right. He knew how bad things had been for him in California before he left, and he was sorry for whatever part he'd played in that. He hoped things were better now. And he hoped Sam would stay in touch and not worry that he'd tell anyone else where he'd gone. He swore he wouldn't. He wanted Sam to know that he wished him well—he said that several times."

Kate held Doc's gaze, waiting, but when he didn't continue, she ventured cautiously, "And that's all he said?"

"Yes." He arched an eyebrow. "Should he have said more?"

"No."

"And *is* Sam all right, Kate? Or is Anderson justified in being worried?"

Kate swallowed hard and answered. "He's a lot better than he was when he left California."

"You've seen quite a bit of him lately, haven't you?"

"Yes."

"Starting the day you hurt your ankle. And the next day—the morning Francis recovered his hearing. And Bob Bradley mentioned to me after church yesterday that Sam was with you at the campgrounds when you were there with Cooney."

Doc paused, and Kate knew what was coming.

"In fact," he added slowly, "maybe I ought to have a talk with Sam about our recent increase in miracles. Maybe he could shed some light on it for me."

Kate felt the tears welling up in her eyes. "Doc...please," she whispered hoarsely. "Please, don't."

He was angry, and she didn't blame him, although his words were not unkind as he asked, "Don't what? Don't talk to Sam?"

He didn't need to hear her answer. With a deep, tired-sounding sigh, he walked past her toward the door, saying, "I think you've got the same problem Martin Anderson has. The man was worried as the devil, and I knew there were things he wanted to say but didn't. And I didn't know how to tell him without saying it outright that he didn't have to protect Sam from me finding out something I already knew."

Pausing with his hand on the doorknob, Doc looked at her. "But I understood Anderson's hesitation. The man doesn't know me from Adam. And he didn't know I'd already been faced with some of the results of Sam's having picked Bourner's Crossing as a good place to...shall we say, hide his light under a bushel? But I have to admit—" he raised his chin in a look that broke Kate's heart "—I'm a little disappointed you don't trust me any better than Martin Anderson does."

"I do," she said quickly, one tear rolling down her cheek. "I'd trust you with my life."

Doc's indignation lasted a second or two longer, then, with a deep sigh, it faded, replaced by the calm understanding she'd grown to expect from him.

"But it's not your life we're talking about," he concluded. "And I don't suppose I can fault you for that, can I?"

She took a step toward him. "Doc, I'm sorry. I... promised."

"And I'm sorry for being impatient." Lifting one eyebrow, he added, "But I would appreciate it if you could get out of that promise sometime soon so we can talk sensibly about this. Or have Sam talk to me himself. Because I'd hate to go blundering into another conversation like this one with Anderson and wind up making a mess of things for Sam...or for you."

"Oh, you shouldn't worry about me. I'm fine and—"

"I don't suppose," Doc interrupted her, "the fact that you came in here this morning looking prettier and happier than I've ever seen you look has anything to do with Sam's Jeep being parked in front of your house all night."

Kate felt a sudden heat creeping into her face. When Doc merely looked at her as if to say, what did she expect, her gaze slid away.

"I guess Sarah was up with the birds this morning, checking," she grumbled.

"I don't know. Probably. But I saw the Jeep myself."

"Well, either way, you're getting awfully personal."

Doc was unabashed. "Maybe I am. Maybe I'm getting *too* personal this time. But maybe I'm a little concerned, because I'm thinking about what it might mean for a woman to be... well, let's say, in love with a man who can do the things you thought I was accusing you of doing."

He waited until she gave him a hesitant look. "It'd be a terrible responsibility, Kate."

"I know."

"Do you?"

She nodded, then ducked her head as she spoke very carefully. "If a woman was... in love with a man like Sam, she'd have to find a way to protect him, if she didn't want to see him broken by people who wanted to use him—people who were so desperate to have what he could give them that they didn't see their demands were too many and too great for him to handle... people who didn't understand it was all still new to him."

Drawing a shallow breath, she raised her head to continue. "So for a while, at least, until he'd had a chance to learn his limits and could handle those people on his own, this woman would try to help the man she loved buy the time and the peace he needed. And she'd feel very, very selfish about it. Because aside from not wanting to see him hurt, she couldn't stand the thought that she might lose him."

"I guess it would be pretty bad if that happened."

"Yes. Very bad."

Doc was silent for a moment, then asked, "Does this woman have any ideas about how she's going to protect this man she loves?"

"A few," she replied. "First, she isn't going to make any demands or requests that he use his gift for her purposes. She's going to trust him to make his own decisions about it. Because the giving has to come from inside him or it isn't a gift at all—it's a duty, and there's no joy in it. And the ability he has to perform this duty becomes nothing more than a burden."

Doc nodded slowly. "Sounds like she's being wise. What else is she going to do?"

Kate held his gaze unwaveringly. "She's going to ask the only other person around her who knows not to tell anyone else."

"I'd say this falls in the category of professional ethics and confidentiality between doctor and patient, wouldn't you?"

"Definitely." Closing her eyes, she added, "And she's going to pray like mad that Marty Anderson means what he says, that he wishes Sam well."

She opened her eyes to find Doc frowning thoughtfully.

"The man sounded sincere," he said. "I don't think he's going to cause trouble." Tilting his head, he added, "By the way, I think tonight would be a good night for me to be on call. Don't you?"

"Doc, you don't have to—" Kate stopped, realizing her foolishness, and instead simply gave him a grateful look and said, "Thank you."

His mouth sloped into a smile of both approval and reassurance. "Don't look so worried, Kate. I think we can cover the tracks this man of yours is leaving behind him. In fact, it could be... well, an interesting challenge." Reaching out to give her arm a pat, he added, "I don't think we could do it forever, but between us we ought to be able to buy Sam the time he needs."

But who would buy her the time she needed? Kate was afraid, knowing what she had to do, that the timer was about to run out.

Chapter Fourteen

At three o'clock Kate closed up the office and started out the old lake road. Yesterday's warm sunshine had disappeared; the sky was overcast, the air chilly, and she reached for the denim jacket on the seat beside her as she hesitated at the turnoff to Sam's, then drove on to the Nielsens'.

She found Lynn doing laundry and sent her straight to bed, ignoring the young woman's protests that she'd been fine all weekend. Then, grimacing in disgust at the Nielsens' ramshackle living conditions, Kate went looking for Erik. She found him putting a roof on one of the camp's small cabins.

No, Erik told her, he'd had no idea Lynn's condition could be really serious. Lynn hadn't really explained. And he guessed he knew why. They didn't have any medical insurance, they were strapped for money, and they had just enough put aside to pay for Lynn's prenatal care and to have the baby in the hospital—provided the hospital stay only amounted to a couple of days. Sheepishly Erik admitted that he'd been worrying out loud a lot and that, in not telling him

the whole story, Lynn had probably been trying not to make
it worse. Kate figured he was right—and promptly told him
he could at least forget her fee.

Erik's pride wouldn't let him accept her offer, but he
promised he'd see to it that Lynn kept her appointment the
next morning with the obstetrician, and Kate left feeling a
tad less worried, after telling him where she'd be for the rest
of the evening, should they need her.

Sam's Jeep was nowhere in sight when she arrived at the
cabin, but the door was unlocked. She started toward the
kitchen with the notion of fixing dinner and found a pot of
fresh string beans in the sink, already washed and snapped.
Stuck in a book, lying on the counter, was a note penned in
straight, definitive strokes: *I'll be back in time to cook. You
relax. Read this, if you want to. Sam.*

Smiling, Kate looked at the book. It was tattered from
numerous readings. The author was a physician with im-
pressive credentials, and the back-cover blurb described the
book as a collection of accounts given to the physician by
people who had experienced death. Thumbing through the
first couple of pages, Kate walked slowly toward the couch.
And there she spent one of the most fascinating, mind-
boggling hours of her life.

Sam, it seemed, was not alone. In fact, he was part of a
growing number of people, most of whom had suffered a
grave physical crisis—heart attack, drowning, or the like—
that by all natural laws should have killed them. Because of
improved resuscitation techniques, however, they had survived. Kate knew about the techniques, but in reading she
realized she'd only considered their physical results; the
body was clinically dead, and then it was alive again. Her
medical training wasn't much different in this respect from
the average cardiologist's. Most health-care professionals
weren't prepared to cope with what a patient might tell them
had happened to their nonphysical being while vital physical functions had ceased.

Except now, it seemed, a few sensitive professionals were
listening to and recording near-death survivors' experiences, in spite of the almost universal claim among those

who'd visited that noncorporeal place that no words existed to adequately describe it. As Sam had told her, there was no language. The first things that struck Kate were the phenomenal similarities among the experiences near-death survivors claimed to have had. In actual content, sequence of events, and detail, each story had elements in common with the others. And a few elements were present in nearly every one.

A tunnel. A vast, dark space. The dying soul moved through the tunnel, beckoned toward a light. A clear, white light. Dazzling, yet not blinding. The gate to heaven, Kate thought, recalling Sam's words to Francis when he'd likened the light to a sunrise seen while flying over the water. As the dying person moved closer, the brightness became a "Being of Light"—a name chosen by the book's author from among the many given by the socially and religiously diverse group of near-death survivors. Although the names the survivors used differed, their descriptions of the Being of Light did not. All were certain they'd met a superior being. And all said that in the being's presence they felt completely accepted and flooded with a kind of warmth and love that defied any description.

The purpose of the encounter for the dying soul also seemed clear. The Being of Light posed a question, not in words, but in pure thought: Was the person prepared to die?

To help answer the question, the soul was given a display of his or her life's events, the events flashing by quickly, yet each remaining distinct. In the review, the survivors claimed they didn't feel they were being judged, but through it they reached an understanding of what had really mattered— what they'd done that *counted*, and what had not. Often, the things the person had thought important appeared, in the face of death, to have been only a waste of time.

A waste of time.

How would a man meet eternity having come to such a conclusion about his life on earth? Would he be glad for a chance to try again? Or would he resent being sent away from that better place? And what would he do differently? Would he plunge into his second chance with enthusiasm and confidence, knowing immediately how to proceed? Or would he hesitate, not so very certain about which pieces of his old life were worth keeping and which, indeed, had been a waste of time or, worse, genuinely wrong?

And suppose the man returned from death with some special gift? For Sam was not alone in this either, Kate discovered; telepathy, visions of the future, uncanny knowledge of subjects never studied, and, yes, healing, too. It didn't happen to all or even most near-death survivors, but it did happen. How would the man who felt his life had been a waste view such a gift? Would he feel compelled to use it to make his "second" life into something better, something worthwhile? Would he experience it as a burden? Or would he simply feel confused?

Kate was tucked in a corner of the couch, her eyes closed in thought, when a rough male voice, coming from behind her, whispered something in her ear that made her blush furiously.

"Sam Reese, you are—"

"Hot." His hands slid down the front of her jumpsuit to cover her breasts. "From thinking all day about you and..."

He muttered something else that made Kate gasp—not in shock but at the instant arousal he sent coursing through her. Her head turned toward him, her fingers curling around the back of his neck, but she caught only a glimpse of windswept hair and clear gray eyes before his mouth found hers and she was wrapped in a sensual, yet tender, greeting.

Finally, with his lips still nibbling at hers, he said, "I'm sorry I'm late. How was your day?"

Kate smiled. "Fine, but why do I get the feeling I'm supposed to ask *you* that question?"

"Because knowing what to say is one of the things you do best."

"You think so?"

"I know so." Giving her another quick kiss, he put a leg over the back of the couch and rolled across it, ending up on his back with his head in her lap. Bending a knee to lay a foot across the top of the couch, he got completely comfortable, then prompted, "So ask me."

Kate chuckled. "How was your day, Sam?"

"Good," he said. But then his eyes narrowed. "No. Make that great. I had a great day. Now, ask me—"

"*Why* did you have a great day?"

"I healed a kid with braces on his legs."

At her burst of laughter, he tugged on her braid. "What? You think that's funny?"

Kate couldn't have said what she thought it was. With his head in her lap, her hand resting on his flat belly, and his fingers leisurely unbraiding her hair, she was suddenly struck by the absurdity of the cozy scene.

And how was your day, dear?

Oh, the usual. I healed a kid.

That's nice.

"I'm sorry," she said, unable to wipe the grin from her face.

Sam's eyes sparkled as he reached up to tap the dimple in her left cheek. "You think you're smart, don't you?"

No, I think I'm in love.

"Where did you find this lucky child? Tell me about it."

His shoulders moved against her thighs as he shrugged. "Well, it wasn't a big deal—that was the great part. I went fishing over at Gogebic, and he was sitting by the lake in a folding lawn chair, with a fishing rod in his hand and a tackle box beside him. His mother was sitting a ways off, reading. He and I got to talking, and a couple of times I unhooked his line when it got hung up in the grass. We both caught a couple of pike, and I had one good size bass—" Sam stopped to give her a quick look. "I've been throwing them back."

"I figured that out." Her finger traced a line down the front of his blue T-shirt. "So, you and this boy were fishing together. How old was he?"

"About ten or eleven. When it came time to leave, his mother came over, and I realized this little squirt of a woman was going to carry the boy the whole three hundred yards to their car because he couldn't handle his crutches in the tall grass and soggy ground."

"And you offered to do it for her."

Sam's eyes closed briefly. "It was perfect. I put him on my shoulders and held on to his legs, and..." His eyes opened, his mouth slanting in a crooked grin.

"And tomorrow he'll be walking by himself," Kate concluded.

"No way. His muscles'll have to develop first."

Her brows drew together. "Then how do you know it worked?"

He started to answer, but hesitated.

"Don't tell me," she said. "You just know."

"Right. I usually know pretty quick when I touch somebody if I can help them or not." He gave her a wink. "The good part of this is that, by the time *they* realize the boy's better, they'll have forgotten about me."

That made him happy. Which made her happy, too. And she relished those moments of happiness as he pulled her down to him, his mouth covering hers in a kiss that promised much more. Lying there, with her arms around him and her breasts and belly and thighs being pleasurably crushed by the provocative movement of his hard, muscled body, she would have given anything to let the moment end as it was meant to end. But there was a small problem in the area of her conscience.

"Sam, I have to tell you something."

"Hmm?" His mouth was trailing in the wake of his fingers as they unbuttoned the front of her safari-style jumpsuit. He'd gotten as far as her belt and was hooking his finger under the front clasp of her bra when her hand covered his to stop him.

"Doc knows," she said.

He hesitated, then went for the clasp again. "Honey, don't fool yourself—by now the whole town knows. But we're both a little old to be sneaking in the back door and—"

"That's not what I meant."

Kate held her breath as Sam went utterly still. Then, slowly, he moved his hand away from her bra and lifted his head to look at her in disbelief.

"You told him?" he whispered hoarsely.

She shook her head. "He guessed. After phone calls from the audiologist, and the surgeon who treated Ray Cooney—who both said what they saw was a miracle—he thought about my ankle and decided they were right. Three in a week was too much for him to pass off as an interesting coincidence."

"Ah, come on!" He levered himself up on an elbow to look down at her. His face was rigid, and his body radiated tension. "Nobody could have guessed without—"

"Sam," Kate interrupted. "I think you've been around big-city doctors and hospitals too long. Old country doctors don't have as many ways to solve their problems, and that probably makes them more inclined to take a leap of faith when the occasion arises. He knew you'd been in all three places at the right time, with me, and he knew darned well *I* didn't do it."

"But still! If you'd just played dumb, he couldn't have—"

"I did. He was convinced before he talked to me." Kate drew a shallow breath. "Something else happened that clinched it. Marty Anderson called, looking for you."

The slight widening of his eyes was the only sign of shock he displayed, yet Kate saw the emotion flickering through those crystal-clear pools; there was no mistaking it for anything but fear.

"He was worried about you, and—" she started to say.

But Sam was off the couch before the words left her mouth. Standing with his back to her, a hand on his hip and the other rubbing the back of his neck, he swore once, crudely. "Of all the . . . How the hell did he find me?"

"The postmark on the letter you sent your dad last week." Kate sat up, buttoning her jumpsuit. "Sam, it's all right. Listen to me a minute." He wasn't listening. He was pacing wildly, muttering curses under his breath. "Anderson asked Doc to give you a message. He's worried about you. That's all. He wanted to know if you were all right. And he swore he wasn't going to tell anyone where you were."

Sam's mouth twisted in a look of derision. "Yeah, sure. And he said that right after he told Doc Cabot he had a genuine healer living under his nose."

"But he didn't tell Doc," Kate persisted. "Doc *guessed*. The things Anderson said—like how he was sorry for his part in making things so bad for you in California, and how he hoped they were better now, how he didn't want you to worry about him calling or knowing where you were—those things only confirmed what Doc was already thinking. Sam, the man's your friend!"

"*Yes*, he's my friend!" Sam pivoted to face her. "And he's done things for me no one else could do. And he's a damned good doctor who cares about his patients and who works like hell twelve hours a day trying to make them well. He's a *good person*!" Leveling a look on her, he finished, "But he's human."

"Yes!" she returned. "And human beings learn from their mistakes!"

Sam drew back, his look becoming suddenly calm—frighteningly calm. He stared at her for a moment, then, very quietly, he said, "They sure do." And without another word, he turned and strode toward the bedroom.

Kate knew what she'd find before she stopped in the doorway to the smaller room. But actually seeing him haul the large canvas bag from beneath the bed, shake it out, and unzip it made every muscle in her body knot with panic.

Her heart was racing in her chest as she said, "And this is learning from your mistakes?"

"No," he muttered, "this is correcting one before it's too late."

"What mistake was that?"

The only answer she got was a harsh laugh as he dropped the bag on the bed.

"I'd really like to know, Sam. What have you done wrong that leaving is going to fix?"

"For starters, how about everything?" He walked to the dresser and yanked open the top drawer, stopping long enough to give her a quick glance. "I went looking for a quiet, out-of-the-way place where nobody knew me. And when I found it, instead of leaving it that way, I wrecked it.''

"I see."

Snatching a stack of T-shirts out of the drawer, he headed toward the bed, where he dumped it, saying, "Everything I've done since I got here was a mistake. It was a mistake to talk to people or to try to get to know them. It was a mistake to get involved with anything or anybody. It was a mistake to pretend to myself I might be able to have something like a normal life.''

"How do you know you can't have a normal life? You haven't tried.''

Apparently, he wasn't going to try to answer her, either. Kate's short fingernails dug holes in the palms of her hands as she watched him pass back and forth from dresser to bed, emptying the drawer. But when he'd snatched the last pile of white briefs out of it, she spoke on a quavering note.

"I suppose last night was a mistake, too."

His hesitation as he closed the empty drawer was barely perceptible, but she knew the question had hit home. The next drawer scraped open, and he gathered up an armful of folded jeans, turning to carry them to the bed. But when he dropped the clothing on the growing pile, he let his arms fall to his sides. And for an instant he simply stood there, his shoulders rising and falling in a single shuddering breath.

"No," he murmured.

But that was all he said. And the stoic lines of his face were in place when he walked into the bathroom, returning a few seconds later carrying comb, brush, razor, shaving cream and a bottle of shampoo.

Kate bit her lower lip. "It wasn't a mistake," she said, "but you can just walk away from it like it didn't happen."

"Dammit, Katie!" The things he held bounced on the mattress as his hands sliced downward through the air. "Do you think I want to?"

Her eyes flickered to the bed, then back to him. "I don't know, Sam. I only know you're doing it."

"God!" Flinging himself away, he halted with his back to her to run both hands through his hair. "*Why?* Why do you need to hear me say what we both know? So you can suffer a little more?''

"No, so I can suffer a little *less*." She hesitated, then added, "Or don't I matter to you at all?"

"That's crazy."

"Is it? I didn't ask you for promises or commitments, but it seems like you might take a minute out of packing to—" her throat tightened "—to say you're sorry you're leaving."

"Would that make you feel better? If I said I was sorry? All right. I'm sorry. I'm sorry as hell."

With that, he pulled open the closet door and snatched a handful of shirts off the rack. And he went on emptying the closet, the nightstand drawer, and the bathroom medicine chest, dumping everything in a heap on the bed, as he continued. "What do you want, Katie? You want me to stick around a while longer, see how far we can stretch this out? Well, forget it. I'm not going to stay another day, another week, just so we can agonize a little longer over what we *aren't* going to have. You want to cry? Fine. That's the way you handle things. But it's not how I handle them."

"Oh, that's right," Kate returned, the bitter tears running down her face. "You're a *man*, aren't you? And men don't cry. And they don't get scared. Men don't *feel*. So, tell me something, Sam Reese, what does that make *you*?"

His hand hovered over the alarm clock beside the bed for all of three seconds before he picked it up and dropped it into the canvas bag.

Kate was beyond caring what he thought of how she handled things, as she sobbed, "How long is it going to be before you admit that men—*real* men—are human beings, and that they *do* get hurt and scared? Or aren't you ever going to admit it? Maybe you plan to keep running away from it forever."

"I'm not running from anything," he mumbled.

"Oh, yes, you are." Taking a step into the room, she insisted, "You're running from me—like you ran from Marty Anderson and everybody else you cared about—because you're afraid I'm going to let you down. I know you've been hurt and that you've had to learn to take care of yourself. But, Sam, can't you trust *anybody*?" And as he scooped up his address book from the dresser top and started toward the bed, she stepped into his path, grabbing his wrists, as she pleaded, "Is it really so hard to imagine trusting me?"

He met her pain-blurred gaze for a moment with eyes that were dry and unrevealing. His voice was especially rough, though, and not quite steady as he said, "I think I made it pretty damned obvious how much I trust you. But I don't trust Marty. And I don't trust Doc Cabot."

Breaking free of her grip, he walked away, and Kate whirled to follow on his heels.

"That's not fair. You don't even know Doc. He's not going to use you, and he's not going to tell anybody."

Sam gave her a cynical look, then began stuffing items into the empty canvas bag.

Kate let out a slightly hysterical cry. "For pity's sake! Look around, Sam! There's nobody here but you and me. Nobody beating at your door. Nobody begging for your help. You healed a little boy today, and you said yourself, by the time they realized it, they'll have forgotten you. And you could go on helping people like that for years without anyone knowing."

"Like Doc Cabot went all of two weeks without knowing?"

"He's the only doctor in a hundred miles! He was bound to find out!"

"Yeah, and I'll keep that in mind when I look for another place to stay."

With a groan, Kate turned away. An instant later, though, she turned back, saying, "Don't you realize the same thing's going to happen no matter where you go? Sooner or later, some smart doctor is going to figure it out. And other people probably will, too. Wouldn't you be just as well off having it happen here as anyplace else?"

Apparently not. He was going to leave without saying a word. He was just going to walk out as if none of what had happened between them meant anything to him. As if she didn't mean anything to him. And she couldn't stop him. She couldn't reach him.

Pacing the distance to the window and back, Kate stopped at the foot of the bed to watch as he jammed his belongings into the canvas carryall. Jeans, toiletries, shirts torn off hangers and given a cursory fold, item after item carelessly thrown in without a moment's hesitation. And as she watched, she felt the cold fingers of hopelessness steal over her, drying her tears and numbing the raw, tearing pain in her heart.

"You're not listening to any of this," she said with almost nerveless calm. "You're not listening because you think I don't understand. You think I can't possibly know what it's like for you. Well, you're right. I'm not ever going to understand how it feels to live with a gift that comes from a place—or from a power—that I only know through faith."

Shaking her head slowly, she added, "But, Sam, there are a few things I do understand—like how it feels to ache inside for other people's pain, and how it feels to be exhausted from trying to meet everybody's needs, and what it's like to wonder if you're ever going to get your own needs met." She paused, her eyes taking in the sight of him silently proceeding with his task. "And something else I understand is that the only mistake you've made since you got here is what you're doing right now."

The last pair of socks was stuffed down the side of the bulging carryall, and he pulled the top edges together, tugging at the zipper. Kate's lower lip trembled, the pain overcoming her numbness, as she watched him gather the handles and lift the bag from the bed.

"But you're not going to believe me," she said. "You're not going to let anything I say matter. So, leave. Go... Go live on some Arctic ice floe, where you don't have to worry about people messing up and hurting you. Or maybe—" her voice cracked as she lashed out "—maybe the hotshot test pilot can go find some big, fast plane and fly away and never have to see another living soul ever again." She met his scowl with defiance. "But no! He can't just fly away from his problems anymore, can he? Because along with everything else, he's scared of flying, too. Scared of the thing he most wants to do. And he's so scared, he'd rather blame the fact that he can't do it on the curse he got in heaven sooner than even *try* to get over it.''

''That does it.'' The canvas bag landed with a thud on the floor beside the bed. With his hands planted on his hips, Sam demanded, ''Who the hell do you think you are, lady? Seems to me you're the *last* person who ought to be accusing me of being too scared to go after what I want.''

''Am I?'' she retorted. ''Well, at least I'm honest with myself about what scares me—which is more than you are.''

''Honest? Ha!'' His eyes raked her from head to toe. ''What's honest about you? Here you are, stuck in this safe little backwoods town, fixing old ladies' dinners and handing out advice on teething rings and looking after women with babies in their bellies. You fill up your days taking care of other people—playing mother—just like you've been doing all your life. But out the side of your mouth you admit that just because you don't have a family doesn't mean you don't want one. And it's so damn clear you want one— that you were *made* for one—that even a stranger can see it! So where is it? Huh?''

With his mouth twisting in mockery, he grated, ''And *don't* tell me you thought you were going to get it with that turkey I met at his father's garage last week. No, while you're busy accusing *me* of being too scared to go after what I want, you tell me why you wasted ten months collecting tight-lipped kisses from a man who wouldn't know what to do with you in bed—*if* he could even figure out how to get you there.'' Shaking a finger at her, he raged, ''If you're not scared of going after what you want, tell me why it took you six years after that jackass hurt you for another man to get to you. And *then* tell me why you picked the man who looked least likely to give you what you *really* want.''

Kate fumed at his arrogance, her eyes flashing as she spoke through clenched teeth. ''Is that what you think? That the reason I'm not married and raising a family is because I'm scared to go after it?''

''You got a better reason?''

"How about sterility."

The silence rolled through the room like a thunderhead, and the force of it made Sam step back, the breath rushing out of him, his face going white with shock. But the shock soon turned to horrified regret.

"God, Katie, I'm—"

"*Don't* tell me you're sorry." She spun away, her long hair swirling in a protective cloud around her shoulders. And with her arms tightly hugging her waist, she stood shaking. Shaking with anger and pain and the strain of keeping the secret for so many years.

But there was no reason to be silent anymore. Sam had melted through every barrier she'd put up around her once-broken heart, and now he was breaking it for her again. And it seemed very important at that moment that he know exactly what his leaving would do to her.

Drawing a shallow breath, she began, "I was involved with a man, another graduate student, during my last year in Ann Arbor. I wanted to marry him. But when I found out I was pregnant and told him, it turned out he didn't want to marry me. And when I wouldn't take money from him for an abortion, he walked out."

Behind her, Sam swore. "Katie, you don't have to—"

"Yes, I do." The simple statement stopped him, and she went on. "I've accused you, more or less, of being a coward, and you've accused me of the same thing. And it may be a case of the pot calling the kettle black, but at least you'll know the facts—as many as I know about you."

"I don't need to know any facts," he muttered, "to know that either of us accusing the other of anything is about the dumbest thing we could be doing right now."

"You're probably right," she replied. "But I'm going to tell you, anyway." And, lifting her chin a little, she went on. "After Rick left, I was... Well, it was pretty bad for a while. But it tells you something about how much I loved him—or didn't love him—that after I'd cried for a couple of days, I didn't care that he'd left. He was expendable. But the baby... the baby wasn't."

When Kate heard Sam start toward her, she took a couple of steps away from him, stopping at the dresser. Without glancing back, she continued. "For four months I walked around trying to figure out what to do. I was close to getting my master's, and I didn't want to quit. I wanted...I wanted to come home, at least to have the baby. But in a small town, being pregnant and unwed is about as scandalous as you can get. And my family—" She broke off, shaking her head. "You've met them. They'd have been devastated to think I'd ever do something wrong. But *I* didn't feel like I'd done anything wrong, and I wanted that baby more than I'd ever wanted anything in my life—except my mother, when she died."

With a flustered gesture, she explained, "So, I felt like I couldn't go home. And I didn't want to quit school. And it got to be pretty hard, trying to go to school and worrying about what I was going to do. But then—" she hesitated, her vision blurring as she watched her fingertip trace a knot in the pine dresser top "—then the problem solved itself. The baby died. I was a little over five months pregnant, and one day, it just . . . stopped moving."

Lifting her shoulders a little, she murmured, "It happens sometimes, for no apparent reason. And when it's early, it's harder to feel the movements anyway—especially with a first baby, when you don't really know how it ought to feel—so it's easy not to notice for a long time. Then, when you do start to miss the movement, you think at first, 'Oh, the baby's just sleeping, and in a while it'll wake up.' But it doesn't wake up, and sooner or later, you have to face it."

Kate closed her eyes briefly, then, as the memories became too chilling that way, she opened them again. "I walked around for weeks, not knowing—or, at least, not admitting it—until I went for my six-month prenatal visit, and the doctor couldn't find a heartbeat. He wanted to do a sonogram right then, and I made up an excuse about not having the time. I was afraid. I knew in my heart what had happened, but I wasn't ready to face it. I just couldn't accept that my baby was dead, because... Well, I'd spent most of my life taking care of my mother's babies. And those babies had grown up and were starting to have babies of their own, and...and it felt like I had to have one of my own." With a tiny wave of one hand, she admitted, "It wasn't a...a good reason. But that's how it felt—like my life would be meaningless if I didn't have that baby."

Kate sighed, a broken, quiet sound. "A week after that doctor's visit, I started having contractions. Then I couldn't pretend anymore. Still, I waited until my water broke before I did anything about it."

Swallowing her tears, she uttered a tiny, humorless laugh. "It was stupid. I knew I was risking infection, but I guess all the information and training in the world don't guarantee a person will do the right thing when they're as emotionally upset as I was. Anyway, I finally called an ambulance, because I couldn't drive, and about twenty minutes after I got to the hospital, I...I miscarried. The baby...it was a boy."

Lifting her watery gaze to the mirror over the dresser, Kate saw Sam standing an arm's length behind her. He was watching her with eyes that held a world of sadness, and she held his gaze as she continued.

"That should have been the end of it. But it wasn't, because the antibiotics they pumped into me didn't keep me from getting an infection—a bad infection. And after it was gone, I kept having problems. So my doctor sent me to a specialist, who did some tests. And finally...finally they told me—" She sucked in a sharp breath, forcing herself to finish. "They told me the problems I was having were related to the infection. They recommended a...a hysterectomy, but I said...I said no. Okay, they said, but I had to...to understand, there wasn't anything else they could do. It was about a hundred percent certain, with all...all the scar tissue the infection had left inside me, that I'd ...never get pregnant again."

Watching in the mirror, Kate saw Sam's eyes rake over her back, then snap up to meet hers once more—crystal-clear eyes that couldn't hide the spark of hope that suddenly flared in them, a spark followed immediately by a look of intense urgency. It was exactly the look she'd expected to see.

"But, Katie," he began, "if it's scar tissue, maybe I—"

"Don't!" Kate jerked away when he reached for her, spinning to face him as she backed toward the doorway. Every nerve and muscle in her body was trembling, and her voice had a hysterical edge to it as she insisted, "Sam, I don't want you to touch me."

"But you could—"

"No!"

"Honey, at least let me—"

"No!"

Her back hit the door frame, and she shrank against it, her hands splaying wide across her belly. Her face tilted to look at him as he stopped in front of her. "I'm going to tell you the same thing I told Rick Sommers he could do with his money for an abortion. Keep it. I wanted him, not his money. And I want you. Not your almighty gift."

Sam stared at her for an instant with a look of baffled disbelief. Then he spoke almost desperately. "Katie, please, don't do this. I know you're mad, and you've got a right to be. But if you let me—"

"No!"

His hands lifted to her shoulders. "Honey, I want to—"

"No!" And when he drew in a breath to argue further, she added quickly, "If you ever put your hands on me again, Sam Reese—for *any* reason—you'd better be ready to marry me."

It was the only thing she could think of to stop him. And it worked. Like a fist in the gut. He looked at her in open-mouthed astonishment, and, an instant later, his hands fell to his sides. She hadn't planned to say it, but she wasn't going to back down.

Shaking inside and out, her arms wrapped tightly around her middle, Kate nodded. "That's right, Sam. Marriage. As in building a good, normal life together. If you want to have children, then I'll let you try to make it so we can. And if you don't, well, I've spent six years thinking I wouldn't have any, and I guess I can go on thinking it. But I'll tell you what

I can't do." She shook her head slowly. "I can't let you make it so I can have *another* man's children. Because after last night, the only babies I'm ever going to want are yours."

The silence that followed her statement was total. They simply stared at each other, Kate feeling as if she'd been cut open and left to die, Sam looking as if he'd just discovered hell. For several long minutes they watched the other suffer, and Kate read in Sam's eyes all the things he couldn't put into words. The disbelief and the loneliness and the aching emptiness that longed to be filled. And the struggle—hope against fear—and, finally, the gut-wrenching ambivalence.

"Katie, I..." He shook his head. Then, with a softly muttered oath, he turned away, taking a few steps out of the doorway, into the main room, before turning to face her. And again he tried. "I don't know—" But he broke off, his chest heaving with the rapid pace of his breathing.

He didn't know what to say, she thought, because he couldn't say what she wanted to hear. He cared. He cared a lot. But he didn't care enough. And somehow, that hurt worse than if he hadn't cared at all.

She started to say she was leaving, but as Sam began to say something else, his breath caught, and his gaze flashed across the room toward the door. Kate heard it, too—the sound of a car door slamming. And a second later, someone banged on the door.

"Forget it," Sam growled. "I'm not talking to anybody until we've finished this."

"It *is* finished. Besides—" she shook her head when he started to protest "—I've got a patient up the road, in the hunter's lodge. I told her husband I'd be here."

The banging came again on the stout pine door, and Sam bit out an angry curse as he strode across the room to answer it.

Kate stayed where she was, wiping the tears on her face while Sam opened the door. But the sight of a wild-eyed Erik Nielsen sent her hurrying toward him.

"Kate!" Relief washed over Erik's youthful face when he saw her. "I'm sorry to bother you, but—"

"It's not a bother." Kate quickly introduced him to Sam, standing stone-faced and silent beside her, then asked, "What's happened?"

Erik stepped through the doorway to grab her shoulders. "Something's wrong," he said. "I went in for dinner, and Lynn was crying and saying she needed you, and—"

"Is she bleeding?"

He shook his head. "No, but everything—her clothes and the sheets—everything is drenched." Running a hand through his blond hair, he rasped, "She just keeps crying and saying it hurts and that she's scared she's going to die, and—"

"Erik, slow down." Kate took his hands off her shoulders and gave them a squeeze. "Now, look. It sounds like Lynn might be in labor, and women say some pretty crazy things when—"

"But she's not due until—"

"I know. But the thing you've got to do—"

"Won't the baby die if it's born now?"

"Erik—" Kate struggled for an instant with her own fear and raw nerves. Then, by act of sheer will, she shoved everything else aside and spoke as calmly as she could. "Thirty-four weeks is early, but babies born even earlier can make it. Lots of factors are involved, and we don't have time for me to explain them. We'll get Lynn to the hospital, and a neonatologist will be right there when the baby's born. But Erik—" her brow furrowed in warning "—no matter what happens, I don't want to hear you worrying in front of Lynn. She's scared enough. Is that clear?"

With a shudder of his big Nordic frame, the young man nodded, his shoulders slumping a little as some of the tension drained out of him.

Kate gave him what she hoped was a reassuring smile. "Okay. I'll follow you in my truck."

But when she started out the door after Erik, Sam's arm blocked her way.

"Sam, I haven't got time to—"

"What didn't you tell that kid?"

"I didn't tell him much of anything. You heard me say—"

"You know what I mean."

Her eyes flashed up to his.

He cast a quick glance at Erik, climbing into the battered truck parked beside Kate's, then looked at her. "Do you want me to come with you?"

Kate returned his troubled gaze steadily. "I did my job alone before you got here, and I'm going to keep doing it after you're gone. So whether you take the time in your hurry to leave to maybe solve one more of my problems is up to you."

And with that, she brushed past him out the door.

Chapter Fifteen

P ant, Lynn. Don't push."

"Kate, I . . . I've got to. I can't . . ."

"Yes, you can, sweetie. Pant—light and high, like a puppy dog. Give me one more second."

Give me long enough to get you to the hospital. But Kate knew, even as she carefully slipped a practiced hand inside Lynn's straining body, that they weren't going to make it.

"Okay, just relax," she said. "I'm going to be very, very gentle. I just need to know what's . . . going on . . ."

The young woman was whimpering and trembling from an hour and a half of bone-racking labor, but at least she wasn't hysterical anymore. The sound of her screams had chilled Kate's blood when she and Erik had walked in the front door of the lodge five minutes ago. Kate didn't blame Lynn for being hysterical. She didn't blame her for anything. What she was feeling made her want to scream a little herself.

"Well," she said, "the good news is, this is going to be over soon. The bad news is, I don't think we're going to make it to the hospital." *And the frightening news is, I can't tell if you might bleed to death before the ambulance gets here.*

With the memory of Lynn's slight bleeding the week before, Kate was very aware that she didn't know the cause of the episode. But if she did a thorough exam, which might verify one or the other of several possibilities, she could start a hemorrhage. The fact that Lynn was almost fully dilated and hadn't started to bleed was somewhat hopeful. And in any case, Kate realized, she couldn't do a thing to stop this baby from being born, and it was happening too quickly to try to take Lynn to the hospital herself.

"Kate, I . . . I want to push again. Please, I . . ."

"I want you to try really hard not to. Give me a minute to get ready here." Kate snapped off the disposable glove, tossed it in the wastebasket beside the bed and looked up to meet Erik's terrified gaze. "Go radio for Doc. Tell him to call for an ambulance and to please get out here."

With one glance at his wife, Erik raced from the room, and Kate flew into action. Talking to Lynn, reassuring and directing her constantly, she checked the young woman's blood pressure and pulse and listened to the baby's heartbeat. She also put an IV needle in Lynn's arm—"Just in case," she said.

Transforming the bedroom into a suitable place to give birth came next, not an easy task amid the piles of plaster dust and peeling wallpaper. The smell of fresh paint from the corridor outside the room burned Kate's nostrils as she replaced the soaked sheets with sterile ones. Another sterile sheet went over a small wooden table, which was then quickly covered with piles of gauze pads, towels, scissors, syringes, clamps and the other tools of her trade. In five minutes' time, she scrubbed and doused everything, including Lynn, with antiseptic. And what she couldn't scrub and douse, she covered with a sterile sheet.

Kate had pinned up her hair and was returning to the bedroom from the adjoining bathroom, where she'd washed her hands and forearms for the second time, when Erik ran into the room.

"I can't get it to work," he announced breathlessly. "The radio... it's broken again."

Stifling the urge to scream, Kate was about to tell him to go use the one in her truck when the look on Erik's face stopped her. Her head snapped around, her gaze followed his to the bright red stain on the white sheet beneath Lynn's hips.

"Lynn, stop pushing and pant" she ordered, sliding quickly onto the bed. "Erik, help me get her head down. That's it. Now lift her hips while I put these couple of pillows under her."

"What's wrong?" Lynn gasped.

"Sweetie, you're bleeding a little. Nothing to worry about. I'm just going to hook up this IV, and...there, that's it. Now, I want to listen for a second and see how the baby's—"

"Kate...I don't know...how long I can— Oh, God..."

"Pant, Lynn. *Don't push.*"

With her forehead pressed to the fetoscope held against Lynn's stomach, Kate counted heartbeats until she was certain the baby was all right—for now.

"Erik." She looked at the young man hovering on the other side of the bed. "Use the CB in my truck. Tell Doc that Lynn's ready to deliver and that she's bleeding. Forget the ambulance—I want a medevac chopper. Fast."

Erik nodded once, then ran for the doorway. At the same time Kate saw Lynn's belly grow taut with another contraction—and another couple of ounces of bright red blood gush out of her.

"Wait! Erik, stop!" Jumping off the bed, Kate ran into the hall, almost colliding with him as he swung around to face her.

"Go get Sam," she told him.

"Sam? You mean, the guy—"

"Yes. The keys are in my pickup. You can radio Doc on the way. Tell Sam . . . tell him I need him."

And, please God, let him still be there.

It didn't matter that the thought of being with him was impossible. Nor did it matter than an hour ago she'd sworn he was safe here and that no one would try to use him. It didn't even matter that she'd told Doc she'd never ask Sam to use his gift for her purposes. Lynn's life, and her baby's, were in grave danger; she'd have sold her soul to save them. And all she was doing in asking Sam to help was selling her future—which she'd already lost.

If he was there, he would come. She didn't doubt that. Because he'd never be able to say no, any more than she would.

Sam's boots clomped on the bare wooden boards as he paced back and forth in front of the open cabin door. He'd headed after Katie half a dozen times, only to turn around and come back. He'd started to fix supper, but he was too agitated to eat. Finally, he'd tried to check on any last-minute packing, but every time he'd walked into the bedroom, Katie's words slapped him in the face: *"The only babies I'm ever going to want are yours."*

Was she crazy? She wanted to marry him? Had she really thought about what she'd be letting herself in for? Hell, forget that. She hardly knew him!

But as he paced to the couch and his eyes fell upon the book tucked behind the cushion, open to the page where Katie had left off, a quiet voice inside him said, *She knows you. And you know her. And she knows better than anybody what she'd be getting into. So stop looking for an easy way out of this and be honest.* Hell, yes. For once in your life, Reese, be honest.

Honest was that Katie wanted to marry him, and she wanted his babies. *His* babies. He knew what that meant; he wasn't *that* dishonest with himself. But he was too scared to put it into words. Yes, scared. Shaking, sweating, pack-and-leave scared. And the worst part was, he wasn't even sure why.

Leaning straight-armed on the back of the couch, staring blindly at the floor in front of it, Sam asked himself what could happen. What was the very worst thing that could happen to him if he stayed here and . . . say it, Reese . . . let himself love Katie, and let Katie love him?

Was it the people who *might* come banging on his door,
asking for his help? Or Marty, whom he frankly missed,
flying up with a patient who was beyond his own skills? Or
Doc Cabot, who practically reeked with integrity, trying to
use him? Maybe it was people finding out what he could do,
then looking at him like he was...like he was God. He hated
that. More than anything else, it made him feel strange and
isolated. But he understood why people reacted that way.
And he thought he could handle it if there was at least one
person who *knew* him—who knew he was only a man. Yes,
he really believed he could put up with the rest if he had just
one person close to him, somebody to whom his being a
man meant more than his being a healer.

So why had he just spent an hour packing to leave her?

Because you're living in the past, that same quiet voice
whispered. *You're leaving her before she has the chance to
hurt you. That's how you learned to survive, even though it
never really gave you what you needed or wanted. But it's
time to let it go, Sam. It's over. You're not the man you were
before. And if you'd give yourself the chance—the chance
Someone else already gave you—you could be a better man.*

It was true, his opinion of himself hadn't been too hot
since he'd had to endure that unearthly replay of his life. It
wasn't that he'd been a bad person. But the next time he
faced that final life review, he wanted to know he'd been a
truly *good* person... The kind of person Katie was. The kind
she should have for a husband and a father for her children.

The rock-bottom truth was that Katie deserved a better
man than the man he'd been. She deserved the man he could
be. The man he felt himself becoming. She deserved a man
with courage that matched her own. Which was not the
courage to risk physical death in an airplane but the courage to risk his heart in love.

It was a risk he'd never taken, and the thought of it chilled
him to the marrow. He honestly didn't know if he could do
it. But he knew he at least had to tell Katie the truth. He
couldn't go running off—yes, running—without saying the

things she wanted to hear about what she meant to him. And
in the meantime...

Sam turned abruptly, one hand diving into his pocket for
his keys, the other snagging his jacket off the hook by the
door on his way out. Maybe Katie didn't need his help—he
figured if she'd really been worried about this woman she'd
have said so. But he wanted to be with her, anyway. Besides, that kid, Erik, had looked about as scared as he could
get. If nothing else, he could lend a little friendly support to
his neighbors.

Sam nearly collided with Erik at the place his drive met
the old lake road. Kate's pickup came bouncing into the
turn, and Sam had to yank the Jeep off the road to avoid a
collision. The pickup swerved, ending up with its front
wheels in a deep rut and its back end blocking the road. Sam
uttered one of his favorite profanities, then drew a steadying breath as he watched Erik run toward him. It was dark
but for the beams of the two vehicles' headlights, the overcast sky making nightfall under the thick cover of leaves that
much blacker, but Sam didn't need to see Erik's face to
know he was wild with panic.

His voice was filled with it as he grabbed the door of the
Jeep and gasped, "Kate said to tell you she needs you!"

"Jump in," Sam ordered. "You can get the truck later."

"Can't!" Erik shook his head. "Gotta get it off the road.
Doc's coming. Probably the medevac crew, too, since the
best place to land the chopper is—"

Sam didn't wait to hear what else Erik had to say.
Throwing the Jeep into gear, he plowed through the under-
brush to get around the disabled pickup. As he hit the old
lake road, he called, "Get that truck out of the way if you
have to take it apart to do it!" And then he was flying.

"Katie! Where are you?!"

Sam hesitated inside the front door of the derelict wooden
building, listening for an answer. It came, faintly, down the
long hall that led past the stairs.

"Here! At the back of the hall off the kitchen!"

He raced down the hallway, through the large kitchen and into a narrow corridor of rooms. Slowing, he heard Katie speaking in that calm, gentle way she had, and he let her voice guide him toward the open door at the end of the corridor. As he approached, he heard her say, "Try to take it easy, Lynn. Pant as much as you can. I know it's hard, but—"

She broke off when he swung to a halt in the doorway, his hand gripping the frame. His eyes went straight to hers, locking for an instant—long enough for him to read the fear in her dark gaze—fear he understood the instant his eyes fell upon the woman lying on the bed.

God, nothing he'd faced before had prepared him for this. Nothing! It wasn't only the blood—and there was enough of that, soaked into the pile of towels and gauze pads on the floor by the bed. It was seeing what should have been a natural, life-giving event turned into a nightmare. Mostly it was the helplessness, the utter vulnerability, of the young woman suffering the nightmare. She was....

"God Almighty...."

Crossing the room quickly, Sam stopped at the foot of the bed, his hand going to Katie's shoulder to give her a squeeze, though his eyes never left the young woman.

"Is she ... ?" he began.

Katie murmured an answer. "She's not in shock, but she's close. The baby's small, and he's coming fast, but I've been trying to hold her back from pushing, because it seems to make the bleeding worse. But the baby's probably losing oxygen with the bleeding, and if I can't get him out soon, he's—"

"Give me a minute."

Moving slowly to the side of the bed, Sam's eyes skimmed the young woman's blotchy face, the dark hair plastered to her head with sweat, the rounded belly that even to him didn't look as large as it should have been. She couldn't have been a day over twenty, and as he saw her face contort with pain and effort, and heard the sounds coming from deep within her as she worked to give birth, it occurred to him he was being given yet another lesson in courage today.

Suddenly, she went all-over limp, her breath rushing out and her face turning ghostly pale. When her dark blue eyes opened and she saw him standing over her, she drew a quick breath, her look instantly becoming wary.

Careful, he thought. You can't go bulldozing your way into this one. She might be bleeding to death, but if you want to help her, you're going to have to win her first.

"Who....Kate?" Her hand fluttered in embarrassment over the blanket covering her from shoulders to hips.

"It's all right, Lynn," Kate put in quickly. "This is Sam. He's a friend of mine, and he was in the Navy medical corps, so he's going to help me. Okay?"

The medical corps? That was a good one. His eyes flashed to Katie's briefly, but she didn't meet his gaze.

Making sure he kept his eyes on Lynn's face, he folded a leg beneath him to sit at her right side, his hand covering hers where it was clutching the sheet. "Hi, there, Lynn. You've been having a bad time of it, haven't you? But Katie and I are going to take care of things, now."

Her frightened eyes searched his face. "Where's Erik?"

"He's down the road, waiting for Doc." Sam reached up to smooth her brow. "But he'll be back soon, and meantime—"

He broke off when her eyes glazed, and a second later, she let out a hoarse groan, her back curling forward. The instant the contraction hit, the trickle of blood coming out of her became a stream. And Sam's response to the sight of the blood was every bit as instinctive as hers had been to the contraction. Without thought, his hand slid lightly across her rounded belly, over the blanket at first, then slipping under the edge until he was feeling her tight, smooth skin.

Watching her face closely, he said, "Easy. Easy, now. Does it hurt to be touched like this?"

"No," she croaked, her eyes squeezed closed. "Feels...nice, but... Oh, Lord. How can it...feel good when...it hurts so much?"

"Hmm, I don't know," he answered slowly, his fingers feathering over her, seeking the source of the bleeding. "Ladies have told me it does, though."

"You've . . . you've seen a lot of babies . . . being born?"

"Hmm, a couple dozen, I guess. In Nam, you know. There was a lot of this sort of thing going around over there."

It was enough to reassure her so she could stop worrying about him and put what little energy she had into pushing. And he could do what he had to do.

His palm was already tingling as it slid downward, like a divining rod seeking water, until it settled over the lower curve of her belly. Immediately, his head started to swim, and his heartbeat slowed to pound in a steady rhythm. Within seconds, the beat of it filled his senses. His breath escaped, his eyes drifted closed . . . and he let it come.

The heat. The bright, burning heat. Let it take over his being. Let it crowd out any thought or wish or need of his own. Let it flood the banks of his soul until it filled every part of him. Until he was lost in it and had no sense of being separate from it. He was the channel, the opening between this plane and the next, the tunnel through which, in this place, at this moment in time, the river of fiery light could flow.

And it flowed out of him, out of his hands, into the body of a woman he didn't know. Didn't need to know. The life was draining out of her, her spirit floating lightly inside her flesh, clinging to her weakening body in a courageous effort to hold on. Her will to live was strong. She grabbed at what he offered her. And a part of him, the part that remained conscious of physical realities, heard her growl with the powerful energy that infused her body. She used it, put it instantly to work.

But suddenly, a warning signal went off somewhere inside him. It wasn't over. Her body was healed—and then it wasn't. And for a moment, he was confused.

"Katie?" His eyes blinked open, and he looked at her. "I don't . . . It keeps—"

Her brown eyes searched his for an instant, then she murmured, "It keeps tearing?"

"Yes."

"You probably won't be able to stop that. But if you can control the bleeding like this—"

"Yes." He didn't know what she was talking about, but somehow her words made sense. Still, there was something else that *didn't* make sense. He hesitated, his eyes losing focus as he let himself be drawn back for a second to that other place. Then, blinking a little to refocus, he met her gaze again.

"Could there be...another place? Something... disconnected. Something I can't get to, like..." He didn't know how to say it—but, again, he didn't need to.

Understanding, and a spark of fear, flashed through Katie's eyes, and she spoke quickly to Lynn. "Come on, now, Lynn. Let's do it this time. Let's get this baby born. One good push. One more. He's coming fast. Push him out...."

Sam's eyes closed again, but he took Katie's voice with him, let her become part of the bond, let her guide him as she guided Lynn....

"That's it. Keep pushing, sweetie. That's it.... A little more.... I've got one shoulder. Now, don't let up. Keep pushing. That's it! You did it, Lynn! You've got a boy!"

"Is he...?"

"Hang in there."

Sam felt the change instantly—felt the draining sensation lessen, felt it ease off with the slowing of the blood, until, a moment or two later, the bleeding stopped and, without conscious effort on his part, his senses came back under his own control.

The first thing he saw when he opened his eyes were the tears hovering on Katie's dark lashes as she clamped the thick cord attached to the incredibly tiny wet body lying in her lap.

"Katie," he began, "do I need to—"

"No." She swiftly covered the baby in a blanket, at the same time she worked to suction his mouth and nose. "The clamp does it. He was bleeding through the cord." Then, in a whisper, she added, "Come on, little one, do it for me."

Out of the corner of his eye, he saw Lynn trying to elbow her way up to see, and he put a gentle hand on her shoulder, saying, "Take it easy, sweetheart. Let Katie get him going." *Take my word for it—you don't want to see him yet*.

But the seconds ticked by and the baby didn't respond to Kate's vigorous efforts, and Sam wondered if Lynn might end up having to look at her boy in this lifeless state. Reaching over, he placed a hand on the baby's wet head, knowing it was useless; he wouldn't be able to heal what hadn't yet grown enough to live on its own. After a few seconds, when there was no intuitive stirring inside him, he lifted his gaze to meet Katie's, letting his eyes give her the answer.

But she wasn't giving up. She bent to her task once more, this time lifting the swaddled baby in her arms to cover his mouth and nose with her mouth as she puffed air into his underdeveloped lungs. It took a couple of tries, but at last he gurgled. Then, with a spluttering cough, his face scrunched into a grimace and he whimpered.

It was a pitiful cry, more like a kitten mewing. And Sam thought he looked damned pale—probably, he guessed, from loss of blood—but pale was better than blue. And he was alive. The sound of his cry was enough to make Lynn start crying—just in time for Erik to come running into the room.

At the sight of the baby, the young man faltered, and Sam used the moment to discreetly remove his hand from Lynn's now-flaccid stomach and get off the bed. He didn't know if she'd start bleeding again when she tried to deliver the baby's life-support system, but for now she was okay. In the meantime, he was having a hard time taking his eyes off Katie and the baby.

While Lynn greeted Erik with lots of tears and kisses, Sam moved to stand by Katie's shoulder, watching the way she touched the infant, listening to the soft, coaxing sounds she made.

"So, you didn't wait for me."

Doc Cabot's voice brought Sam's gaze snapping to the doorway as the older man walked in, carrying his black bag.

"This one hardly waited for me," Kate returned, cutting the newborn's umbilical cord, then quickly wrapping them up in the blanket. "I only got here about forty minutes ago."

Stopping beside her, Doc took in the scene in a glance. "And I'll bet it feels like it's been an eternity," he murmured.

"Several," she murmured. "And it's not over."

"Hmm. Well, let me get washed up." He set his bag down and walked quickly toward the bathroom, rolling up his sleeves.

The room was silent. Too silent, Sam thought. Erik had propped Lynn against his chest so she could see their son; the infant now had an IV in his arm and a baby-size oxygen mask on his face that was attached to a portable tank sitting on the floor. It was pretty clear what the score was: this baby might die. And Sam hated knowing there wasn't a damned thing he could do about it.

When Doc returned, he watched for an instant as Katie checked the baby's lungs for maybe the tenth time in the past three minutes. Then he filled two syringes out of different bottles on the worktable, picked up a couple of other items, and sat himself down with a grunting complaint about his old bones on the opposite side of the bed beside Lynn.

"What's the ETA on the chopper?" Kate asked him, scribbling notes on a clipboard.

"About thirty minutes, I'd say," Doc answered as he gave Lynn one of the shots he'd prepared. "I sent Scott over to the old McCarron place with his van to wait for them. I'd give it another ten, after they land, before they get here."

Sam caught the look the two of them exchanged. It was too long. And with ten minutes to the chopper, then forty-five minutes to Marquette, they were looking at almost two hours before they could get the baby to the hospital.

"How many miles is it to Marquette?" he asked.

Kate's reply was distracted as she finished the note she was writing. "About a hundred."

"Steve could have him there in a half hour—maybe less."

Her head jerked up, and Sam saw the spark of hope flicker in her eyes as they collided with his.

"I can have you at Steve's in ten minutes, tops—except what about..." He hesitated, his eyes flashing to Lynn, who along with Erik, was listening intently.

Doc cleared his throat, and Sam glanced down to see him giving Lynn the second injection he'd prepared. Sam didn't understand what Doc was trying to say, but when he looked at Katie, it seemed she did.

"We can go," she told him. Then, as her gaze dropped to the baby, she added, "I'll need something to keep him warm. I can take the stethoscope and the oxygen tank, but...Ah. Got it." She stood quickly, saying, "Here. Hold him for a second."

Sam reached automatically, but it startled the hell out of him when she put the blanket-wrapped bundle in his hands. Damn, for all the infant weighed, it could have been *just* the blanket he was holding. Katie had cut a tubular gauze bandage and tied one end closed to make a funny-looking hat for the infant's head, and all he could see was the wrinkled little face. He stared at the baby, fascinated, for several moments. Then Katie's movements caught his attention, and his gaze snapped up. In the next instant, his mouth went dry.

"Kate, what are you doing?" Lynn's tone was slightly horrified.

Erik uttered a strangled sound and quickly turned his head.

Doc answered. "She's keeping him warm, young lady— the best way there is."

That was the truth, Sam thought, but ... God, it took his breath away to watch Katie strip off her clothes without a second's hesitation, until she was bare to the waist. Her breasts swayed as she moved close to him—close enough that her nipples brushed the backs of his hands, and he felt them pucker and harden from the contact.

"Okay," she said, unwrapping the infant until he was naked, too. "Now, lay him up against me like ... like this. That's right. And if you can take one of those sheets and tear it ... Hurry, though, before he gets cold."

Sam's hands shook as he snatched a white sheet off her worktable, found the middle of it, and gave it a hard yank. Half of it was still too big, and he folded the piece in half again before wrapping it under the baby, like a sling, being careful to avoid the oxygen and IV tubes.

"That's good," Kate said as he brought one end of the sheet over her shoulder, the other end under her arm and tied the ends in the middle of her back. "His head's up, and I can still get to him in a hurry this way. Help me put my arm . . . Good."

One at a time, he pulled the sleeves of the jumpsuit up her arms, then buttoned it up over the small lump the baby made. When he got to the button just below her breasts, he paused, his eyes lingering on the deep valley between them that the sling and the baby's head didn't hide. Then his eyes rose to meet hers.

Three aching heartbeats later, he spoke. "Is that good?"

She nodded once, slowly.

Sam knew it was crazy. The baby belonged to somebody else, and those somebodies were watching every move he and Katie made. Everything in sight was bloody, they were in a terrible hurry, and the whole damned situation could hardly have been worse. But he wanted her—right then, right there, he wanted every sensual inch of her. He wanted her gentleness and her sense of harmony with life and her unaffected, earthy sexuality. He wanted to take her and claim her and protect her. . . .

But he'd hurt her. The pain was there, in her dark eyes. Pain that the past half hour had only made worse. It was torturing her just to be with him, and he knew what it must have cost her to ask for his help. But the only choice either of them had was to play out the scene. And somehow, when it was over, he swore, he'd find a way to make her stop hurting—or he'd die trying.

Bending quickly, Sam snatched the portable oxygen tank off the floor, easing the strap over Katie's shoulder.

"Let's get going," he said.

She nodded, then turned to kneel on the bed beside Lynn.

"Oh, Kate..." The young woman reached out, her hand fluttering over the tiny lump of her baby.

"I'll take good care of him," Kate told her. "I promise."

"I know you will. I just..." She lifted her eyes to meet Kate's. "I'm just scared."

"I know." Kate smiled a little, looking at Erik, then at Lynn. "But he's bigger than I thought he'd be, and that's a good sign. Let me get him to the hospital, where they can give him what he needs. He'll be waiting for you when you get there."

Erik and Lynn both nodded, and Kate quickly gathered up a suction cup, a stethoscope and her clipboard, telling Doc she'd leave her notes on Lynn for him to bring. Sam draped her jacket over her shoulders, then motioned her ahead of him out the door.

"Sam."

Lynn's voice stopped him when he reached the doorway, and he swung back to meet her gaze across the room.

"Thank you."

He shot her a wink and a lopsided smile, but as he started out again, he caught the look Doc was giving him. It was knowing and wise and...amused. Sam couldn't figure what the hell was so funny about any of this, but he got the message: He didn't have anything to worry about as far as Bill Cabot was concerned.

Giving Doc a brief nod, Sam followed Kate down the hall.

Chapter Sixteen

You're sure Lynn's going to be okay?"

"Yes, I think so." Kate hung on to the seat with one hand and the baby with the other, watching the headlights bounce on the rutted dirt road as Sam tore through the pitch-black woods. "You stopped the bleeding—all of it that I wouldn't have considered normal, anyway. And Doc gave her a shot of blood coagulant, just in case. She should be fine."

"Hmph. So, is this baby going to make it?"

That was a harder question. "I don't know," she replied. "He has a collapsed lung. But I didn't want to try to do anything about it—not under the conditions back there—unless I had absolutely no choice." Looking down, she touched the top of the infant's stocking-capped head. "He needs a lot of work, but I think if we can get him to Marquette quickly, he's got a good chance."

"Well, let's hope Steve hasn't left yet," Sam muttered.

She shot him a quick look. "Left to go where?"

"Pittsburgh. He talked about flying the Mentor down tonight, but I'm guessing he'll put it off because of the cloud cover."

Kate braced herself as they came to the end of the track and Sam swung onto Main Street with barely a pause, ran the stop sign at the intersection, and shot out of town over the straight, even road.

"Sam?"

"Hmm?"

"Were you in Vietnam?"

"Nope."

"Have you ever seen a baby born besides this one?"

"Nope . . . And I was never in the medical corps, either."

They exchanged a glance in the darkness, and Kate half expected to hear him growl something about not needing her to lie for him. She didn't feel a scrap of guilt about it; the end had more than justified the means. But when he didn't say anything, she figured it was because he'd decided he could put up with her protecting him *this* time. After all, he wasn't going to give her the chance to make a habit of it.

"Steve's not home."

Standing on the Fourniers' front porch, Sam listened in grim silence as Cressie explained her husband's where-abouts.

"He came in from work and did his ground checks and whatnot, then decided not to leave tonight because of the weather. Then he got a call from the garage to go tow somebody out of—"

"Is the plane fueled up?" Sam interrupted her.

"Yes, he did all that, but—"

"Did he get a report from the weather service?"

"Yes," she said. "He always writes it down and puts it in his flight case. But I don't understand what—"

"Where's the flight case?"

Cressie waved her hand in a vague gesture. "In the plane, I think, but what's this all about?"

Sam glanced across the dark yard to his Jeep, where Katie sat, waiting. Then he looked at the plane—a hazy shadow looming in the field beside the barn.

Drawing a ragged breath, he turned to Cressie. "Katie's got a premature baby that she has to get to Marquette. And that's all I've got time to tell you."

That was enough to put a look of horror on her face. "Oh, no! Whose is it? Not Lynn Nielsen's!"

He nodded, asking, "Where are the kids?"

"Asleep, but—"

"Can you drive a Jeep?"

"Yes, but . . . Sam, wait!"

"I haven't got time to wait." Taking her by the elbow, he pulled her down the steps and across the yard, saying, "I want you to drive my Jeep to the far end of the field and park it, with the lights facing straight at this end. Back it up to the edge of the trees—but not under them. You can do that, can't you?"

"Sure," she said, stumbling a little in the wake of his rapid strides. "But what about—"

"Good. After I take off, drive it up here and park it for me, will you?"

"But you're not going to—"

"Yes. I am. Tell Steve I'll pay him back for the fuel."

"He won't mind about *that*, for heaven's sake! I mean, it's a *baby*, and it's... Oh, Lord, I... It's so dark and cloudy, and they said it might storm! Isn't there *some* other way?"

Some other way that won't make me scared. That was the problem, Sam thought. Fear would look for any excuse to get out of doing the right thing.

Swinging around to face her, some twenty feet from the Jeep, Sam grabbed her shoulders. "Cressie, do you want to see your sister happy?"

Her eyes widened. "Of course, I want to see her happy! What kind of question—"

"Take my word for it. This'll do it. Now you go do what I said, and just keep telling yourself you're making Katie happy." *And I'll tell myself the same thing.*

Catching her hand, he pulled her along, letting go of her to yank Katie's door open, as he said, "Let's go."

With a glance at Cressie, Kate took the stethoscope out of her ears, reached for the hand he offered her and climbed out. "Hi, Cress. Did Sam tell you what happened?"

"Yes. Is Lynn okay?"

"So-so. I'll tell you about it later."

"Where's the baby?"

"In here." She patted the front of her jumpsuit as Sam put an arm around her and guided her toward the plane.

A few seconds later, when the Jeep roared by them and took a turn around the corner of the barn, she hesitated, glancing over her shoulder, then at him.

"What's Cressie doing?"

"She's marking the end of the runway."

Several steps farther on, she glanced over her shoulder again.

"Where's Steve?"

"He's not home."

Her head jerked toward him, but she didn't say a word. And she remained very silent as they hurried the rest of the way to the plane.

When they reached it, he hopped onto the wing to open the clear plastic canopy, then pulled her up beside him. He started to lean around her to move the helmet off the seat, but when she lifted a hand and laid it against his face, his head turned sharply toward her.

Their eyes met in the darkness of the chilly spring night.

"Sam, I love you," she said.

And for a moment he was paralyzed. No air, no sound, no strength to move. Only the words, stealing softly into his heart. Then her name—an aching gasp. And he kissed her. A hard, rough, desperate kiss. A crushing of her lips, a driving sweep of her mouth, a moment of breathing the same air she breathed. Enough to tell her, *Wait. Wait until this is over.* Enough to lock her words inside his heart.

Then he was helping her climb into the back seat of the narrow fuselage and making sure the IV and the oxygen tank and the baby weren't in the way of strapping her in. He didn't like it, but he didn't waste time arguing when she refused the helmet, saying she wouldn't be able to use the stethoscope with it on. It would be noisy, he told her, and they wouldn't be able to talk because the headset was built into the helmet. The seats were too far apart for her to reach him over the console that separated them, and he wouldn't be able to see her, either, so she was going to be back there completely on her own.

She'd be fine, she said. He shouldn't worry about her. But it stunned him the way she calmly put her life into his sweating, shaking, terror-numbed hands.

He slid the back half of the canopy closed over her, then swung into the front, his long legs straddling the stick, his hands reaching back to pull the canopy closed over his head.

The motions were automatic. Procedures learned years ago. This was the first plane he'd ever flown, and it would be the first again. The difference was that, then, he hadn't had the sense to be scared. And now he was too scared to have any sense. Then, he'd taken off as fast as he thought his flight instructor would let him get away with. Now, if he let himself stop and think for even a second, he'd freeze up solid, and they'd never get off the ground.

Swallowing constantly against the urge to throw up, Sam strapped himself in, pulled on his helmet, and took hold of the stick. A quick thumb on the boost pump brought the fuel pressure up, and a touch on the starter made the engine roar to life.

You know what you're doing. You've done it thousands of times before. There's not a single good reason to be afraid of doing it again.

The words sounded good, but all the reasoning in the world didn't keep the memories from flooding his mind as he flipped on the lights and ran through the sketchiest checklist he'd ever performed in his life.

Switches and green glowing dials blurred before the image of the earth and sky tumbling out of control, until the earth won out and everything around him—and in him—exploded. The sound of his bones snapping, the smell of his flesh burning, the ungodly howl of his own screaming. The

pain—the mindless, blinding, shattering pain. And the
dying. Oh, yes, that. Floating out of his body, looking down
to see it there, on the operating table—crushed and burned
and bloodied beyond recognition, and cut wide open with
all those gloved hands trying to piece his insides together.
The sadness that he should look that way. The aching sadness that it should end like this . . .

Those were the memories that swamped his senses as he
brought the power up and the plane began to roll forward.

The ground was rough beneath the wheels, nothing like
concrete, and the plane jostled and bounced its way along.
It's a piece of cake, kid's play, no big deal, he told himself.
But by the time he'd jockeyed into position, he was ready to
reach for the oxygen mask, because he was so dizzy he
couldn't see straight and he couldn't breathe for the tightness in his chest.

Then he saw lights. The lights of his Jeep. Way off, at the
end of the long, black field, bright spots of white and amber beneath the shadows of the trees. And somehow, seeing
them there, made something inside him snap.

So he was scared. Out-of-his-mind scared. But what was
he really scared of? Flying the plane—or dying again? The
answer was pretty simple; he'd never been scared of flying
anything he could get off the ground. He didn't used to be
afraid of dying, either. There was nobody he'd let himself
care about too much, or who he'd thought cared about him.
He'd had no commitments, no goals, no sense of the future
being any different from the past. And so he'd had no reason to care whether he died or not.

So he'd thought.

Never again did he want to meet the white light with
empty hands and nothing he felt was worthy to show for
anything he'd been or done . . . And he wouldn't have to; he
had five months of making people's lives better that he
could look at and say, "This is what I've done. This is who
I've been." And the only reason he had to be afraid of dying
right this minute was if this baby died without his at least
having tried to do the only thing he *could* do to save him. He

couldn't heal him. But he could damned well fly him to somebody who might.

And in doing so, he'd be healing himself. Finally and completely. Because right here, in this dark field, with this old any-kid-can-fly-it plane, he had the chance to reclaim that piece of his past that was worth keeping and to meld it with his present in a way that made sense. He had the chance to have everything he'd ever wanted. And suddenly it was very clear to him that the thing he wanted most was sitting in the back seat, waiting to see if he would let her down.

A man might be afraid, Sam decided. Afraid of being hurt. Afraid of having his heart broken. But no real man would let his fear stand in the way of having the woman he loved—or of giving her everything he was capable of giving her that she might ever need or want.

"I love you." The words pulled him forward, through the darkness, toward the lights. And they steadied his hand as he loaded the stick, coaxing the nosewheel off the ground. Forward a little more...and a little more...more, until the mains came up, and suddenly the jostling along the rough field became a smooth glide in the air.

"I love you." Unfamiliar words. Never-spoken words. Words that took the plane, and his heart, soaring over the tops of the trees and upward, into the starless night.

It was going to be all right. Oh, God, it was going to be all right. If he'd thought it wouldn't worry the daylights out of Katie, he'd have laughed. Shouted. Hollered a little. He didn't try to fool himself; the jumping in his stomach wasn't all excitement, and he was damned glad he was in a plane as forgiving as the Mentor, because his hands weren't all that steady on the controls. Yeah, he was still scared. But he was flying the plane, and God almighty, it was going to be *all right*.

There was one thing, though—a naked little bundle wrapped up against Katie's warm skin—that might not be all right, if he didn't find out where the hell he was going and get there. Fast.

With a silent thanks to Steve for having had the sense to give his old war bird an extra dose of horsepower, Sam headed the plane east, immediately contacting Marquette radio, who scrambled to respond to the situation. Heck, yes, bring it in, they said; they'd have an ambulance waiting, and they'd tell the hospital what to expect. They gave him the emergency frequency for his transponder that would put him on their radar screen, and from that moment on he was never alone. Flying became a matter of following Marquette's precise instructions. And in a few minutes' time— about twenty from the time he'd taken off—the lights of the airport appeared dimly below.

Chapter Seventeen

Kate lifted a hand in thanks to the state trooper pulling away from the curb, then turned to trudge through the door of the Marquette airport. It was 5:30 A.M., she could barely walk for exhaustion, and the cup of coffee and sandwich she'd had at two o'clock weren't doing much for her growling stomach. On top of that, she was a hundred miles from home. And as she made her way through the sparse, pre-dawn airport crowd she didn't know what she should hope to find: that her ride had waited or left without her.

The last time she'd seen Sam, he'd been standing on the wing of the Mentor, watching the ambulance tear off with her inside of it. There'd been no question of his coming with her; it wouldn't have been allowed. And for most of the night, she'd been too busy to think about him. But when she arrived at the information desk and discovered he'd left her a message to look for him in the pilots' lounge, other people's crises faded with the night and she was forced to face her own.

Why had Sam kissed her when she told him she loved him? Was he saying he loved her, too? Or was it a kiss goodbye? It could have been either or both. And it could have been only a reaction to the moment. Hadn't her impulsive words been just that? She'd simply had to tell him she loved him. And after she'd already said she wanted to have his children...well, what was "I love you" saying that he didn't already know?

Probably his kiss had been the same sort of impulsive gesture. *One last kiss before I die*—he'd been that terrified when he climbed into the plane. As hard as he'd been shaking, she didn't know how he'd gotten them off the ground. But he had. And she'd never had a flight like it in her life. Encased in a bubble of plastic yet unable to see through the darkness, the roar of the engine nearly shattering her ears, and her anxiety over the baby, and over Sam, roiling inside her. It could have been a hellish experience, but Sam hadn't let it become one. In spite of all he'd been through and was going through then, he'd gotten them to Marquette without a waver of a single wing tip. And she was fairly certain he'd done it at a speed that would make Cressie, and maybe even Steve, faint if they knew.

Kate stopped in the doorway to the dimly lit pilots' lounge, her gaze falling upon the lanky male form stretched out on the couch along the opposite wall. His denim-clad legs were crossed at the ankles, and an open magazine covered his face. He was the only one in the small room, and as she listened to the faint sound of his snoring, she wondered if he'd already made plans to go back to Rutger. It seemed like a real possibility....

She should be happy for him. She *was* happy for him. But it was hard not to think that, in beating the demons that had kept him earthbound, Sam had given her one less reason to believe that his last, fierce kiss had meant anything at all. Her love hadn't been enough for him yesterday; today, it was hopeless to think it might be, when he could go back to doing what he liked and did best: flying never-flown-before airplanes—alone.

Crossing the room, she stopped by the couch. An instant later, she heard his breathing change, his breath catching a little, then rushing out as his hand rose to move the magazine off his face. Blinking a couple of times, Sam's eyes were fully alert as they met hers.

"The baby?" he asked immediately.

Kate managed a tired smile. "I think he's going to be fine. It'll be a while before the doctors will say that, but they sound hopeful. You have to learn to read between the lines."

"And Lynn?"

"Erik had her in a wheelchair outside the nursery window when I left. They were discussing names."

"You've got to be kidding."

"You'd never know she'd almost bled to death last night."

Passing a hand over his beard-shadowed face, Sam swung his feet to the floor and sat up, mumbling, "God, to be that young and foolish again."

Kate was feeling ancient herself as she replied, "I think they're a little less young and foolish than they were yesterday. Erik's talking about selling the camp and going to Ironwood to work for his dad, and Lynn's saying she's not taking the baby back to 'that place' once they let him out of the hospital." Hesitating, she added, "Both of them asked me to thank you, but I don't think they realize how much they have to thank you for. Sam, it was an hour before the medevac chopper got to Lynn."

His head snapped up, his startled gaze flashing to hers.

"I'm sure the baby wouldn't have lasted that long," she said. "Not without a respirator. You bought him a fighting chance to survive. A good chance. And no matter what happens now, I want you to know that."

His eyes held hers a moment longer, then, with a faint smile, he lowered his gaze. "Well, I guess he and I are even."

Before she could respond, he tossed his magazine aside, glanced at the clock on the wall, then stood to let his eyes skim over her. "You've got to be beat," he said quietly.

"Probably no more than you are," she replied. Although, in fact, she thought he looked wonderful—sleep-hazy and unshaven and kind of glowing. The way he'd been when they'd woken up together, yesterday morning...

"I'm fine," he told her. "I went to sleep somewhere around midnight. I didn't know how long you'd be, and I knew I'd have to fly back, so..."

He trailed off, and when his hand came to her face to brush aside a long strand of hair—one of many that had escaped the pins she'd stuck in it so many hours ago—she stiffened at his touch. *Don't do this to me,* she wanted to cry. *Don't touch me or be warm and tender, when you're only going to take it away. Please, just don't make it hurt any worse than it already does.*

Sensing her response, Sam hesitated, the backs of his fingers grazing her cheeks. Kate couldn't meet his gaze but stared at the blue T-shirt molded to his chest.

Finally, he dropped his hand and sighed. "I know. I've got a couple of other scores to even, don't I?"

Kate's brow twitched into a wary frown, and she glanced at him. But he turned to snag his jacket off the couch and sling it over his shoulder. Then, catching her hand in his, he started toward the door.

"Come on, Katie. What you need is a dose of Sam's Special Elixir. I guarantee, it'll cure whatever ails you. And we've got just about enough time to catch the show, too."

Special elixir? The show? Her look became pained when he shot her a wink. Did he expect her to respond to his lighthearted attitude? Was she supposed to put on her usual cheerful face and play along? Kate couldn't have done it if her life had depended on it. And as she allowed herself to be towed through the terminal, she wondered if Sam knew how hard it was for her right then simply to speak to him ... But he *must* know.

Her confusion deepened when he gave her a sideways grin and asked, "So, how'd it go with the hospital? Did you spent the night explaining away another miracle—or was this just a 'highly improbable'?"

Tossing an apology to a lady she'd bumped into, Kate replied, "Neither. But if Doc hadn't been there, I might have had trouble."

"Oh?" Sam swerved around a couple of people ahead of them.

"He'd altered my notes on the delivery. As he pointed out to me, you may be a miracle worker, but you're not an X-ray or a sonogram—meaning, your intuition about what was going on inside Lynn shouldn't have been the basis for my making a diagnosis."

"But you knew, when I told you—"

"Yes, I knew."

Stopping in front of a door that read FLIGHT SERVICE STATION, he waited for her to finish.

She avoided his gaze as she admitted, "But I have no idea how I knew. I just..."

"Read my mind."

She hesitated. "Somehow it seemed almost like that. But not words. Just images."

Sam opened the door, motioning her through it, then led her across the room to a long, high counter. Leaning on the counter he turned toward her, saying, "Images are all I get. I never know what's happening in a technical sense, unless I can see it or it's explained to me. And I've never had bleeding stop, then start again, like that—like it wasn't working. It worried me, Katie, and if you hadn't been there to give me the clues I needed, I might have given up." His eyes skimmed her features, then met hers in a look that was far too intimate for her nerves. "I thought we did pretty good together," he murmured.

She'd been trying not to think about how good they'd been together—it would only be one more thing to miss.

Deliberately avoiding his clear, knowing gaze, Kate said, "But Doc was right. Officially, we don't know the cause of the hemorrhage. So, instead of saying Lynn had a partial previa—"

"A what?"

"A condition where the placenta covers part of the cervix. It usually requires a C-section." Kate shook her head a little, adding, "Anyway, the chart now reads, 'cause of bleeding unknown.' Since previas aren't a chronic or genetic thing, the chances of Lynn having another one are extremely slim, so..."

"What they don't know won't hurt them," Sam concluded. Picking up a flight plan form off the stack on the counter and a pen from the holder in front of him, he began filling in blanks.

Kate watched him write as she continued, "That's about it. Whatever it is you do to a person when you heal them seems to act like a...a..."

"A megadose of vitamins?"

"Yes. The obstetrician was very impressed with what good condition Lynn was in, all things considered." A small smile tugged at the corners of her lips as she added, "Doc had a great time, acting smug in front of all those hospital doctors, saying what a *fine* day it was that he decided to take me on as his associate, and how some OBs he's met would do well to take a lesson from me in labor and delivery management."

Sam glanced up from his writing to look at her, and Kate expected to see him scowl. But a second later, to her utter amazement, he began to chuckle.

"So, the old fox handed you the rap, huh? How'd you get out of it?"

"I stammered a lot."

His earthy laugh turned into a bad-boy grin, and he touched a finger to her cheek. "Honey, if you'd just flashed your dimples, they'd have been eating out of your hand."

Flashed her dimples? How insensitive could he be, making fresh remarks, flirting with her, like he'd been doing since the day they'd met? But as Kate felt the pain—and the anger—slice through her, a voice said, *wait*. Sam wasn't insensitive or cruel—not deliberately, like this. Maybe, though, he was feeling so good about flying again that he didn't realize what his obvious happiness was doing to her. And she almost could have forgiven him for that... Almost.

* * *

Ten minutes later, strapped in and helmeted in the back seat of the Mentor, Kate listened on the headset to the confusing radio chatter as Sam got clearance for takeoff. She didn't understand most of what was said, but she understood something more important: Sam wasn't scared. He was excited, though. And despite her exhaustion and heartache, his excitement was starting to affect her, too.

It was still dark as they zipped down the runway, but the weather had cleared, and as the plane climbed, Kate saw the first blush of dawn starting to pearl the eastern horizon. The view was breathtaking, sitting high in the low fuselage of the old military plane, with nothing in the way of seeing the pink and lavender shades creep into the sky off to her right. Below, the lights of Marquette rapidly disappeared, replaced by an unrelieved inky blackness. And finally it occurred to her that the inky blackness was the deep, chilly waters of Lake Superior.

Confused, Kate glanced to the left, then down, then to the right again, where the sky was growing brighter. When Sam did a banking turn to the right to head due east, she adjusted the microphone on her headset and spoke on a tentative note.

"Sam?"

"Huh?"

"Can I ask you a very dumb question?"

"Katie, you can ask me anything you want."

"Aren't we headed in the wrong direction?"

"Oh, I don't know...." he drawled. Then, in the next instant, when the first piercing ray of sunshine shot over the horizon, he added quietly, "Are we?"

But she knew he didn't expect a reply.

It came fast. Much faster than if you were level with the horizon. The top of the sun's fiery arc appeared first, in a sliver at the watery edge, its golden beams rippling over the water's surface, reflecting in its mirror. The arc grew, swelling over the rim of the earth, the light racing ahead of it. Glittering light. Blinding light. Higher it rose, above the horizon, a throbbing ball of golden-white fire.

It was glorious. A breathtaking display so powerful, so pure, it could make a person forget everything else. Before long, though, the sheer physical impact of such blinding light became overwhelming, and Kate had to shut her eyes.

She was reaching up to pull down the black visor on her helmet when she heard Sam mutter, "So much for the show." Then the nose of the plane took a swing upward and blocked out her view of the horizon.

Instead of turning, though, Sam kept going—straight up...and over, until the plane heeled onto its back. For several long seconds, the waters of Lake Superior became the sky, and the sky, the ground. Then, with a flip, they sky was where it belonged again—and Kate's heart was down somewhere around her feet.

"Katie?"

"I'm still here."

"The important thing is, is your stomach still here?"

"Definitely. It's been growling for hours. Which I have a feeling is about to become a real advantage."

"Lets you appreciate the full effects of—"

"Don't tell me. Sam's Special Elixir."

"Honest, honey, you could use a little of it. But let me know if it gets to be too much. Okay?"

But it wasn't too much. It was wonderful. Easy, slow rolls and great swooping loops, and heart-stopping dives where the glistening waters of Lake Superior rushed to meet them, drawing closer and closer until she was sure they couldn't pull out of it in time. But they did, in a twisting roll, and suddenly they were climbing again, leaving Superior in their wake.

On and on it went. The little plane playing in the early-morning sky over the "shining big sea waters." And somewhere in the middle of it, Kate forgot she was tired. Forgot the strain of the long night. Forgot everything but the moment—and the man who was sharing it with her.

It was a lark. A pure outburst of joy. It was also a gift. A baring of his soul. As intimate a gesture as any he could have made to her. The sunrise, and now this romp in the quiet solitude of the northern sky. *This is who I am. Take it. Take what I want to give you.*

And, oh, how she wanted to. But it was only a moment. And what she wanted was a lifetime.

When the plane finally leveled out, the Michigan coast appearing in the canopy ahead, Kate's heart was aching. It ached even more at the ardent, slightly breathless way he said her name.

"Katie?"

"Yes, Sam."

"Let's go home."

Home. . . . She thought about the way he'd said the word as they flew westward, across the green carpet of the wilderness far below.

A light morning mist still hovered over the empty field when they landed.

Kate managed her straps and helmet while Sam brought the plane to a stop by the barn. She wanted to get out on her own, didn't want him to help her. Didn't want even to look at him. For the ride, as he had known it would, had worked its magic. She was feeling raw and vulnerable, and she knew the first tender word or gesture from him would have her crying hysterically for him not to leave her. Before Kate could climb out, though, Sam was reaching for her, and she couldn't avoid giving him her hand.

She felt the difference in him the instant he touched her, his hand enclosing hers in his strong grasp. Energy, excitement, and that underlying urgency she was coming to recognize—it radiated from him as he helped her climb onto the wing. Their bodies brushed, and his hands went to her waist to steady her. It was completely unnecessary—the wing wasn't that far off the ground—but he kept hold of her hand, stepping down, then turning to wait for her to follow.

He didn't speak, but in a quick glance she caught the intense, compelling look in his gray eyes as they searched her features. She was afraid she knew what he was thinking— that now they could pick up where they'd left off, with him

trying to convince her to let him make it so she could con-
ceive. He wouldn't give up until she let him try, for then he'd
be able to leave with a clear conscience, having given her the
only pieces of himself he could give her honestly.

Maybe she was being a fool not to take what she could
get. But if she let him heal her, what would she have when
he was gone that she didn't have now?

Nothing. His gift would be wasted on her. For she could
never have another man's child without knowing it had been
Sam who'd made it possible. And without wishing the child
were his.

As Kate walked beside Sam toward the Jeep parked by the
back door of the house, thoughts of another confrontation
like yesterday's sent shivers of dread racing through her.
When the screen door banged, she glanced up, relieved to
see Steve and Cressie coming out to meet them. And it
flashed through her mind to simply stay and get Steve to
take her home later. It didn't surprise her, though, after
they'd given Steve and Cressie a bare-bones account of the
night's events, to hear Sam say they had to go. Cressie offered to fix them breakfast, and Kate was about to say she'd
love some. But Sam said, thanks, anyway, he had something he had to take care of.

Kate's thoughts—and her insides—were in turmoil as she
let him guide her, with a hand on the small of her back, toward the Jeep. She was vaguely aware of Cressie's curious
looks and of Sam telling Steve he'd be back later to "settle
up." But it wasn't until they were headed out the long
driveway that the strangeness of the men's conversation
bothered her.

She waited until they'd turned onto the road and were
headed toward Bourner's Crossing—at a speed that made
her wonder if Sam thought he was still flying the plane—
then she spoke, more to break the unbearable tension than
out of any real curiosity.

"I thought Steve was flying to Pittsburgh today."

Sam's voice was especially rough as he replied. "He decided not to go."

"Did the man change his mind about buying the plane?"

"No." He paused, then added, "Steve got a better offer."

"Oh, really?"

"Mmm...from me."

Kate turned her head slowly to look at him. "*You* bought the plane?"

Sam's eyes remained fixed on the road as he nodded. "Last night, over the phone, when I called to tell Cressie I'd gotten you to Marquette in one piece."

Her eyes searched his profile, taking in the set line of his jaw, the sharp angle of his cheekbone; they'd never been less revealing. His white knuckles on the steering wheel told her something, though.

"But...but why?" she asked.

"Why do I want a plane?"

"Why do you want *that* plane?"

"Oh, I think it's just about perfect for what I want to do with it."

"Which is?"

"Have fun. Mostly... What are you looking at me like that for?"

Kate glanced away. "No reason, except..."

"You liked all that monkey business over the lake, right?"

"Yes, I—I liked it... A lot."

"It was fun."

"Yes."

"So...?"

"I guess, it just seems, if you were going to...to buy a plane, you'd want something—" she waved her hand in a flustered gesture "—newer? Faster?"

Sam took his eyes off the road to give her a steady look. "Am I in a hurry?"

She held his gaze as she answered. "Aren't you?"

"Only to get you out of this Jeep and behind a locked door."

Kate swallowed hard, panic tightening the knots around her heart. But as he continued, the panic washed away, and her aching heart began to swell with a very different emotion.

Turning back to the road, Sam told her, "There might be other times I'm in a hurry, too. Like last night. But a plane wouldn't always do the job—like if there was snow on the ground, or if you needed room for a stretcher. Or, say, I wanted to haul packages, like medical supplies—or people, like a fishing or skiing party. Between the swamps and the mountains on the coast and all the trees, there's not enough places to land to make a plane practical. So the T-34's mostly for fun, and maybe—" his eyes raked over her once "—maybe for teaching a certain friend of mine—a friend who could stand to have a little fun now and then—to fly... if she's interested. For work, I need a chopper. And a place to keep them both. A big place—like the one we just passed with those pink trees and the For Sale sign on the lawn. Katie, who owns that boarded up farm?"

Kate had the back of her hand pressed to her mouth and could hardly speak to answer. "The McCarrons. They moved to... to Chicago. About th-three years ago."

Sam reached to catch her hand, wrapping it in his as he brought it over to rest on his thigh. "The property starts here, at the edge of town?"

"Yes."

"Hmm. Well, I guess it's a good thing I've spent the last ten years living on a quarter of what I made."

With her lower lip caught between her teeth and her senses focused entirely on the warmth of his hand holding hers against the rock-hard muscles of his thigh, Kate struggled against the burning tightness in her throat. No, not yet. She couldn't start crying yet. But her heart was crying, *Hurry,* as they passed her house, paused at the intersection of Main and Bourner's Mill, and took the turn onto the old lake road.

"Later..." Sam paused to let out a shuddering breath. "Later on, after everybody's had a chance to rest up, we'll go have a talk with Doc. And the two of you better start looking for another associate to work with you."

"That . . . could be a while. It's really hard to find people . . . w-willing to live this isolated."

"It better not take too damned long." He flashed her a heated look. "This town's about to find out your priorities have been rearranged."

Kate's vision suddenly became very watery.

Sam continued. "I bet Marty could come up with somebody. He's good at solving problems nobody else can solve. Besides, then I'll owe him one, and that'll make him feel better. Can't have my friends waiting around feeling guilty."

"Sam, I don't think I can wait anymore to hear—"

"Hang in there, honey." He slammed the Jeep to a halt in front of the cabin and, seconds later, was pulling her out of it and into his arms. "I know the next line's mine," he said. "And I know you've waited all night to hear it, thinking you weren't going to hear it. I'm sorry for that, Katie. I'm sorry you had to go all this time hurting." Swearing softly, he added, "But I couldn't have done this right in an airport. And I couldn't have done it yesterday at all. If I'd tried, I'd have ended up hurting you worse than I did."

"Oh, Sam . . ." Kate bit back a sob, her fingers digging into his arms to keep from falling as the last scrap of courage and strength drained out of her.

"Katie, honey, it's all right," Sam tried to tell her.

But the tenderness in his husky voice only made her cry harder. When her knees buckled, he lifted her to carry her inside, kicking the door shut and carrying her straight to the bedroom. Standing her beside the bed, he tugged off her jacket, shrugged out of his own and wrapped her against him once more.

The morning sunshine, filtering through the green leaves, lit the room with a soft, golden light, but the only light Kate saw was the clear light in Sam's eyes as he tilted her face to kiss the tears as they ran down her cheeks.

"Katie . . . Katie, please don't cry," he said. "I promise, it's going to be all right."

She hadn't a coherent thought in her head, yet she was exquisitely aware of the difference in textures as she touched his face, his hair, the broad expanse of chest against which

her face was buried. "Sam, I h-have to cry. I won't b-believe
it if I don't."

"Then you go ahead," he murmured, "and I'll just keep
kissing you.... God, I love kissing you."

His gentle, stirring kisses were being laced more and more
with passion, his mouth opening on her skin, his lips tugging at her earlobe, his teeth nibbling at her shoulder. Finally, Kate had to ask, "Why? Sam, I don't . . . understand
why you . . ."

"Why I'm standing here kissing you instead of . . ." Instead of finishing the statement, Sam gave the suitcase sitting beside them on the floor a shove with his foot. Then
with one arm around her waist, he leaned to pick it up and
toss it behind him. It whacked against the closet door and
landed with a thump.

When he straightened and his gaze met hers, Kate caught
her breath. She'd wanted the man. But she'd never truly
seen him—not all of him. Not like this. His eyes, those
beautiful prisms of gray light, had always given her glimpses
of a man she'd come to love. But now they reflected a certainty, a sureness of heart she'd never seen. This was a man
whole and intact, who knew his mind and who had a purpose. And that purpose . . .

Her fingers trembled as she lifted them to touch his face
and he covered her hand with his own, turning his head to
bury his lips in her palm.

"Yesterday," he began, "you said, if I ever put my hand
on you again, for any reason, I'd better be ready to marry
you. But, Katie—" his eyes squeezed closed "—I *wasn*'
ready. Not until I realized that, of all the things I was scared
of, the worst would be facing the rest of my life, and all of
eternity, knowing I'd lost you."

"No . . ." Kate slid both her arms around his waist, holding him tightly. "You'll never lose me. I promise, yo
won't."

"I'd have lost you if I'd left," Sam muttered. "And I'
afraid I would've if last night hadn't happened. But sittin
in that plane, staring down that damned black field, I rea-
ized, if I walked away from you, it wouldn't just be th

worst mistake I'd made since I got here. It'd be the worst mistake I'd ever made in my life.''

Taking her face in his hands, meeting her gaze, he told her, ''Katie, nobody's ever said they loved me. Nobody.'' And when her eyes widened a little, he shook his head. ''Not because there haven't been people who might have. But because I've never given anybody the chance.''

How could she have been so blind? She'd always known he'd probably never said the words himself, but surely, she'd thought someone—some woman who thought she could tie him to her—had said them to *him*. But, no. When Kate thought about all the times she could have told Sam she loved him, all the times she'd thought he wouldn't accept it—the times she'd been afraid to tell him for fear of having her love rejected—she saw how it could be that he'd gone thirty-eight years without hearing the words. And suddenly that last, fierce kiss that she'd thought meant goodbye came to mean something else. Something precious.

She started to say, ''I should have told you when we—''

''No.'' Sam touched a finger to his lips. ''You picked the right time. Hearing the words then, when I most needed to hear them—'' He took a ragged breath. ''I can't explain what it did to me. But I can tell you I'd never have gotten that plane off the ground if you hadn't said it. I swear, Katie, nothing in this world has ever made me feel as good inside as knowing you love me—nothing, except...'' He watched his fingertip trace her lips, then met her gaze as he finished. ''Except, maybe, knowing that I love you.''

Kate's lips formed his name, but no sound escaped past the tightness in her throat. The look in her tear-filled eyes spoke for her, though, and she held his gaze as he reached to pull the pins from her hair. He caught the heavy curtain as it fell, angling her head as he lowered his. And then he kissed her, his mouth taking hers with a devastating tenderness that made the tears stream down her face and left her weak and trembling.

''I love you.'' His lips tugged at hers in between rough-spoken phrases. ''And I love kissing you...and making love to you...and being with you... I love having you fly with

me. And I love helping people...the way we did it together, last night. But most of all—'' his mouth covered hers
for a brief, deep joining ''—mostly I'm going to love telling
you I love you and having you melt like this, all over me.
Marry me, Katie. Let me tell you I love you for the rest of
my life.''

''Oh, Sam...'' Kate turned her face into the pocket of
warmth where his neck met his shoulder. ''Yes, I'll marry
you. And I'll move to the desert with you, if you want to go
back. I'd never ask you to fly helicopters when you really
want to fly planes with names like Pegasus.''

''We're not going anywhere,'' he growled. ''And I don't
want you thinking it's some big sacrifice on my part, either.
I came here thinking I needed some temporary peace and
quiet. But I'm starting to see it's got to be permanent. I
think I'm always going to need a place like this now—a quiet
place I can call home, where I can pay attention to what's
going on inside me without a lot of distractions from the
outside.''

A trace of humor crept into his voice as he added, ''If I
feel like I'm getting lazy and need a challenge, I'll make a
trip down to Mojave and tell Chris I want to take his latest
toy up for a spin. But, honest to God, I think the chances of
that happening are next to none, because I've got all the
challenges I'm going to need or want right here.''

His hands roamed her back and hips, lingering on the
curves. ''This is a good place, Katie, with good people. A
good place for a pilot to make a living or to be useful in an
emergency—or just to enjoy flying for its own sake. And it's
a good place for me to meet kids with hearing problems or
braces on their legs—and to learn more about this new envelope I've been given. I think I'm ready now to see how far
I can make it stretch—which, from what they told me at the
research center, might eventually be a hell of a lot farther
than I've stretched it up till now.''

As his lips nuzzled at her temple, he added, ''I think I'm
going to be able to stretch myself in all sorts of new directions, being married to a woman who loves me and under

stands what I'm about, and who seems to know just what it takes to keep me sane. And besides all that—'' his hand slid down her sides to tighten on her waist ''—she likes to fish . . . and to mess around in planes . . . and she makes love like no other woman I've ever known. And from what she tells me—'' his hand slipped between them to slide across her belly ''—yeah, I've got a feeling she's going to give me the prettiest, dimple-cheeked babies a man could ever want.''

Kate squeezed her eyes closed, whispering breathlessly against the pulse in his neck. ''Sam . . . Oh, Sam, can you really . . . ?''

''Oh, yes,'' he whispered back. ''I can really.''

She hadn't dared ask. Hadn't dared hope or even let herself think about it for fear she'd be one of those his touch wouldn't heal. But hearing the certainty in his voice brought the words, and the tears, pouring out of her.

''Sam—Oh, Lord, I *do* love you. And I'll make you such a good wife! I promise, I will!''

''You think I don't know it? You think I'm not going to wonder every day how I got this lucky? Katie, I swear to God, I'm going to do my best to be the kind of husband you deserve.''

''Oh, I know. I know you will.''

''I'm going to take such good care of you.''

''Sam, please, kiss me. Please, I—''

He kissed her again and again, hot kisses, abandoned kisses, luscious, deep, swirling kisses. He kissed her until she was gasping for breath. But he didn't give her time to breathe, and she didn't care. She didn't need to breathe. She only needed him. She was aching, melting . . . burning with a need fueled by a staggering, almost blinding happiness, after so many long hours of heartache.

Her hands shook as they tugged at his clothes, and she made a tiny, frantic sound when her efforts got her nowhere. Finally, she simply clung to him as he swiftly undressed them both, peeling the clothes from her trembling body, then tearing off his shirt at the same time he kicked his jeans and briefs aside. His eyes held hers as he lowered her to the bed. But when he came down to lie on top of her, his breath caught and his eyes closed, a look of almost tortured pleasure crossing his features at the first full contact of their heated flesh. Settling onto her, he whispered her name, and she wrapped him close, sinking into the mattress beneath the marvelous, vital weight of his body.

He was warm and hard and male. He was hers. And she needed him desperately. But the only word she could speak was his name, and so she tried to tell him with her hands and the movement of her body against his to come inside her, to take her before she died of this terrible, throbbing emptiness.

But he wanted her in flames. That's what his hands told her as they raced over her, stroking her, molding every soft curve and hollow. He said, it, too, in words—dark, erotic words muttered hoarsely against her lips, her thighs, the curve of her belly. Finally, when his mouth opened over the rosy peak of one breast, his cheeks going hollow beneath her fingers as he drew her inside, she cried out.

"Sam . . . Sam, please . . . I can't wait, I—"

"It's going to happen, Katie. Right now. All of it."

And then he was kneeling between her legs, settling back on his heels with his knees spread wide to drape her thighs over his. He pulled her down the bed toward him, lifting her until she felt his hardened flesh testing the wet heat at the entrance to her feminine depths. Whimpering, she arched her back, her body quivering, already wavering on the edges of fulfillment. But he didn't complete the union, and she let out a throaty, almost agonized moan.

"Easy, honey," he soothed.

She gasped, squeezing her eyes closed. *"Sam . . ."*

"I know. Me, too."

Yet he held back. And she opened her eyes to see him watching his hands, splayed across her skin, his gaze following their path as they traveled slowly up her thighs, across her belly, her breasts, her shoulders, then, just as slowly down again.

"Sam, please, you're—"

"Shh, it's okay. Feel me . . . there?"

"Yes!"

"I'm not going anywhere. But I need a minute to do this right. And, honey, that's the only way I'm going to do it."

She couldn't imagine anything being any more right. But then she began to feel it: that shimmering warmth, emanating from the palms of his strong, long-fingered hands. Like the first flickering tongues of flame, it began to lick at her skin, sensitizing it, bringing it to life. And she realized suddenly, with a small, startled gasp, that his hands flowing over her were telling her that he'd meant what he said—it was going to happen. Right now. *All* of it. And he wanted *all* of her with him when it did. He didn't intend simply to make love to her, he intended to heal her. He wanted—needed—to do both at once, whether it was possible or not. And she could only let him.

With her body completely vulnerable, Kate lay panting and shaking, her hands clutching the bedspread, watching the sweat appear on Sam's forehead and upper lip. His concentration was total, an astonishing thing to witness, as his hands continued to move over her with exquisite care and deliberation. The warmth built slowly, sinking into her, sinking deep inside to awaken her soul the way he'd awakened her body; it grew slowly until, finally, it equaled the liquid heat he'd kindled in her loins.

Remembering the other times she'd seen him this way, she didn't expect him to speak. Yet he did, in a rasping, broken whisper.

"Seeing you with that baby last night . . . both of you naked like that . . . it was the sexiest thing I've ever seen in my life. The most beautiful thing I've ever seen anybody do. And I'll never be able to say . . . to say how it made me feel to hold that tiny little body up against you." He drew a shallow breath and let his eyes drift closed. "There aren't any words to describe what it was like to feel your soft skin and his soft skin touching . . . touching my hands. And to see . . . to see his head lying there, between your breasts."

He didn't need other words to describe it, Kate thought; his voice and his touch alone were imbued with all the feeling the experience had evoked in him. And she knew what he was going to say before she spoke again.

"I want to see you do that with *our* baby." His hoarse whisper was barely audible. "I want to come inside you and see your belly get big and know there's part of me growing in you. And I want—" He broke off, his hands coming together in her abdomen, drifting lower to settle over her womb. "I want to see that baby slide out of you and hear it holler—loud, like it ought to sound. And I want to hold it and touch it . . . and know that it's mine."

"Sam . . . !"

"Take it, Katie. Take it all. Everything I want to give you. Let my love work a miracle on you the way yours has worked one on me."

And with a gasping sob of absolute surrender, she yielded herself, and every desire or hope she'd ever had, to him.

He came into her slowly. Filling her body as he filled her soul to bursting with the flesh and the spirit of his being. Filling her so entirely that, for a moment, she felt as if she'd never be able to accept the full, shattering power of what he was giving her, for her body and soul together didn't seem enough to hold it.

She cried out once more, a little frightened. And then, it was as if some part of her did burst open, for suddenly there was no sense of being separate from him. No limits between them. No limits at all. There was no *him* or *her*. No needs or wants or thoughts or emotions. Certainly no fear.

There was only the heat. Throbbing white heat. They were dissolved in it, lifted by it, floating in a radiant, glowing beam of it. Like the beat of a pulse. It thrummed in a rhythm that was the measure of all time. And it was sexual and spiritual and mortal and immortal. It was all things possible. It was the best of what can exist between a man and a woman when they open themselves to each other and to the power of love. . . . It was the piece of heaven that can exist on earth when human hearts allow it a place to dwell.

She wanted to stay there forever. To remain in that place of total rightness. To stay there with him, with the essence of life flowing from him into her in a steady, endless stream.

The knowledge that she was bound, body and soul, with a man from whom it seemed she was drawing her very life's breath filled her with awe. So much so that she began to wonder how she would ever give it back to him. How could she, a mortal woman, ever hope to satisfy the needs and desires of a man who could give her this most unearthly gift?

That thought came with the awareness that the energy was shifting. Reality was breaking up into its different planes and separateness, returning. Slowly, her senses were being given back to her, gradually coming under her own control. And with the awareness of her flesh being distinct from his, of his hands still lying low on the curve of her belly, came the intuitive answer to the question: She knew how she would give back to him the gift he'd given her. She would return it in kind. A perfect gift for a perfect gift, both gifts born of love and joy.

But he would have to wait for his. And as her senses began to clear, sharpening to a level of clarity that was acute, she realized he hadn't yet given her *all* that was necessary to make her gift to him possible. He might be able to evoke the light of heaven, but he still lived and breathed in this world. And he would go on living and breathing in the world—with her—for a long, long time.

At that moment, she was very aware—and very glad—that the hands now gliding over her breasts were simply a man's hands. And that the muscled, hair-dusted body coming down to cover hers was a man's body. That the steely hardness filling the depths of her feminine passage was the flesh that rose from a man's loins. And when she opened her eyes to the morning sunlight, the face she saw above hers was a man's face.

The face of the man she loved.

He gazed down at her with eyes still warm with passion and the trace of a smile curving his lips. And he said, "Now, Katie . . . let's see if we can make a miracle—together."

* * * * *

Silhouette Special Edition

Now appearing
in a special return engagement, Nora Roberts's
bestselling 1988 miniseries featuring

THE O'HURLEYS!
Nora Roberts

And making his debut in a brand-new title, a very special
leading man . . . Trace O'Hurley!

In 1988, Nora Roberts introduced THE O'HURLEYS!—a close-knit
family of entertainers whose early travels spanned the country. The
beautiful triplet sisters and their mysterious brother each experience
the triumphant joy and passion only true love can bring, in four books
you will remember long after the last pages are turned.

Don't miss this captivating miniseries—a special collector's edition
available now wherever paperbacks are sold.

OHUR-1A

Take 4 bestselling love stories FREE

Plus get a FREE surprise gift!

PASSPORT TO ROMANCE
SWEEPSTAKES RULES

1. **HOW TO ENTER:** To enter, you must be the age of majority and complete the official entry form, or print your name, address, telephone number and age on a plain piece of paper and mail to: Passport to Romance, P.O. Box 9056, Buffalo, NY 14269-9056. No mechanically reproduced entries accepted.

2. All entries must be received by the CONTEST CLOSING DATE, DECEMBER 31, 1990 TO BE ELIGIBLE.

3. **THE PRIZES:** There will be ten (10) Grand Prizes awarded, each consisting of a choice of a trip for two people from the following list·
   i) London, England (approximate retail value $5,050 U.S.)
   ii) England, Wales and Scotland (approximate retail value $6,400 U.S.)
   iii) Carribean Cruise (approximate retail value $7,300 U.S.)
   iv) Hawaii (approximate retail value $9,550 U.S.)
   v) Greek Island Cruise in the Mediterranean (approximate retail value $12,250 U.S.)
   vi) France (approximate retail value $7,300 U.S.)

4. Any winner may choose to receive any trip or a cash alternative prize of $5,000.00 U.S. in lieu of the trip.

5. **GENERAL RULES:** Odds of winning depend on number of entries received.

6. A random draw will be made by Nielsen Promotion Services, an independent judging organization, on January 29, 1991, in Buffalo, NY, at 11:30 a.m. from all eligible entries received on or before the Contest Closing Date.

7. Any Canadian entrants who are selected must correctly answer a time-limited, mathematical skill-testing question in order to win.

8. Full contest rules may be obtained by sending a stamped, self-addressed envelope to: "Passport to Romance Rules Request", P.O. Box 9998, Saint John, New Brunswick, Canada E2L 4N4.

9. Quebec residents may submit any litigation respecting the conduct and awarding of a prize in this contest to the Régie des loteries et courses du Québec.

10. Payment of taxes other than air and hotel taxes is the sole responsibility of the winner.

11. Void where prohibited by law

COUPON BOOKLET OFFER TERMS

To receive your Free travel-savings coupon booklets, complete the mail-in Offer Certificate on the preceeding page, including the necessary number of proofs-of-purchase, and mail to: Passport to Romance, P.O. Box 9057, Buffalo, NY 14269-9057 The coupon booklets include savings on travel-related products such as car rentals, hotels, cruises, flowers and restaurants. Some restrictions apply. The offer is available in the United States and Canada. Requests must be postmarked by January 25, 1991 Only proofs-of-purchase from specially marked "Passport to Romance" Harlequin® or Silhouette® books will be accepted. The offer certificate must accompany your request and may not be reproduced in any manner. Offer void where prohibited or restricted by law LIMIT FOUR COUPON BOOKLETS PER NAME, FAMILY, GROUP, ORGANIZATION OR ADDRESS. Please allow up to 8 weeks after receipt of order for shipment Enter quickly as quantities are limited. Unfulfilled mail-in offer requests will receive free Harlequin® or Silhouette® books (not previously available in retail stores), in quantities equal to the number of proofs-of-purchase required for Levels One to Four, as applicable.

PR-SWPS

OFFICIAL SWEEPSTAKES
ENTRY FORM

Complete and return this Entry Form immediately—the more Entry Forms you submit, the better your chances of winning!
• Entry Forms must be received by **December 31, 1990**
• A random draw will take place on **January 29, 1991**
• Trip must be taken by **December 31, 1991**.

3-SSE-2-SW

YES, I want to win a PASSPORT TO ROMANCE vacation for two! I understand the prize includes round-trip air fare, accommodation and a daily spending allowance.

Name_____

Address_____

City_____ State_____ Zip_____

Telephone Number_____ Age_____

Return entries to: **PASSPORT TO ROMANCE**, P.O. Box 9056, Buffalo, NY 14269-9056

© 1990 Harlequin Enterprises Limited

COUPON BOOKLET/OFFER CERTIFICATE

Item:	LEVEL ONE Booklet 1	LEVEL TWO Booklet 1 & 2	LEVEL THREE Booklet 1, 2 & 3	LEVEL FOUR Booklet 1, 2, 3 & 4
Booklet 1 = $100+	$100+	$100+	$100+	$100+
Booklet 2 = $200+		$200+	$200+	$200+
Booklet 3 = $300+			$300+	$300+
Booklet 4 = $400+	_____	_____	_____	$400+
Approximate Total Value of Savings	$100+	$300+	$600+	$1,000+
# of Proofs of Purchase Required	4	6	12	18
Check One	_____	_____	_____	_____

Name_____

Address_____

City_____ State_____ Zip_____

Return Offer Certificates to **PASSPORT TO ROMANCE**, P.O. Box 9057, Buffalo NY 14269-9057

Requests must be postmarked by **January 25, 1991**

- ✂ - - - -

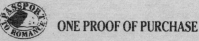

ONE PROOF OF PURCHASE

3-SSE-2

To collect your free coupon booklet you must include the necessary number of proofs-of-purchase with a properly completed Offer Certificate

© 1990 Harlequin Enterprises Limited

See previous page for details.